A RELIC (

Sammel, Garander discovered, was stocky and white-haired, his face worn and wrinkled, and his left hand was missing two fingers. He was wearing a thigh-length leather vest over a dirty white tunic and well-worn black breeches. He marched into the room, Landin on his heels, then stopped dead and glared at Garander. He did not look friendly. "You're the one who claims to have found a Northerner talisman?" he demanded.

"No," Garander said. "My sister found it. I just brought it here. And I don't know if it's a Northern talisman or not."

"Well, where is it?"

Garander pointed at Azlia, who held out the glowing object. Sammel strode over and snatched it from the wizard's hand, then studied the talisman intently, holding it up to catch the sunlight just as Azlia had. The hostility in his expression faded, to be replaced with intent interest.

"It's Northern, all right," he said. "See these glyphs in the crystal? That's Shaslan military cipher. This was part of some soldier's equipment."

Garander had no idea what a Shaslan military cipher might be, but apparently that was what those shifting shapes were. "What's it for?" he asked.

Sammel frowned. "Don't know," he said. "It's not standard issue. I've never seen one like this."

"Is it dangerous?" Azlia asked.

"Sorcery is almost always dangerous," Sammel said, studying the object.

LEGENDS OF ETHSHAR

RELICS OF WAR
A LEGEND OF ETHSHAR

LAWRENCE WATT-EVANS

WILDSIDE PRESS

Published by Wildside Press, LLC
www.wildsidebooks.com

CHAPTER 1

Garander Grondar's son looked out the barn's loft door at the forest beyond the north field. The first traces of autumn color were starting to appear, and what had been a solid wall of green was now speckled with gold. Soon enough the leaves would fall, and the snows would come, and he and his parents and his sisters would spend most of their time huddled around the hearth.

Garander suspected that far too much of that time he would be listening to his parents argue about where the border should be drawn, and who they and the nearby village would owe allegiance to. He was not looking forward to that.

At least the harvest had been good, and they had gotten it all in; barring disaster, they would have more than enough bread to last the winter. He had learned the winter before last that listening to the adults argue politics was even less fun on an empty stomach.

He braced himself with one hand on the door frame and leaned out, looking up at the northern sky. It was clear and intensely blue. He lowered his gaze again, down across the sky, across the changing leaves, to the shadows beneath the trees—and there he caught a flash of color that was not turning leaves. That distinctive splash of red and white was his little sister's tunic, he was sure.

"Ishta, you little idiot," Garander muttered to himself. He turned away and half-climbed, half-slid down the ladder to the dirt floor, then trotted out the door and around to the east side of the barn, where he stopped and looked north.

He spotted her immediately. There was his youngest sister, Ishta Dark Eyes, just emerging from the line of trees that marked the farm's northern limit.

"*Hai*!" he called. "Ishta!"

She started at the sound of his voice, then froze. He started toward her.

She spotted him, and relaxed slightly when she saw it was her brother, and not her father, who had seen her. "Hello, Garander," she said. "Look what I found!" She held out her hand.

He did not look at it immediately; he was looking her over, making sure she didn't have twigs in her hair, or marks on her clothing that would give her away to their parents. She was wearing her favorite red-and-white tunic belted at the waist, a pair of oxhide slippers on her feet, and nothing else—she was still too young to have added a woman's skirt, so her legs were bare from knees to ankles. "If Father found out you'd been in the woods again…" he began.

Then he finally noticed what she was holding out toward him. His eyes widened, and he drew in his breath. "By all the gods, Ishta," he said. "What *is* that?"

"I don't know," she said cheerfully. "I found it in the forest." She held it up to his face, to give him a better view.

The object was about the size of a plum, but a little flatter and wider. Most of it was as smooth as glass, and as black as their mother's onyx pendant, but on one side was a golden oval, and that oval was glowing, as bright as the finest candle. Garander stared at it in wonder.

"If you look closely, you can see things moving in there," Ishta said proudly.

Garander peered at the glowing oval, and he saw that his sister was right—there were small shapes dimly visible through the golden light, sliding back and forth.

"Where did you find it?" Garander asked.

"That way," Ishta said, waving in a generally northeasterly direction. "It was under a pile of leaves."

"There wasn't anyone around who might have put it there?"

"No, silly. I'm not a thief. It was all dirty; it must have been there for ages. I cleaned it off." She pulled her handkerchief out of her tunic pocket with her other hand, and Garander saw it was smeared with black dirt. The glowing thing itself was as shiny and clean as if it had just been polished, but he did not doubt his sister for an instant; she would not have thought to dirty her handkerchief. Whatever the glowing thing was, dirt didn't stick to it very well.

"Oh," he said.

Ishta looked down at the mysterious object, then up at her brother. "Do you think it's magic?" she asked.

"Of course it's magic," he said. "How could it glow like that if it wasn't magic? The question is, what *kind* of magic? Is it dangerous?"

Ishta looked down at the thing again, and asked, "How could it be dangerous?"

Garander snorted. "It's magic, Ishta. It could do anything. Maybe it explodes when moonslight hits it, or maybe if you say the wrong word it'll turn you into a toad, or maybe it's poisoning you right now, just because you're holding it."

Ishta immediately dropped it, then looked closely at her hand. "It looks all right," she said. "I feel fine. I don't think it's poison."

"Probably not," Garander admitted, "but we don't know."

"If it's poison, why would it have those shapes in there?" Ishta asked, transferring her gaze from her hand to the magical object.

"So you'll look into it to try to figure them out," Garander suggested. "Maybe it makes you go blind if you stare at it."

Ishta frowned, then stooped and picked the thing up again. "I don't think that's it," she said. "Why would a magician make something like that? Why not just cast a spell?"

"*I* don't know," Garander said. "*I'm* not a magician. Maybe the kind of magician who made it can't cast spells that way."

Ishta considered that for a moment, turning the glowing thing over in her hands. "You think it's Northern sorcery?"

"Well, it certainly might be," Garander said. "I mean, look where you found it. No one from Ethshar ever lived in those woods!"

"I know I said it must have been there for ages, but it's been twenty years since the war! It can't have been lying there that long."

"Why not? It's magic, isn't it?"

"But it looks new!" Ishta protested. "It *can't* be left from the war. There must have been scouts and people like that who explored the woods after that. Maybe one of *them* dropped it."

"Maybe," Garander admitted. "I never saw any, and we've lived here for a long time, but I suppose there might have been some. Still, I think we should tell Father. We shouldn't be messing around with magic when we don't know what it is; it's too dangerous."

Ishta considered this, then ventured, "Maybe we could tell Mother, instead?"

Garander turned up an empty hand. "Why? She'll just tell Father."

Ishta could not deny this; she slumped. "All right," she said. "If we have to."

"Come on," Garander said, beckoning to her.

"Do we need to tell him I found it in the woods, though?" Ishta asked, as they started toward the house. "Can't we say it was, you know, just over there, somewhere?"

"*I* didn't see where you found it," Garander said. "That's what I'll tell him."

"Thank you."

After a few silent steps, Garander asked, "Why do you keep going into the woods, anyway? What's out there that's worth making Father so angry?"

"I don't know," Ishta said. "It's just nice. I like the shade, and the trees are so pretty, and there are all these places to explore. There are birds, and squirrels, and chipmunks…"

"And there might be dragons, or bears, or mizagars," Garander replied.

"I don't think bears are *real*," Ishta said. "I've never heard of anyone who ever saw a live one, except in nursery rhymes."

"That still leaves dragons and mizagars. You aren't going to claim *those* are imaginary, are you?"

"No, of course not. I know about Uncle Gror and Great-Aunt Sirina."

Those two family legends were hard to avoid. Their mother's eldest brother had served in a dragon's company in the Great War, and had a scale the dragon had shed to prove it, a shiny dark green scale the size of a dinner plate; he had brought it out and shown it to them when he had visited several years ago. As for mizagars, their paternal grandfather had seen his older sister devoured by a mizagar when they were children, and the story, with all its gruesome details, had been retold many times.

"But that was a long time ago," Ishta added, "and it wasn't around here."

Garander sighed with exasperation. "That doesn't mean there aren't any here!" he said.

"I've never *seen* any," Ishta insisted.

But then they were at the door of the house, and there was no time to worry about a reply. Garander opened the door, wiped his feet on the mat, and stepped into the kitchen.

Their mother and sister, Shella of the Green Eyes and Shella the Younger, were standing by the big iron stove, taking turns scooping something from a steaming pot into clay jars. The air in the room was warm and damp and smelled of cooked apples.

"*Hai*," the elder Shella said, without taking her eyes off her ladle. "Stay back, this is hot."

Their sister threw them a quick glance, then returned to her work.

"Is Father around?" Garander asked.

"He's in the smokehouse, I think," their mother said. "Did you get the hay stored?"

"Yes," Garander said. "The loft's only about two-thirds full, though." The family should have enough food for the winter, but some of their livestock might not be quite as fortunate.

"That should probably be enough," she said, as she put down her ladle and clapped a lid onto the jar she had just filled. She swung the steel band over the top and pressed down hard, putting most of her weight on it, until she was able to hook the loop and seal the jar.

Garander was not entirely sure whether her comment had been about the hay supply or the jar of apple preserves, but it didn't much matter. "Come on," he told Ishta.

A moment later they were at the smokehouse, where their father had just finished hanging the remains of a butchered hog. He turned when they entered, wiping sweat from his face with a dirty handkerchief. "Done with the hay?" he asked.

"Yes, sir," Garander said. "Ah...Ishta found something."

"What kind of thing?" Grondar asked.

Wordlessly, Ishta held it out.

Grondar leaned over to stare at it. "What in the World is that?" he demanded.

Garander glanced at Ishta, but she seemed frozen in place, displaying the glowing object. "We don't know," he said. "Ishta found it."

Grondar looked up from the mysterious thing at his son's face. "It must be magic," he said.

"We thought so," Garander agreed.

"It might be valuable," his father said.

"Or dangerous," Garander said.

"Or both." Grondar frowned. Garander noticed that he made no move to touch the thing. "We'll want to have a magician look at it."

"I could take it to Rulura tomorrow," Garander suggested.

Grondar grimaced. "That doesn't look like witchcraft to me," he said. "They go in more for herbs and potions."

"I know, but she might be able to tell us what kind of magic it is, even if it isn't witchcraft."

"Why would a witch know anything about other magic?" Grondar replied. "No, I think we should send it to the baron, and let his magicians figure it out."

Garander's insides seemed to tighten. "The baron?"

His father looked him in the eye. "I'm not making any secret of my loyalties, son. We're north of the river, and as far as I'm concerned, that makes us Sardironese."

"Some of the neighbors—"

Grondar cut him off. "Some of our neighbors are fools," he said. "Ethshar of the Sands is fifty leagues from here."

"And Sardiron of the Waters is thirty!"

"Which is much less than fifty, and the Baron of Varag's stronghold is only five, which makes it the closest place you're likely to find real magicians. Besides, it won't hurt us to treat Lord Dakkar with respect. Tomorrow you'll take that thing to Varag and let the baron's magicians take a look at it."

"*Me?*"

"Yes, you."

"But Ishta found it!"

"Don't be ridiculous, boy. I can't send a little girl to Varag by herself. You'll take it and see what the baron's people make of it."

Garander looked helplessly at Ishta, who was still standing there, holding the magical object out. She looked miserable, but said nothing.

"Can I bring Ishta with me?" Garander asked. "I'm sure she'd like to see the baron's court, and she *is* the one who found it."

Grondar shook his head. "No, she'd slow you down, and it wouldn't be safe, taking a girl her age. Besides, I can spare *one* of you from your chores, but not both. You'll go alone, right after breakfast."

Garander looked from his father to his sister and back, but saw no help in either of them—Grondar had made his decision, and Ishta was not going to argue. His shoulders sagged.

"After breakfast," he said.

CHAPTER TWO

The magical thing was tucked in a leather pouch, inside a wooden box, inside a leather bag, which Garander then stuffed into a traveling pack, along with a change of clothing, a waterskin, and a parcel of bread. He had his knife on his belt, and a purse with six bits in copper and five in iron—the sum total of his savings. Preparations made, he sat down to breakfast with his mother and sisters.

"I wish *I* was going," Shella the Younger said, as she cut herself a slice of ham.

Garander made a noise.

"When you get back you'll have to tell me what the ladies of the baron's household are wearing," she continued.

"Don't get any fancy ideas," their mother said, before Garander could respond. "We can't afford silks and velvet."

"I know, but are they cutting their sleeves full or tight? Are they wearing veils? Do their hats have brims, if they wear hats at all? Just because we're out here on the edge of civilization doesn't mean we can't *try* to look fashionable!"

"It *does* mean we don't need to worry about it," her mother retorted. "Oh, I don't suppose it will do any harm to know what's in style; you can spend all winter sewing new clothes that will be out of fashion by spring."

"Do styles change that fast?" Shella asked.

"Well…sometimes," her mother replied. She glanced at her youngest. "You're being quiet this morning, Ishta."

Ishta pointedly said nothing, but glared at her brother.

"It wasn't *my* idea," Garander protested.

"It's *mine*," Ishta said. "I found it."

"I know!" Garander said. "I'll give it back to you as soon as I can."

"The baron may not allow that," their mother remarked.

Garander glowered at her. "You aren't helping," he said.

"I'm just speaking the truth!"

"It's still not helping." He turned to Ishta. "I'm really sorry about this, but Father's right—it's too dangerous for a girl your age."

"I don't see why we need to take it to the baron at all," Ishta said. "We should at least *ask* Rulura."

"Father doesn't think Rulura knows anything about any magic that isn't witchcraft."

"She might."

Garander turned up an empty palm. "He doesn't think so."

"If he really wants to find magicians," Shella the Younger said, "he should send you to Ethshar. They have dozens of magicians there. Probably hundreds."

"Yes, but it's fifty leagues to Ethshar. I'd be gone all winter."

Shella snorted. "You think that's a *bad* thing?"

"Maybe not for me," Garander said, "but you'd miss me." He clapped a hand on his heart, smiling at his sister. "Especially when it came time to fetch in firewood."

"There is that," Shella conceded. "But at least we wouldn't need to feed you; you eat as much as Ishta and I do put together."

"He's not going to Ethshar," their mother said, wrapping up the remaining ham. "He's taking that thing to Varag, and he should be back in a day or two, at most."

"It's mine," Ishta muttered. "I shouldn't have shown it to you at all."

Garander did not argue with that.

Ten minutes later they were done eating. While the women cleared the plates, Garander pulled on his good boots and slung his pack on his shoulder; then he gave both Shellas, mother and sister, hugs. A glance at Ishta made it clear that she would not welcome his embrace, so he merely waved to her, then marched out of the house and headed west.

Garander knew that a league was supposed to be an hour's walk, which would make it a five-hour journey to Varag, but he was tall for his age and pushed hard, taking few rests, hoping to get there fast enough to have some hope of getting home that night.

He crossed his family's farm quickly, and then dodged around the wheat fields that Felder the Ill-Tempered farmed—they had been harvested, but he did not want to be accused of trampling anything that might have been left lying out, so he followed the drainage ditch Felder had dug along one side. That took him to old Elkan's place, and beyond that were the lands of three more neighbors whose names he was not quite sure of, though he had seen them often enough, in the village or at neighborhood gatherings; he hurried across them all, not wanting to stop and talk. Fortunately no one was close enough to his path for courtesy to require him to do more than wave in passing.

He reached the road in about an hour, and picked up the pace even more, trotting through the village of Ezval without stopping. He turned right at the fork, onto the smaller of the two roads leading west, trotting past more farms.

When he finally glimpsed the top of the Varag watchtower in the distance, he took a break. He sat down on a large rock by the roadside, took a long drink of water, and unwrapped the loaf of bread he had brought. He was not sure just what would happen when he tried to see the baron's magicians, so he wanted to arrive reasonably rested, with a full belly.

The day was sunny and pleasantly cool, and Garander thought the gods of weather must be favorably disposed toward him—if they had noticed him at all, which they probably had not. A walk like this would have been far less pleasant in the rain, or in the sweltering heat that they had been through a month earlier. He tore off a chunk of bread and ate it, casually watching three men with scythes cutting hay a hundred yards away.

He had only been this far from home half a dozen times in his life, and this was the first time he had made the trip to Varag alone. No one had even mentioned that before he left, though; apparently his parents recognized that he was almost a grown man, and felt no need to remind him of his youth and inexperience. That gave him a warm feeling of pride. He knew he would be expected to take on more responsibility in coming seasons, perhaps clear some fields of his own to work. The woods where Ishta had found her mysterious toy might become his own farm.

He would inherit his parents' land eventually, of course, but he was in no hurry to see that day. His sister Shella would most likely marry one of the neighbors' sons—probably that annoying Karn Kolar's son, down by the ford, though Garander had no idea what she saw in him—and move to her husband's farm, and start a family there.

Ishta, though—Ishta said she didn't want to be a farmer. She had been asking their parents about arranging an apprenticeship, though she kept changing her mind about what sort of apprenticeship. Garander looked down at his open pack, at the bag holding her magical find; was there some way to make a living out of being insatiably curious? If so, Ishta certainly qualified.

Well, she was not quite eleven, and apprenticeships had to begin between one's twelfth and thirteenth birthdays, so she had some time yet to decide what she wanted. Perhaps she would settle down and decide that farming was a good life after all.

Garander wrapped up the rest of the bread, took a last drink of water, then got to his feet, hefted his pack, and marched on toward Varag. A glance at the sun told him it was not yet midday; he had made good time thus far.

Perhaps half an hour later he arrived at the town gate. More of the structure was stone now than he remembered, presumably a result of the baron's efforts to replace the original wood with stronger materials; the right-hand tower was now stone for its entire height, though the roof was still thatch, and two of the left-hand tower's three stories were stone. The open gate itself was still wood, of course, as was the lintel above it, but a new catwalk now connected the upper floors of the towers on either side, and Garander guessed that the baron someday hoped to have a stone arch and rampart there.

He wondered why the baron was putting so much effort and expense into defenses; who did he expect to fight? The Northern Empire was gone, utterly destroyed, and the World was at peace. Did Lord Dakkar think the overlords of Ethshar were going to invade, to reclaim the northern lands they had let slip from their grasp?

Garander knew that many people, including his own mother, did think exactly that, but he found it very hard to believe. They really didn't have anything to fight about. If the overlords had wanted to rule Sardiron, why had they let the barons go in the first place? And if they *did* want to conquer the baronies, Garander suspected they would come with wizards and theurgists, not soldiers and siege machines. After all, it hadn't been mortal men who destroyed the Northern Empire; it had been the gods themselves.

Besides, the Baron of Varag might be spending a fortune building walls and towers and arming his soldiers, but the guards at the gate stood by and watched as Garander strolled into the town without so much as asking his business. Those defenses weren't keeping anyone out, and if the overlords of Ethshar really wanted to take the town, their soldiers could just walk in with swords under their coats.

On the other side of the gate Garander paused and looked around at the square. It wasn't a market day, so there were no tents; the inn stood to one side, the smithy to the other, and half a dozen shops ahead. A plank-paved street led up the hill from the square to the baron's house—not big enough to be called a palace, nor fortified enough to be called a castle, it was still the grandest building in town. Garander headed directly for it.

A bored-looking guardsman stood by the door, and Garander greeted him. "I am Garander Grondar's son," he said, "and I've come to see Lord Dakkar's magicians, to see if they can identify a piece of magic."

The guard perked up. "Magic?" he said. "What kind of magic?"

"I don't know," Garander said. "My sister found it on our farm, northeast of Ezval."

"Well, what is it?"

"It's…it's an object, about this big." He held out his hands to indicate the thing's size. "It glows."

The guard cocked his head, frowning. "What else does it do?"

Garander blinked. "Nothing, so far as we know. We were hoping the magicians could tell us."

"You have it with you?" The soldier held out a hand.

Garander hesitated. "No offense, sir, but I came to find a magician, not a soldier."

The guard lowered his hand. "Let me see it, and I'll fetch Azlia, Lord Dakkar's court wizard."

"Why do you want to see it?"

"Because I need to make sure it's not dangerous."

"You can tell that from looking at it? Did the magicians train you?"

The guard glared at him. "Just let me see it, all right?"

Reluctantly, Garander unslung his pack. He pulled out the leather bag, unwrapped the box and opened it, lifted out the inner pouch, and opened it to show the guardsman the thing inside. The soldier peered into the pouch, eyes wide.

"It *does* glow," he said. "Looks like sorcery."

"Is it dangerous?"

"*I* don't know; I just wanted to see it." He turned his head for a better angle.

Annoyed, Garander closed the pouch. "You said you would fetch a wizard?"

Equally annoyed, the guard said, "Right. Wait here." Without waiting for Garander to reply, he turned, opened the door, and vanished inside, closing the door behind him.

Garander stood by the step, unsure what he should do. He was not particularly inclined to pack the magical object away again, since he hoped to be bringing it out for inspection soon, but he felt foolish standing there holding the pouch. He lowered it and pulled the drawstring tight, but kept it in his hand as he closed the box and returned the box and the outer bag to his pack. Then he looked around.

There were a few townspeople in sight, going about their business; some of them glanced in his direction every so often, but no one stared or pointed or tried to get his attention. Garander shifted uncomfortably. He was not used to being around strangers.

Then the baron's door swung open again, and the guard reappeared, beckoning. "This way," he said.

Garander followed him into the house, and then stopped, stunned, to stare at his surroundings. He was in a large room, and he had never seen such opulence. The floor was not earth, nor wooden plank, but polished stone in black and white squares. The walls and ceiling were all smooth plaster painted gleaming white, without a single exposed beam anywhere, and no fewer than five large tapestries were on display, hanging on three of the four walls. Half a dozen gilt-edged little tables of dark polished wood stood scattered about, and two of them held grand vases finished in bright enamel and mother-of-pearl. The sconces on the walls held gleaming copper-bottomed oil lamps with glass chimneys so clear as to be almost invisible, though of course at midday they were not lit.

"This way," the guard repeated, and Garander followed him down a wood-paneled passage to a small sitting room where a woman sat waiting. She was small and slender, with long black hair—not quite his mother's age, Garander thought. She wore a blue velvet gown embroidered with gold, and a brimless blue velvet cap that curled back to a sort of point. A silver dagger gleamed on her belt.

A pointed hat, a silver dagger… "You're a wizard?" Garander asked.

"Azlia the Wizard," she replied. "And you are…?"

"Garander Grondar's son," Garander said, with an awkward bow.

"Landin tells me you have something you want me to see?"

"Oh," Garander said, embarrassed. He held out the pouch, and pulled it open.

Azlia leaned forward, reached into the pouch, and pulled out the object. Her eyes widened. "Northern sorcery," she said. "Where did you find it?"

"My sister found it," Garander said. "On our farm, near Ezval."

"Were there any other talismans with it?" the wizard asked, turning the object over in her hands.

"No," Garander said. "Ishta said it was under a pile of dead leaves." He cleared his throat. "Did you say *Northern* sorcery?"

"I did," Azlia replied, holding the thing up to catch the light from the room's only window.

"But…the war's been over for twenty years, and it looks almost new."

She turned and smiled at him. "Oh, twenty years is nothing to a Northern sorcerer. We've found talismans a century old that look as if they were conjured up yesterday. In a pile of leaves, you said?"

"That's what Ishta told me."

"Then someone probably just dropped it there during the final retreat." She looked down at the glowing thing in her hand. "I wonder what it's for?"

"We were hoping you could tell us that," Garander said.

Azlia shook her head. "Not I," she said. "You need a sorcerer." She looked past Garander to address the guard. "Landin, would you please go tell Sammel we need his services at his earliest convenience?"

The guard nodded, then turned and vanished, leaving Garander alone with the wizard. Garander looked around uneasily.

Azlia noticed. "Calm down," she said. "I'm not going to turn you into a worm or anything."

"No, of course not," Garander said. "It's just…I'm just a farmer. I'm not used to magic, or to places like this." He gestured at their surroundings.

"I understand," she said. "I suppose you've lived your entire life on your farm?"

"Yes, of course," Garander said. "Where else would I go?"

She smiled wryly. "Wherever you want," she said. "You know, during the war people moved around more, fleeing from the fighting, or following the troops. Now it seems everyone wants to stay on their own little piece of ground and never go anywhere."

"Well, farmers can't exactly wander around like tinkers or witches," Garander said. "The land doesn't go anywhere, so neither do we."

"Well, if you're satisfied with that, who am I to argue?" She smiled. "You walked here from Ezval?"

"Yes."

"Then please, sit down! You must be tired."

Reluctantly, Garander took a seat two chairs away from the wizard.

"How old are you?" Azlia asked, looking up from Ishta's find.

"Eighteen," Garander said. He was unsure why the wizard wanted to know, but he didn't dare refuse her.

"You said your sister found this thing?"

"That's right."

"How old is she?"

"Almost eleven."

"Ah." She nodded. "Is that why you're here, and she isn't? She's too young to make the trip?"

"Yes. Father said he couldn't spare both of us."

"Who else is in your family?"

"Our mother, and our sister Shella."

"Three children? No aunts, uncles, or grandparents?"

Garander shook his head. "Our parents came here after the war, and the rest of the family stayed in Ethshar."

"Any magicians in the family?"

The question astonished Garander. "No!"

"You needn't sound so shocked," Azlia said with an amused smile. "Magicians are just people—we have families and friends like anyone else. I have four brothers, and my father's a tanner; I didn't spring full-grown from some spell."

"Oh," Garander said, trying to absorb this. He had never thought of magicians having families. It didn't fit his mental image of a wizard. They sat silently for a few seconds while Garander considered the idea of witches and theurgists being people, with parents and siblings, and Azlia studied the glowing talisman. Then she looked up, and Garander realized he could hear approaching footsteps.

"That will be Sammel," Azlia said. "He's quite knowledgeable about Northern sorcery. Perhaps he'll be able to tell you what this thing is for."

"I hope so," Garander said. By this point, though, what he really hoped for was that whatever was going to happen would happen quickly, so he could go home, away from this strange place and these strange people.

Sammel, Garander discovered, was stocky and white-haired, his face worn and wrinkled, and his left hand was missing two fingers. He was wearing a thigh-length leather vest over a dirty white tunic and well-worn black breeches. He marched into the room, Landin on his heels, then stopped dead and glared at Garander. He did not look friendly. "You're the one who claims to have found a Northerner talisman?" he demanded.

"No," Garander said. "My sister found it. I just brought it here. And I don't know if it's a Northern talisman or not."

"Well, where is it?"

Garander pointed at Azlia, who held out the glowing object. Sammel strode over and snatched it from the wizard's hand, then studied the talisman intently, holding it up to catch the sunlight just as Azlia had. The hostility in his expression faded, to be replaced with intent interest.

"It's Northern, all right," he said. "See these glyphs in the crystal? That's Shaslan military cipher. This was part of some soldier's equipment."

Garander had no idea what a Shaslan military cipher might be, but apparently that was what those shifting shapes were. "What's it for?" he asked.

Sammel frowned. "Don't know," he said. "It's not standard issue. I've never seen one like this."

"Is it dangerous?" Azlia asked.

"Sorcery is almost always dangerous," Sammel said, studying the object. "But I don't think it's a weapon, and I doubt it's poisonous. I'll check. Wait here." Then he turned and marched out, taking the talisman with him.

Landin and Azlia stayed, though. Garander turned to them and asked, "How long will he be?"

Azlia turned up both palms, meaning she didn't know. Landin said, "It depends. It could be quite some time, though—would you like something to eat while you wait?"

Garander glanced at Azlia before admitting, "I'd love something to eat." It had been a long, hungry walk from the family farm, and his bread and water had had time to settle, leaving room for more.

CHAPTER THREE

Garander ate the generous lunch Azlia and Landin provided, surprised to be served good sliced ham when he was a mere guest and there was no particular cause for celebration. The small beer they provided was pleasantly frothy, and tastier than the stuff his mother brewed. Sammel had still not returned by the meal's end.

After lunch Landin returned to his duties at the front door, and Garander waited through the afternoon in the sitting room, chatting with the wizard, but growing ever more concerned, casting ever more frequent glances at the door. Still there was no word from the sorcerer.

The lamps were lit, and a page came to invite Azlia to join the baron at supper, and Sammel had yet to reappear.

"Would you care to dine with us?" Azlia asked, as she rose to follow the page.

"With the baron?" Garander asked, shocked. "No, I couldn't."

Azlia looked as if she was about to argue, but then paused, and Garander realized she could see on his face his terror at the idea of dining with Lord Dakkar. He tried, belatedly and unsuccessfully, to hide his fear, but he knew she was not fooled. "Shall I have something sent back to you, then?" she asked.

"No, I'll be fine," Garander said. "I have bread."

Azlia hesitated, then turned up an empty palm and followed the page out the door.

Garander sat silently for several minutes, watching the daylight outside the window fade, and wondering how he had wound up in this strange and awkward position, sitting alone in the baron's house, awaiting the return of his sister's find. Finally he let out a sigh and unwrapped his remaining bread.

He had finished every last crumb, and the sky outside the window was thoroughly black and speckled with stars, when the sitting room door finally opened again and startled him out of a doze. He jerked upright to see Azlia and Sammel entering the room. He rose to meet them.

"Garander," Azlia said. "I'm sorry we've kept you waiting." She held out a small bundle, a napkin wrapped around something, and for a moment Garander thought she was returning Ishta's discovery. When he accepted it, though, he found that the napkin held an apple and a wedge of hard cheese.

"Thank you," he said, but he looked past Azlia at Sammel.

The sorcerer gazed back calmly and said nothing. His hands were folded across his belly, and if he had Ishta's talisman anywhere, Garander could not see it. That was worrisome. "What about the thing my sister found?" Garander asked.

"Ah," Sammel said. "You will be glad to know that it is not poisonous. No one in your family will sicken from handling it."

"Yes, but what *is* it?"

"I'm afraid we still don't know," Sammel admitted. "I have spent the entire day testing and analyzing it, with only very limited success. It does not appear to be a weapon, nor is it obviously dangerous in any other way. My best guess is that it is intended to communicate with its user, but whether it relays messages from somewhere else, or answers questions, or warns of impending danger, or something else, I have been unable to determine. It does not appear to be working at present, but whether that's because it's damaged, or because it can tell we are not its rightful owners, or because it simply has nothing to say, I don't know."

Garander absorbed this, then said, "So it's harmless, and useless?"

"So it appears, yes."

That was a relief. Garander held out a hand. "May I have it back, then? My sister is waiting for its return."

Azlia and Sammel exchanged glances. "Garander—" Azlia began.

"The baron took it," Sammel said, interrupting her. "He's keeping it for himself."

Garander's mouth fell open. "But it's *Ishta's*!" he said.

"Not anymore," Sammel replied.

"But that's…that's…"

"Consider it a tax," Azlia said, as Garander groped for words. "I think we can see to it that your family will be credited with a year's taxes."

A year's taxes, as Garander well knew from his father's complaints, came to six copper bits or the equivalent in grain. Garander knew nothing about magic, but he was fairly sure a Northern talisman would be worth many times that amount—and besides, the thing wasn't Grondar's to give away, it was Ishta's.

"That's not right," he said.

Azlia turned up her empty hands. "It's Lord Dakkar's will," she said.

"He's just *taking* it?"

"He's the baron. He has the right."

"What am I supposed to tell Ishta?"

"She's just a little girl," Sammel said. "Tell her whatever you like; you aren't getting the talisman back."

Azlia threw her fellow magician an angry glance, then told Garander, "I'm sorry. There's nothing we can do."

Garander stared at the magicians in helpless anger for a moment, then fell wordlessly back into his chair.

"Do you have anywhere to sleep tonight?" Azlia asked. "It's clearly much too late for you to go home."

He shook his head silently.

"I'll get you a bed at the inn for tonight, then," she said. "Come, I'll take you there." She held out a hand.

Garander accepted her hand and allowed himself to be led out of the sitting room, out of the baron's house, and down the hill to the inn by the town gate. He stood in miserable silence as the wizard bargained with the innkeeper.

What would he tell Ishta when he got home? Her discovery was gone, and they still didn't even know what it was! She would be furious. Not only that, he had come to visit Varag, he had seen the baron's house and met two magicians, and Ishta, the one who wanted to get away from the farm and see the World, had stayed home and seen none of it. She would be jealous, and angry about that, as well—and with good reason!

But he said none of this aloud. It wasn't any of the innkeeper's business, and Azlia had already made plain through her silence that she was not going to help him get Ishta's talisman back. She said nothing about the talisman when she bade him good night and left.

He spent the night curled back to back with a wool merchant in one of the inn's cheapest beds—apparently the wizard's generosity had not extended to anything better. He did not sleep well, and at dawn he rose, careful to not wake the merchant, resolved to do what he could on his sister's behalf. He gathered his things, brushed off his clothes, waved farewell to the innkeeper, and slipped out the front door into the morning mist.

He made his way back up the hill to the baron's house, moving slowly and uncertainly. He could not bring himself to simply walk home without making at least one more try to recover Ishta's magical device, but he had no clear idea of how he could convince the baron to return it. He had hoped some brilliant inspiration would strike, but none did.

The guard at the door was not anyone he had seen the day before; presumably this was the man who had the early shift. It took a moment before Garander could get up his nerve to tell him, "I need to speak to one of the magicians—Azlia or Sammel."

The guard looked him over from head to toe, then asked, "Are they expecting you?"

"No, but we spoke yesterday. They have something that...well, really, I suppose the baron has it, but I need it back."

"The *baron* has it? Lord Dakkar?"

"Yes. At least, that's what they told me."

"And what is this mysterious thing Lord Dakkar has?"

"It's a sorcerer's talisman, left from the war. My sister found it."

The guard frowned. "Are you a sorcerer, then? Or your sister?"

"No, we just *found* it. We don't know how to use it."

The man studied Garander for a moment, and was about to say something else, when the door behind him opened and Landin looked out.

"Who are you talking... Oh, Garander! What are you doing back here?"

"You know this man, sir?" the guard asked.

"Met him yesterday. Well, Garander?"

"I came to get Ishta's...the thing Ishta found. I hoped that Lord Dakkar might have tired of it, or thought better of keeping it."

Landin shook his head. "That won't happen, Garander. The baron is still asleep, and will be for another hour, but it doesn't matter. Lord Dakkar does not part with his acquisitions, most particularly magical ones. Go home. There's nothing you can do here; the baron won't give you back your talisman."

"But I...I really..." His voice trailed off as he saw the unyielding expressions on both guards' faces. "It's my sister's," he finished weakly.

"Not any more. Go home."

Reluctantly, Garander turned away, and went home. He trudged down the hill through the town, and out the city gate with his pack on his shoulder, ignoring the guard who leaned against the tower wall.

He had no reason to hurry now; in fact, the longer he could put off telling his sister what had become of her prize, the better. He also hoped that if he thought hard enough while walking he might eventually think of something to tell her other than admitting that the baron simply stole it. He devised wild tales about Northern sorcerers traveling through time from the past, or dragons with a taste for sorcery, but he knew none of them would do—they wouldn't fool Ishta for a moment, and he did not think he could bring himself to tell them in the first place.

He ate the last crumbs of his provisions and drained the last of his water before he had gone two leagues. He knew that would leave the remaining three leagues a hungry, thirsty, journey, but he was so disconsolate he simply didn't care.

He hadn't wanted to go to Varag in the first place, he told himself; it had been his father's idea. He hadn't wanted to take Ishta's magical toy away. He knew, though, that none of that would matter. He had taken the talisman to Varag and given it to the baron, and he was quite sure that Ishta wouldn't acknowledge *why* he had done it. It had been Garander who first said they should tell their father about the glowing thing, and that was quite enough for Ishta to blame him for everything that had happened since.

He wasn't even sure he would disagree with her. He plodded on, past farms and fences.

The sky was overcast, and a cool breeze blew against his back, but no rain fell, and the long walk kept him more than warm; he would definitely want to give his clothes a thorough washing once he got home.

He finally stepped into the family house an hour after noon, to be greeted by a worried mother who had wondered why he was gone so long and feared he had been kidnapped by bandits or eaten by a dragon, and an angry father who was certain he had dawdled intentionally, to enjoy his freedom and avoid his chores.

Shella the Younger was neither worried nor angry; her entire response to her brother's return was, "Oh, you're back."

And Ishta, as he had expected, was furious once she learned that her discovery had been confiscated. "It was *mine*," she said, once he had told the entire tale over dinner. "I found it! They had no *right* to keep it!"

"I know," Garander said miserably. "I'm sorry, Ishta."

"He's the baron," their mother said. "He can do what he pleases."

"It was Northern sorcery," their father agreed. "It was probably dangerous."

"The sorcerer said it *wasn't* dangerous," Garander objected. "Lord Dakkar took it anyway."

"If it was Northerner military equipment, it's tainted with evil," Grondar persisted. "It may not be explosive or poisonous, but it isn't anything I want in my house."

"It's too bad we couldn't *sell* it, though," their mother said. "We could use the money."

"We're getting a year's taxes, if that wizard can be trusted," her husband said. "That's good enough for me."

"But it was *mine*," Ishta repeated.

"So go find another one," her sister told her. "The woods are probably littered with them."

"The woods are *not* littered with them," Grondar said, with surprising forcefulness. "We never found any talismans when we were clearing this land. Besides, you know I don't want you girls going in the woods in any case. There may not be any Northern magic to worry about, but there still could be mizagars."

"Mizagars *are* Northern magic," his wife corrected him.

"They were *created* by Northern magic," Grondar argued. "That doesn't mean they're magic themselves."

"*I* think it does."

"That only shows…" Grondar stopped in mid-sentence, catching himself before he could say something he would regret.

Ishta ignored her parents and muttered to Garander, "This is all your fault." She kicked his shin under the table—not hard, just enough to demonstrate her anger.

"I'm really sorry, Ishta," Garander replied. He knew better than to try to argue, even though he didn't think it was *entirely* his fault. Or even mostly.

Enough of it was his fault that he was not going to try to convince Ishta of anything, though, at least not until she had gotten over her initial outrage.

By the end of the meal Ishta had subsided into sullen silence, her arms folded across her chest, no longer speaking to anyone. Her parents did not seem to notice—or perhaps, Garander thought, they were humoring her, pretending to be unaware of her distress. Sometimes, he knew, that was the best way to deal with this sort of thing. He could remember when Ishta was very young and prone to tantrums; back then, simply ignoring her outbursts had been the best way to cope with them, since what she had really wanted was attention.

This time, though, he thought that what she really wanted was justice, or at least an acknowledgment that an injustice had been done. Pretending nothing was wrong did not seem to him as if it ought to be the best approach, but their parents presumably knew what they were doing. They were the adults here, after all.

Then Shella distracted him, demanding descriptions of what the women in Varag wore, and Garander was kept busy trying to recall details he had hardly noticed in the first place. The only woman he had seen for more than a few moments had been the wizard Azlia, and he very much doubted that her garb was the height of fashion; even Shella admitted that magicians wore whatever they pleased, whether it was in style or not.

By the time Shella let him escape Ishta had gone to the room the two girls shared. Garander knew better than to intrude there; that was exclusively female territory.

He did not see her again that evening.

The next day Ishta refused to speak to Garander. In fact, it was three days before she once again acknowledged his existence in any way. Even then she said as little to him as possible, and ignored everything he said except for direct questions or requests. She was not much friendlier with their parents; only her sister, who had taken no part in the disposition of the Northern talisman, was treated with the usual consideration.

Garander did not press Ishta. He assumed she would come around in time, and things would return to normal. If she wanted another apology he was ready to provide one, but he was not going to force one on her. Besides, he had enough to keep him busy with preparations for winter.

He certainly hoped that Ishta was over her anger by the time the snows came; being cooped up in the house for days at a time was bad enough even when the whole family was getting along. Huddling around the hearth with an angry girl, ready to find fault at every opportunity, would be utterly miserable.

CHAPTER FOUR

The cold autumn rain and wind had swept most of the trees bare, and had covered the sodden ground beneath their branches in a slick brown mat of fallen leaves. A month and a sixnight had passed since Garander's return from Varag, and he and Ishta had reached a state of silent truce. She had tacitly acknowledged his apology, but was not yet ready to forgive him completely. She spoke to him only when necessary, telling him nothing unless he specifically asked.

For his part, he did not try to force the issue. He spoke to her as he always had, but made no complaint and took no offense if she said as little as possible in reply. He did not spy on her, or follow her around, or make any attempt to supervise her; he was her brother, not her parent. It was pure accident that he happened to be coming around the corner of the barn just as she slipped into the woods.

"Oh, death," he muttered to himself.

He wasn't really surprised. After all, Ishta had been sneaking off into the woods for years, even when she was getting along with everyone; when she was angry with her family, she had all the more reason to disobey. She was probably hoping to find more Northern sorcery.

He didn't think she had seen him; she had been looking into the woods, not back toward the barn. He hesitated, trying to decide what to do. If he did nothing, just let her go, and something went wrong, if she got lost or hurt, he would be responsible *and* their father would be furious. The odds were that she would be fine, but the risk was more than he wanted to take.

But if he tried to stop her, that would undo all the peacemaking he had managed since he got home from Varag.

Besides, he was curious. Where was she going in such damp, dismal weather? He stuck the shears he had been carrying in his belt, and turned to follow his sister into the gloom of the forest.

The wet leaves underfoot were slippery and required caution, but they did not rustle or crunch like dry leaves; even though he was just a farmer, untrained in any sort of wilderness skills, he was able to move almost silently through the woods. He was also able to follow Ishta's trail readily, by seeing where her feet had flattened the leaves.

She was not wandering randomly; she was walking in a straight line, or as near to a straight line as was possible among the trees, into the forest. Garander thought she clearly knew where she was going. That worried him, though he could not say why. He quickened his pace, and before long he spotted Ishta's green jacket moving through the woods ahead of him.

She didn't look back, didn't see him; all her attention seemed to be focused forward. Then she raised an arm and called, "*Hai!*" For a moment Garander thought she had spotted him, but she had still not turned her head, or slowed her own steps. Then he saw movement ahead of her, something dark and quick, and he stopped walking, slipping quickly behind a tree and peering out to see what his sister was up to.

Then there was a man there, standing in front of Ishta. Garander had not quite seen him arrive, but he was definitely there.

Garander did not recognize him. He was still fifty yards away, but even at that distance Garander was fairly certain this man was a stranger. He did not dress or move like anyone Garander had ever seen before.

He was tall and slender, and dressed entirely in black. His tunic was cut tight and short; if he had followed tradition and set the length for life at the distance from shoulder to knee when he was twelve, this man had clearly been a small child, but made up for it later. His black leather breeches were also cut tight, and tucked into his boot-tops.

That was unusual, but the *really* strange part, the part that immediately let Garander know that something out of the ordinary was happening, was that he wore a round black helmet that gleamed like glass even in the shadowy woods. It covered his head from just above his eyebrows to the nape of his neck, hiding both ears. Garander had never seen anything remotely like it.

The stranger wore a pack on his back, held in place by wide straps over both shoulders rather than the more usual single shoulder-strap; these in turn connected to the widest belt Garander had ever seen, and the belt and both straps were adorned with various pouches and other attachments. There were several other unfamiliar objects slung here and there, protruding from his harness; they looked like tools of some sort, but Garander could not identify a single one of them with any degree of certainty.

And all of this equipage was black. Some was drab, some was glossy, but all was black.

The man's skin, on the other hand, was unusually pale, and his beard a lighter shade of brown than Garander had ever seen on a human face. Garander was unable to judge his age, except that he was a grown man and not yet going gray.

"Ishta," the stranger said. Then he looked directly at Garander and said, speaking loudly but with a thick, unfamiliar accent, "Did you know someone followed you?"

"What?" Ishta turned, staring into woods behind her. Garander did not think she had spotted him, but there was no point in pretending any further—the stranger was obviously not going to be fooled. Garander stepped out from behind the tree and moved a few steps toward Ishta and the stranger, to make conversation easier, but stopped when he was still several yards away so as not to seem threatening.

"Hello, Ishta," he said. "Would you like to introduce me to your friend?"

"Garander?" Ishta said, shocked. "You *spied* on me?"

"I followed you," Garander said. "I don't think it was spying, exactly."

"You were *spying* on me!"

Garander sighed. "Fine, I was spying on you. Are you going to introduce me, or not?" As he spoke he was keeping a careful eye on the stranger—and the stranger, he saw, was watching him just as warily. He had not, however, reached for a weapon, and almost certainly some of those mysterious tools were weapons; that was encouraging. It was still suspicious for a grown man to be meeting a girl of eleven in the woods without her family's knowledge or permission, though.

Ishta glared at him for a moment, then said, "Fine. Garander, this is my friend Tesk. Tesk, this is my brother Garander."

"I am pleased to meet you," the stranger said. Garander had never before heard anyone pronounce simple Ethsharitic so strangely.

"Yes," Garander said, rather than making a polite response that would be a lie. "Tesk, is it?"

The stranger smiled. "Ishta calls me Tesk. My real name is Tezhiskar Deralt aya Shatra Ad'n Chitir Shess Chitir."

Garander listened to this jumble of meaningless syllables and said, "Tesk it is, then."

"Yes," the stranger said. "Gorandaar?"

"Garander," Garander corrected him.

"Garander. Yes."

"Why are you here?" Garander asked.

The stranger glanced at Ishta. "Here? Where do you mean?"

"In these woods. What are you doing here? Who are you?"

"I live here."

Garander looked around for a house, or shed, or lean-to, or tent, or even just a hole in the ground or a hollow tree. He saw none. "Where?" he asked.

"Anywhere," Tesk replied. "I do not have a shelter. I sleep in any tree that is handy."

"In a tree?"

"Yes."

"Any tree?" Garandar was trying to make sense of this bizarre claim.

The stranger did something with his shoulders. "One that is strong enough to hold me, with branches to climb," he replied. "That one, for example." He pointed to a nearby oak.

Garander wanted to be sure he understood this. "So you don't have a home?"

"I do not."

Even if that was true—and Garander was not yet convinced—it left the stranger's origins a mystery. "Where did you *come* from, then?" he asked.

"I do not know. I do not remember. I have always lived in the forest."

Garander frowned. "I don't believe that. You must have come from *somewhere*."

"Garander, you're being rude," Ishta said.

"He merely wishes to protect his family," Tesk said. "That is good of him."

"He doesn't need to protect *me*! He stole my talisman!"

"*I* didn't steal it! The Baron of Varag did."

"Well, *you* gave it to the baron!"

"Father made me!"

"But you did it!"

Garander glared at her helplessly, then turned to Tesk. "I'm sorry," he said. "It's a family disagreement; we shouldn't be speaking of it here in front of you."

"I am not troubled," Tesk answered. "I am glad to hear human voices. I have been alone a very long time."

"You have? How long?"

Again, the stranger made that curious movement, lifting his shoulders and then dropping them. "I do not know," he said. "Several years."

"That's why he talks funny!" Ishta said.

"Is that right?" Garander asked.

The stranger hesitated.

"He's forgotten how to act normal!" Ishta insisted.

"Or he wasn't normal in the first place," Garander said. "It sounds to me as if he grew up speaking another language, and hasn't learned Ethsharitic very well."

The stranger smiled, a tight, humorless little smile, but he did not say anything; he neither confirmed nor denied Garander's guess.

"If you've lived alone in the woods for years," Garander asked, "how do you keep your clothes so neat? Why haven't they worn out?"

"They were very well made to begin with," Tesk said. "I am careful with them. I wash them and I repair them when necessary."

"Who made them for you?"

Tesk stared at him without blinking for several seconds before replying, "I do not remember."

"You don't know where you got that hat?"

"No. I have had it for as long as I can remember."

"Stop asking him silly questions!" Ishta said, stamping a foot. "He's my *friend*, not some stranger who's planning to steal our things."

"How do you know he isn't?" Garander asked.

"Because he hasn't done it yet! Garander, he's been living out here for *ages*, but he hasn't taken anything."

"So what does he *eat*?" Garander demanded of his sister.

She looked at Tesk, who said, "I catch animals for meat. I gather berries and nuts and apples when they are in season."

"You can live on that?"

"I do not need much. I do not exert myself needlessly."

Garander had no evidence that this was anything but the simple truth, and in any case it didn't really matter. He dropped the subject and got to the important point. "What do you want with my sister?"

Tesk looked surprised. "Nothing," he said. "We met by chance. We spoke. We enjoyed the conversation, so she has returned several times to speak again."

"That's *all*?"

"I have been alone a long time. Any human contact is welcome."

"Then why haven't you come out of the woods and found a place for yourself among other people?"

Tesk blinked. He took several seconds to consider before answering, "I do not know."

That surprised even Ishta. "You don't?" she asked.

"I had not thought about it."

"You can come home with us!" Ishta exclaimed.

"Hold on," Garander said, before Tesk responded. "I don't know about that. Father probably doesn't want us bringing strangers home."

"We could ask him."

"Please do not," Tesk said. "I am content as I am. I do not wish to intrude on your family."

"I don't—" Garander began.

"Are you sure?" Ishta interrupted.

"I am quite certain, Ishta. I do not wish to inconvenience anyone."

"If you're willing to work, it might not be an inconvenience," Garander suggested.

Tesk shook his head. "No. I am content living in the forest."

"I should tell our father you're here—" Garander began.

"No!" Ishta and Tesk exclaimed simultaneously.

"I do not wish to worry anyone," Tesk added. "He would be concerned about my presence."

"He'd want to drive Tesk away!" Ishta said.

Garander could not argue with either of these statements, but he said, "I don't like keeping things secret from him."

"*I* do!" Ishta said. "You saw what happened when you showed him that talisman! You still owe me for that, Garander, and I want you to promise not to tell Father about Tesk!"

Garander bit his lip as he glowered at his sister.

"You won't do anything stupid?" he asked her.

"No!"

"You'll tell me if Tesk does anything he shouldn't? If he steals anything, or tries to hurt anyone?"

"I promise."

"I will not steal anything or harm anyone," Tesk said. "But I understand why you do not take my word."

Garander glanced at him, then turned back to Ishta.

"And after this we're even? No more apologies or demands or anything?"

"If you keep this secret I'll forgive you for the talisman. I'll even owe you a favor!"

Garander smiled. "Then how can I refuse? But I *will* tell Father all about Tesk if you go missing, or anything."

Ishta glanced at Tesk, then nodded. "That's fair."

"Then we're all set." He turned back to the black-clad stranger. "So what's your native language? You don't sound as if you grew up with Ethsharitic."

"I have not spoken much," Tesk said. "For as long as I can remember, I have had no one to speak to."

That did not actually answer the question, Garander noticed. This Tesk apparently had some secrets of his own. "I'm told that up in Sardiron people mix their Ethsharitic with the old Northern tongue," he remarked.

Tesk looked puzzled. "Sardiron?"

"Sardiron of the Waters. It's north of here. The Council of Barons meets there."

Tesk looked politely blank. "Council of Barons?"

Garander sighed. "Some of the commanders of the old army don't accept the authority of the overlords of Ethshar," he said. "They each claimed a piece of land, and they call themselves barons, and they have a council where they meet to decide what to do."

"And what do the overlords of Ethshar say about this?" Tesk asked. Garander thought he heard a note of concern in the stranger's voice.

"They say the Northern taint in these lands has driven these men mad, and it's not worth fighting over, and they'll come to their senses in time. At least, that's what I've heard. I've never seen any of the overlords myself."

"No, of course not."

"Have *you* ever seen an overlord?" Ishta asked Tesk.

He smiled. "No, I have not. I live in the forest; what would one of the mighty rulers of Ethshar be doing in such a place?"

Garander smiled in return. Although he still had no idea what the man was doing here, he was starting to like Tesk.

They chatted for a few more minutes, and Garander grew steadily more comfortable with the stranger. His speech was awkward, but he seemed pleasant and calm. At last, though, Garander said, "We should be getting back, before our parents miss us. They'll want us to help with supper."

Ishta opened her mouth to protest, but Tesk said, "Yes. You should. But I will see you again?"

Garander nodded, and Ishta said, "Of course!"

They turned and headed back toward the farm. Garander glanced over his shoulder to see Tesk standing there, watching them go—but then the stranger moved, so fast that Garander thought he must be imagining it, and leapt for a tree branch. A moment later he had climbed up and vanished among the treetops.

Garander looked down at his sister, who had missed the whole thing. "How did you find him?" he asked.

"The first time? I don't know. He was crouching on the ground looking for something, and I asked what it was he wanted."

"What *was* it?"

"He wouldn't say. He said it wasn't important."

"When was that?"

She turned up an empty palm. "Maybe a month ago?"

"How often have you been out here, then?"

She gave Garander a disgusted look. "I've been playing in the woods since I was a baby!" she said.

That was true—and their parents had been trying to put an end to it ever since they first noticed. Warnings about dragons and bears and mizagars had not deterred her; neither had spankings, withheld meals, or anything else. Garander did not really understand why she was so determined; *he* had never been so obsessed with the forest. He kept hoping she would outgrow it.

"I meant, how often have you been meeting Tesk?"

"Oh. I don't know, maybe five or six times, counting today."

"So what do you know about him that he didn't mention today?"

She turned up her palm again. "I don't know," she said. "I think he's a halfwit, the way he talks, and he says he doesn't remember anything about his family, or where he grew up, or anything."

"He seems smart enough to me," Garander remarked.

"But he doesn't *know* anything!" Ishta said. "He *looks* smart, and everything, but he doesn't know anything!"

Garander considered that for a pace or two. He suspected that this Tesk knew plenty of things he did not admit to, and there was probably a reason for that. "I'm not sure it's safe, talking to him," he said. He spoke mildly; he did not want to antagonize his sister now that they were finally speaking to one another freely again.

"Oh, don't be silly," Ishta replied. "He's not a *bear*, or anything."

"No, he's not a bear, or a mizagar or a dragon, but he's a man, and men can be dangerous."

"He's a *nice* man," Ishta insisted. "He talks to me like a real person, and he's interested in everything, not just in farming like you and Father, or clothes like Shella, or food like Mother."

"I'm interested in other things!" Garander protested.

"Well, yeah," Ishta conceded. "But I was mad at you about my talisman."

"So what do you talk about?"

Ishta looked down at her feet as they walked. "Oh, trees, and sunlight, and dragons, and throwing rocks, and the neighbors, and, you know, stuff."

Garander nodded. "Sounds nice," he said.

"I told you he was," Ishta said, raising her head.

Garander did not argue—for one thing, they had reached the edge of the forest, and he did not want to answer any awkward questions should one of their parents overhear their conversation. Neither of them spoke again until they reached the house.

CHAPTER FIVE

That night Garander lay awake in his bed, staring at the dark beams overhead and thinking about what he had seen and heard.

Tesk *did* seem pleasant enough, but why was he there, in the woods? Why was he dressed all in black? Why did he move and speak so strangely?

That clothing was unlike anything Garander had ever seen before. So were the tools Tesk carried, whatever they were. Those weren't anything he found in the woods, and Garander didn't see how Tesk could have made them without a workshop of some sort. They were much too *finished* for anything made by hand out of materials found in the forest.

In fact, they looked downright magical.

Tesk did not admit to remembering any family, or any origins. If he was lying, then he was hiding something. If he was telling the truth, then something very strange had happened to him at some point. After all, he must have had parents once—parents, or a creator.

Tesk's tools, his clothing, his way of moving—they all smacked of magic. It was possible he had been *created* by magic. He might be something a magician had made in the shape of a man, or something a magician had *turned into* a man—a snake, perhaps, from the way he moved. Garander didn't know enough about magic to say with any certainty what sort of magician could have done such a thing; he thought a wizard probably could and a witch probably couldn't, but sorcerers and theurgists and demonologists, well, he just didn't know. Tesk could be a clay statue brought to life, a creature conjured out of thin air, a transformed beast...

Or a ghost. Maybe he could survive in the woods because he was already dead, and didn't know it. That would explain why he wasn't worried about finding enough food, and his missing memories fit with some of the ghost stories Garander had heard.

But he had certainly looked solid enough, even in bright daylight. That didn't seem very ghostly.

And of course, he might just be a human being, despite the strangeness.

But if he was human, why was he living in the forest? Why did he talk so oddly? Where did he get those clothes, and the things he carried? Why wouldn't he say where he had come from?

Garander tried to find some way of avoiding the obvious conclusion, but he couldn't. Tesk was living in territory that had belonged to the Northern Empire right up to the very end of the Great War, in an area where that talisman Ishta had found proved Northerners had been active. He spoke like someone whose first language was something very unlike Ethsharitic. He wouldn't say who he really was or where he was from.

However unlikely it seemed after so long, he might be a Northerner. He might have somehow survived the war, and hidden out in the forest ever since. Yes, the gods had blasted the Empire out of existence, and the armies of Ethshar had wiped out the remnants of the Northern military, but that didn't mean every single Northerner had died. Garander had never heard of any Northern survivors, but that didn't mean much; he was a farmer's son on the edge of civilization, not anyone who heard all the latest gossip. For all he knew, hordes of captured Northerners had been paraded through the streets of Sardiron, or sold into slavery in Ethshar.

But if Tesk was a Northerner, then he was evil, wasn't he? The entire Northern Empire had been evil—that was why Old Ethshar had fought against it for a thousand years, and why the gods finally destroyed it. That was why killing all the Northerners had been a good thing to do, when killing anyone else was a horrible crime—Northerners were evil by their very nature.

Tesk didn't seem evil.

But appearances could be deceiving; Garander knew that.

And there were exceptions to every rule; Garander knew *that*, too. Maybe Tesk really was a Northerner, but still wasn't evil; maybe that was why the gods had spared him when they destroyed the Empire. Maybe he was an exception.

Or maybe not. Maybe Tesk really *was* a demon-worshipping monster. And Garander's little sister had been meeting him in the woods and chatting with him.

But if he was a Northerner, then he must have been living out there in the wilderness for *twenty years*, ever since the war ended. Thinking about Tesk's appearance, Garander judged him to be in his thirties, which would mean he had been a child when the war ended—but then why did he have clothes that fit him as an adult?

Maybe he was older than he looked, or maybe he had salvaged the clothes somewhere later. A more important question was what the things he carried on his back were.

Ishta had found a Northern military talisman in the woods where Tesk lived. Maybe he wasn't just a Northerner; maybe he was a Northern *sorcerer*. Maybe that had been *his* talisman. Maybe those things on his back were all sorcery, and his magic kept him young.

That was a frightening thought.

Garander wondered whether he should tell someone about Tesk. He had promised not to, but if Tesk was a *Northern sorcerer*...

And if he was a harmless halfwit who had wandered off from a farm or camp, as Ishta thought, then what? In that case, telling others wouldn't accomplish anything except angering both Ishta and Tesk.

Or what if he really was a squirrel or a snake some passing wizard had enchanted in the waning days of the Great War? What good would it do to tell anyone?

Destroying Tesk's privacy and ruining his own relationship with his sister before he was *sure* that Tesk was dangerous did not appeal to Garander. He decided that he needed to find out more about Tesk, and more about Northerners, and see how well they matched up. Having reached this decision he tried to get to sleep, with only intermittent success.

At breakfast the following morning Garander was so obviously not at his best that his mother asked if he was feeling well.

"It's nothing," Garander mumbled.

Shella considered this, then turned away. Grondar eyed his son for a moment, then continued eating.

A moment later Garander asked, "Father? During the war, did you ever meet any Northerners?"

"*Meet* any? No. How could I meet any?"

"I thought there might have been prisoners you spoke to."

Grondar shook his head. "We never took any prisoners."

"Did you ever *see* any Northerners, then?"

Grondar snorted. "More than I wanted to."

"You did?"

"Of course. Mostly at a distance, though—I didn't see much close combat, thank the gods!"

"So you didn't get a good look at them?"

"Not when they were alive. I helped strip and burn some of the bodies a couple of times, and *that* certainly let me see more of them than I wanted."

"So they really were human?"

"Oh, is *that* what this is about? Yes, they were really human. Once the uniforms were off, you couldn't tell a dead Northerner from a dead Ethsharite."

Garander nodded.

"You were wondering how ordinary people could serve an evil empire?"

"Well, that," Garander said. "And I heard stories in Varag that made me wonder. One of the soldiers there said that Northerners didn't move like ordinary people—he said they were faster than we are, and their movements were…funny. Really smooth and graceful."

His father turned up an empty palm. "The ordinary Northerners were just people, and they moved like anybody else. But according to the stories, *shatra* moved the way that soldier said." Grondar shuddered. "I never saw any *shatra*, thank the gods!"

"What are *shatra*?" Ishta asked. Garander had not realized she was listening; he threw her a nervous glance, wondering whether she had realized why he was asking about Northerners.

Something about the word "*shatra*" was troubling him, but he was unsure what. He had heard it before, in stories about the war, but that wasn't it…

"*Shatra* were half man, half demon," Grondar told his younger daughter. "According to what our magicians told us, it took a demonologist and a sorcerer working together to turn a man into one, and no one on our side could do it. *Shatra* were stronger and faster than humans, and they could move so silently that no one could hear them coming; there were stories about sentries who turned around and found *shatra* had come up right beside them, or behind them, and they hadn't heard a thing. The stories said that *shatra* were inhumanly efficient, that they never wasted any motion, and could hold so still that they blended in with the background. They didn't have any scent—watchdogs couldn't smell them—and they could see in the dark. They dressed all in black, and they were all sorcerers, carrying dozens of powerful talismans, including a big wand that was some kind of magical weapon that could spit fire."

Garander listened to this description with mounting horror.

"I never saw one myself," Grondar continued. "I just heard stories. But they were definitely real, because we had orders about what to do if we saw one. We weren't supposed to try to fight it, even if it was just one of them against our entire regiment; our orders were to retreat and call for magicians and dragons to tackle it. One *shatra* was a match for at least a hundred Ethsharitic soldiers."

Garander looked at Ishta, who was staring at their father, fascinated.

This was horrible, even worse than Garander had feared. It sounded as if Ishta's friend in the forest was not just a Northerner, or even a Northern sorcerer, but a half-demon *shatra*. In fact, Garander realized what had been troubling him about the very word—hadn't it been a part of Tesk's *name*? Right in the middle of that string of syllables? That really didn't leave much room for doubt.

Surely, Garander thought, there must be some sort of mitigating element that would make this less of a disaster! "If they were so dangerous," he asked, "then how did we win the war?"

"Because there were only a few of them at any one time," Grondar replied. "Maybe a few hundred, at most. Maybe only a few dozen. For some reason the Northerners couldn't make very many of them." He turned up an empty palm. "Maybe the demons they used to make them didn't like it, or maybe there were only a few of the right kind of demon available. Besides, they weren't *impossible* to kill; a dragon had a pretty good chance against a *shatra*, at least a flying dragon, and a good wizard could usually find a spell that would get through even a *shatra*'s defenses. There was even supposed to be at least one magic sword powerful enough that an ordinary soldier could kill a *shatra* with it, though I sure wouldn't want to be the one to try it. A *shatra* might do a lot of damage, but sooner or later they all got stopped somehow. If they hadn't, we *wouldn't* have won the war!"

"I suppose the last ones were all killed by the gods," Garander said. "I mean, at the end of the war, didn't the gods kill all the demons?"

"You can't *kill* a demon," his father corrected him. "All you can do is send it back to the Nethervoid. And that's what the gods did—they cast all the demons out of the World, and I assume that would have included half-demons like the *shatra*. But I don't know for sure, and I don't know whether anyone really does."

With that, Ishta finally looked at Garander, and for a moment he feared his sister was going to say something stupid, such as telling Grondar that the *shatra hadn't* all been destroyed, but instead she held a knuckle to her lips, indicating that her brother should keep his mouth shut.

So she did understand what they had just been told, Garander thought. She *did* know now that her friend Tesk was a half-demon monster left from the Great War, one that had somehow survived the destruction of the Northern Empire.

The question was, what was she going to do about it?

"Are you done eating?" Grondar asked his son. "Because if you are, there are chores that need doing."

Garander looked down at his plate, then called to his mother, "Is there any more hash?"

By the time he had finished breakfast and completed his chores the morning was almost gone, and Garander was growing steadily more worried. What if Ishta went out into the woods to ask Tesk what it was like being a *shatra*? The Northerner might kill her rather than risk exposure.

At last, though, Garander was able to go looking for his sister, and he found her in the barn, petting the old gray tomcat that kept mice from overrunning the place. She looked up at his approach, but stayed seated on the barn floor.

The cat looked up as well, but stayed sprawled comfortably where he was.

"Ishta," Garander said, "I wanted to talk about what Father told us at breakfast."

Ishta turned her attention back to the cat. "What is there to talk about? Tesk is a *shatra*; so what?"

"So he's dangerous," Garander replied. "*Very* dangerous. You should stay away from him."

"Why?"

"Because he's a half-demon Northerner!"

"So? If he wanted to hurt me, he would have done it already."

That was an excellent point, but Garander said, "We don't know that. He's half-demon; we don't know how he thinks. Maybe he's waiting for something—waiting until he can get all of us, perhaps."

"He asked us not to tell anyone he's there. You offered to bring him in to meet the family, and he said no."

"Fine, maybe he's not trying to get all of us, but we *don't know*, Ishta! We don't know what he wants, or why he's there, or *anything*. We don't know whether we can believe a single word he says."

"Why would he bother lying?" Ishta's expression made it clear that she thought her brother was being silly.

"Because he's a *shatra*!" Garander exclaimed. "He's a Northerner! Even if that doesn't mean he's evil, what do you think Father would do if he found out? He fought in the war, remember? If Father found out there's a *shatra* in the woods he'd tell the baron, or maybe send a message to Lord Edaran if he doesn't think the baron can handle it. You heard what he said; they would bring dragons or wizards to kill any *shatra* they found."

"Where would Father find a dragon or a wizard?" Ishta demanded. "There aren't any around here!"

"That's why he'd tell the baron or the overlord! They have *lots* of wizards in Ethshar of the Sands."

"That's fifty leagues from here! Why would they care what's in *our* woods?"

"Because he's a *shatra*!"

"He's not bothering anyone! The war's been over for twenty years!"

"Honestly, Ishta, I don't think that matters. If anyone finds out he's there, they're going to send for help. They're going to send magicians to kill him. And Tesk is going to fight back, and a lot of people could get hurt."

She lifted the hand that had been stroking the cat and turned up an empty palm. "So we won't tell anyone he's there!"

"All right, we won't, but you *can't visit him* again. Someone might see you."

"Nobody has yet!"

"*I* have!"

Ishta hesitated. She obviously wanted to say that Garander didn't count, but at the same time, he *had* followed her without her knowledge, and if he could do it, so could Shella, or their father, or one of the neighbors.

"I'll be more careful," she said. "I didn't know it was important before. Now I do. And you can tell people things so they won't follow me."

"I don't want to lie for you," Garander protested.

"But you're my brother! And Tesk was nice to you!"

"Yes, he *was* nice to me, which is why I don't want us to get him in trouble."

"He'll worry if I don't come back."

Garander hesitated. He had not thought of that.

"All right," he conceded. "You can visit him again, so he won't worry, but you should tell him you won't be back."

Ishta didn't answer; she just looked silently stubborn.

"Come *on*, Ishta, can't you see how dangerous this is?"

"I'll be careful," she said.

"Talk to him about it, if you insist on visiting him," Garander suggested. "See what *he* thinks." Tesk was an adult; he would probably have the sense to realize how difficult his position would be if anyone else found out he was in the area.

"I guess I should," Ishta grudgingly acknowledged. "But I don't want to upset him. If he's really half-demon, upsetting him really *might* be dangerous."

Garander decided not to point out that this more or less contradicted Ishta's earlier assertions. "Good," he said. "Just be careful."

"I will," Ishta said, as she bent down to scratch the tomcat under his chin.

Garander hesitated, then turned away. Any more argument would just make her more stubborn, he was sure.

He really, *really* hoped she would be sensible and break off her contact with the *shatra*.

CHAPTER SIX

A sixnight later, while the two of them were feeding the chickens, Garander asked Ishta if she had spoken to Tesk.

"About what?" she asked.

"About him being a *shatra*," Garander said, struggling not to shout.

"Oh. No. We talked about when we were likely to get snow, and whether he needed a winter coat, and stuff like that."

"But you've talked to him since we found out he's a *shatra*?"

"Sure. Twice, I think."

"And you didn't *mention* it?"

"It didn't come up. I didn't want to bring it up out of nowhere, as if I'm accusing him of something!"

Garander flung the last handful of grain, upended the bucket, then turned and told his sister, "We are going to go talk to Tesk right now."

"What?"

"We are going to talk to him. Both of us. *Now*. He needs to know about this."

Ishta blinked uncertainly, then said, "All right."

Garander hung the bucket on its hook, pulled his jacket tighter, and marched out of the barn.

The weather was cold, the wind biting, but as yet there was no snow on the ground. A brief flurry had fallen two evenings before, but nothing had stuck. Garander's feet crunched on frozen leaves as he headed for the forest.

"Not that way," Ishta said, tugging at his sleeve.

Garander stopped.

"Father could see you," she said. "Come this way." She pointed to the north.

Garander followed as his sister led him around the barn, behind a woodshed, across a ditch he had forgotten was there, and then behind a big oak—a route that he realized kept them hidden from the house and most of the farm almost the entire way. Ishta had clearly given this matter some thought, and had not just been ducking into the forest from wherever she happened to be. Garander was not sure whether to be relieved at her sense, or worried by her deviousness.

Ishta moved through the woods with surprising stealth; she was obviously familiar with her surroundings. Here and there she paused and looked at something, usually a tree or stone, and after a few instances Garander realized that she was following signs of some sort, presumably markers Tesk had left so she would know where to find him.

He looked for the signs himself, and now that he knew there was something to find, he could usually locate them. Sometimes it would be a forked twig hooked over a branch, or a rolled-up leaf stuck in a crotch, or some other bit of debris that would not have looked at all out of place if Garander had not known there were markers; sometimes he could not find the marker at all. There was never anything as obvious as a mark carved into bark.

He did not have all that much time to look, though, because Ishta was hurrying deeper into the woods, not waiting for him. They were a good hundred yards or more into the wilderness, perhaps more, when Ishta waved—not to Garander, but to someone ahead.

A moment later Garander spotted Tesk, sitting comfortably in a tree, about eight feet off the ground and a hundred feet deeper in the forest. The *shatra* waved, but stayed where he was.

The two humans made their way through the wood until they were almost beneath the Northerner; then suddenly Tesk dropped off his perch, seeming to glide down the tree's trunk until he stood on the ground beside them.

"You have brought your brother," he said.

Ishta glanced at Garander, then nodded.

"I wanted to talk to you," Garander said.

"About what?" Tesk asked.

Now that the opportunity was here, Garander's nerve failed him; he could not bring himself to speak directly. "About the war," he said.

Tesk tilted his head slightly, and his eyes seemed to lock onto Garander. "The war?"

"The Great War, between Ethshar and the Northern Empire," Garander said. "You...you're old enough to remember it, aren't you?"

"Yes. I am older than I look, I think. I remember the war."

"You said you didn't remember anything before you lived in the woods."

Tesk moved his shoulders in that odd way of his. "Perhaps I did not tell the exact truth."

Garander was relieved that Tesk was admitting that—but then he immediately tensed again, as he knew the questions would not get any easier. "But you're admitting that now?"

"I think I must trust you, Garander and Ishta, if I am to remain in this area and continue to enjoy your company. If you meant me harm, you have had sufficient time to incur it."

For someone who spoke Ethsharitic as poorly as Tesk did, he certainly knew some fancy words, Garander thought. He ignored that and tried to get back to the point.

"Did you fight in the war?"

Tesk threw a quick glance at Ishta, who was not saying a word. "Yes. I fought," he agreed.

"I…you were a soldier?"

"I was a scout," Tesk said. "I patrolled the border between the armies, to warn my commanders if the enemy tried to move through the forest. I lived in the woods, unseen. When the war ended, I remained in the woods, unseen—I had nowhere else to go. My home was destroyed in the fighting when I was only a boy—my entire *village* was destroyed, and my family killed."

Ishta made a little whimpering noise at that. Garander refused to be distracted. "So you fought in the war," he said. "On which side?"

"The war has been over for many years, Garander. There are no sides now."

"But there *were* sides," Garander insisted. "Which side were *you* on?"

"The Northern Empire was destroyed. That side is gone."

"But you *were* a Northerner, weren't you? That's why you talk so strangely."

Tesk remained absolutely still for a moment before finally replying, "Yes. I was a Northerner."

Garander noticed that he said "*was*," not "am." Emboldened, he continued, "You weren't just an *ordinary* Northerner, were you?"

Tesk did not answer; he simply stared at Garander.

He was not reaching for a weapon. He was not fleeing. He was not attacking. He was not grabbing Ishta as a hostage. He was simply standing there, silently staring at Garander.

"You're a *shatra*," Garander said.

"I did not realize you knew that word," Tesk replied. "I had hoped you did not."

"Our father told us about *shatra*," Garander said. "They dressed all in black, as you do, and carried talismans on their back, as you do, and moved strangely, as you do."

Tesk nodded. "I am *shatra*," he said.

"You aren't human."

"Not entirely."

"Are you going to kill us because we know?" Ishta asked.

Tesk blinked, once, then looked down at her. "Why would I do that?" he asked.

"I don't think people around here are going to tolerate a *shatra* near them," Garander said.

Tesk raised his head and met Garander's gaze. "Are you going to tell them?" he asked.

"I...I don't know," Garander said.

"Why would you tell anyone?" Tesk asked calmly.

"Because...because you're dangerous. I think...I have a duty to warn my family, and my neighbors."

"I *could* be dangerous," Tesk admitted. "Very dangerous. But I have lived here for twenty years and I have not harmed anyone. Why would you choose to change a situation that has been comfortable for everyone for so long?"

"You've lived here for *twenty years*?" Ishta asked, startled.

Tesk looked down at her again. "I have. Or in this vicinity, at any rate."

"Then why didn't anyone see you until I found you?"

"I did not choose to be seen. And I admit that I have often retreated into the hills to the east. I have not always lived this close."

"But why did you let Ishta see you, then?" Garander asked. "Why did you talk to her? Even if she saw you, you could have slipped away— aren't you supposed to be able to run faster than a human?"

"I could have fled," Tesk agreed. "I did not want to. I am *tired* of living alone in the woods, with no human contact whatsoever. I knew a child could be no threat to me, and I hoped to develop contacts slowly. This is why I did not flee when *you* saw me—it was the next step."

"But you didn't want us to tell our parents."

"It was too soon. Your parents undoubtedly remember the war too well to accept me without preparation."

For a moment none of them spoke. Then Tesk said, "I had hoped that your people might have forgotten what *shatra* are."

Ishta and Garander exchanged glances. "I hadn't heard of them until Garander figured out that *you* were one," Ishta said.

"I'd only heard a few stories," Garander said. "I didn't know much about them until I asked Father."

"Has your father ever met *shatra*?"

"No," Garander replied. "He just heard stories. And he says that in the war, his company had orders for what to do if they ever *did* see one."

That seemed to catch Tesk's interest; for a moment his expression was much more animated than usual. "What were those orders?" he asked.

"They were to call in the nearest magician or dragon. Or both."

Tesk nodded. "Those were good orders."

"So you *were* evil?"

"No," Tesk said patiently. "I was *dangerous*. It is not the same thing."

"Everyone says that Northerners were evil!" Ishta said. "I thought maybe you weren't, and that's why you're still here."

"And during the war, *my* people said that *Ethsharites* were all evil."

"Ethsharites aren't evil!" Ishta protested. "Northerners were evil!"

"Which side exterminated the other?" Tesk asked. "Is not such indiscriminate slaughter evil?"

"It isn't evil to kill bad people!" Ishta insisted.

Tesk and Garander exchanged glances. Neither of them was quite so certain of Ishta's argument.

After a moment, Garander broke the silence. "If you're a *shatra*, you're part demon," he pointed out. "Doesn't that mean you're evil?"

Tesk took a moment to think before answering that one. "My people did not think demons were inherently evil," he said. "And it is the human part of me that controls me, in any case. It is the human part you are speaking with. My demon portions give me magical speed and strength and sight and hearing, and other magic, but my thoughts are still human. I do not *think* I am evil. I have done nothing to harm anyone since the war ended."

"How do we know you're telling the truth about that?"

Tesk did that odd shoulder movement again. "How do we *ever* know whether someone is lying?"

Garander had no good answer for that.

"I have even done some good," Tesk said. "There are mizagars in this area, and I have ensured they did not trouble anyone. I outrank them, so they obeyed when I told them to stay hidden and harm no one."

Garander blinked. He had no way to know whether the *shatra*'s claim had any truth to it or not. It *could* be true, for all Garander knew, or it could be a complete fabrication—but why would Tesk lie about *that*? It didn't seem like a sensible lie, and Tesk, however strange he was, did seem sensible.

"Why would you bother?" he asked.

"Because I do not wish anyone to be harmed," Tesk said. "I understand that the war is over, and my side lost; there is no point in inflicting any further damage. Mizagars do *not* understand this; they are little more than beasts. They will take orders from Northern officers, though, to the extent they understand those orders, and *shatra* are officers."

"How can they tell?" Ishta asked. "How would a mizagar know *I'm* not an officer?"

Tesk smiled. "You do not speak Shaslan. You do not carry a talisman of rank. You do not know the magic words that force a mizagar to obey you."

"A talisman of rank?" Garander asked.

"Yes," Tesk said. He held out a hand, and something gleamed red and gold on his wrist. "This is one. It glows when I wish it to, and is bound to me—it will not glow for anyone else. I have others."

"Do you have a lot of talismans?" Ishta asked, staring at the one he displayed.

Tesk smiled and withdrew his wrist. "Yes," he said.

"Do you know about the one I found? I mean, I told you about it, but do you know what it was for, or how it got there?"

"That was mine," Tesk said. "I discarded it. It relayed orders from my superiors—but my superiors are all long dead, so I had no further use for it. I thought it might be an entertaining toy for you, and left it where you might find it. I am sorry your baron took it for his own."

"He's not *my* baron!" Ishta said.

"Yes, he is," Garander told her. "Whether you like it or not."

"Hmph."

"Now what?" Tesk asked.

"What?" Garander said, startled.

"Now that you know what I am, and you have heard my account of myself, what will you do about it?"

Garander hesitated. He had not yet decided, and was unsure whether he would want to tell Tesk if he had. "What would you do if I told our father?" he asked. "Would you kill everybody?"

Tesk sighed. "No. The war is over, I do not want to harm anyone, and I am fast enough to escape any non-magical pursuit. If your father sought to destroy me, alone or with others, I would retreat into the hills where I would never be found. I would advise against this, however, because if I leave this area the mizagars may return. They obey my orders, but only for a limited time—two or three months, usually—and they move around, so that ones I have not instructed may wander into the area."

That was a reason to lie about the mizagars—to keep from being sent into lonely exile in the mountains. But that assumed he had not lied about wanting human company.

"There, you see?" Ishta said. "He won't hurt us!"

"So he says," Garander retorted. "We don't know he's telling us the truth."

"*I* think he is!"

"I think he probably is, too," Garander admitted, "but we can't be sure."

"You must do as you think best," Tesk said. "You should consider this, though—if I am not telling the truth, why am I here now, and not years ago? Perhaps when you were Ishta's age?"

"You could have been trapped somewhere, and only recently escaped," Garander said. "Maybe a wizard captured you during the war, and the spell he used on you has only just broken."

Tesk nodded. "That could be. But if I meant you harm, why are you still alive?"

"I don't..."

Then Tesk moved, so abruptly and so fast that Garander could hardly see him; he was little more than a dark blur, like a shadow among the trees, and then he was standing behind Garander's right shoulder, a knife at the youth's throat.

Then he was gone again, only to reappear a few feet away, where he ostentatiously sheathed his knife, sliding it slowly into a scabbard on his belt, deliberately making an audible scraping sound.

"You see why your father's orders were to call in magicians or dragons?" he said.

Garander swallowed, then nodded.

"And I have not yet shown you what the sorcery I carry can do."

Garander was about to say that that wouldn't be necessary when Ishta said excitedly, "Oh, can you show us?"

That seemed to catch Tesk off-guard, but he recovered quickly and smiled. "A small demonstration, perhaps," he said. He reached around and brought forward one of the black rods he carried on his back, then asked, "Would that stump make a satisfactory target?" He pointed.

The "stump," perhaps fifteen feet away, was the remains of a dead tree, seven or eight feet tall and about a foot and a half in diameter for most of its length. It was quite obviously hollow. Garander looked at Ishta.

She met his gaze and nodded.

"It'll do," Garander said.

Tesk said, "Observe." He ran his fingers along the rod in a quick pattern of short strokes, then pointed it at the dead tree.

To say that the hollow stump burst into flame did not, Garander thought, convey what he saw; the stump *exploded* into flame with a loud "thump," red and gold sparks showering in all directions. In an instant the entire thing was a column of fire.

"We do not want to draw attention," Tesk said. He waved the rod, and a sudden mist appeared; the flames quickly died away until only flickering red embers lingered on the greatly-reduced remains of the tree.

"*Hai, hai, hai!*" Ishta shrieked, clapping her hand. "That was wonderful!"

Garander nodded. "Impressive," he said.

"You do not want your father and his friends to seek me out," Tesk said. "Either I would flee, which would make it all a waste of time and might allow mizagars to harass your people, or they might catch me, and I would defend myself." He lifted the black rod. "Even if they win in the end, and kill me or capture me, some of them will be hurt or killed in the process. You see?"

"I see," Garander agreed. He looked at his sister. "I think I'm convinced," he said. "What about you, Ishta?"

"I was never going to tell anyone in the first place, Garander!"

"Then we are decided," Tesk said, "and I am pleased. I did not want to leave."

"May I try that black stick?" Ishta asked, pointing at the rod.

Tesk smiled. "No," he said. "It would not work for you. But I have other things I can show you."

Garander hesitated, then admitted, "I'd like to see them, too."

"Of course," Tesk said. He reached around and tucked the black rod back into place. "Let us find somewhere more private, away from the smoke of the stump, and I will show you."

Together, the three of them retreated deeper into the woods.

CHAPTER SEVEN

Just a sixnight after Ishta and Garander visited Tesk, the first real snowfall arrived. It began in the night, and Garander woke up to a dimly-lit world covered in white, with big fat flakes swirling outside the window.

At breakfast Grondar said, "The clouds are thinning. It should stop by noon, I'd say."

Garander nodded, and stuffed another chunk of bread in his mouth.

"You'll need to feed the livestock, of course, but anything else can wait until the snow stops."

"Yes, Father."

"May I play outside?" Ishta asked.

Their parents exchanged glances; Grondar turned up an empty palm. "Why not?" he said. "But stay close, in case the storm gets worse."

"You just said it was stopping!"

"Am I a wizard, then, to foresee the future? It *looks* to me as if it's stopping, but I could be wrong, so don't go far."

"Yes, Father."

"Shella, we can work on the mending," their mother said.

The elder daughter looked up from her plate. "Yes, Mother."

"Don't *you* want to play in the snow?" Garander asked her, teasing.

Shella shuddered. "I have no desire to be cold and wet, thank you," she replied.

Accordingly, once the table was cleared Ishta and Garander bundled up in their boots and winter coats, while Shella and their mother pulled out the mending bag and settled by the hearth. Garander was still filling a bucket with table scraps for the hogs when Ishta dashed out into the snow. He glanced after her, then continued with the task at hand.

It occurred to him that she might plan to pay Tesk a visit, to see what he thought of the snow; he hoped not. Still, it should be safe enough, since their parents were staying inside. Garander attended to his own business—seeing that the hogs and chickens were fed.

He was done with his rounds and was putting the unused chicken feed back in the bin before closing up the barn when he heard the house door slam. He thought at first it must be Ishta going in, which was unexpected—he had expected her to stay out for hours, enjoying the weather. In fact, he was mildly surprised he had not yet been hit by a snowball. He looked up.

A figure was standing at the door, and it was much too big to be Ishta. Startled, Garander peered through the snow, and realized that his father, Grondar, had just emerged, and was looking around the yard. He seemed to spot whatever he was after, and began trudging northward, past the barn.

Puzzled, Garander was about to call out when he heard Grondar shout, "Ishta!"

Garander turned and looked, noticing that the snow was coming down more thickly now, but he did not see his sister anywhere. "What's going on?" he called.

Grondar spotted him. "Oh, your mother wants Ishta for a fitting," he called. "She's cutting one of Shella's old tunics down for Ishta, and wants to get the size right."

"Oh," Garander answered.

"Do you know where she is?"

"I haven't seen her," Garander replied. "Do you want me to look?"

His father waved him off. "No, I'll do it. I've found her tracks here. You finish up your chores and go on in."

Garander hesitated. He was afraid Ishta's tracks would lead into the woods, but he could not think of any reason he could use to insist on being the one to follow her.

And then it was too late; his father was marching northward through the snow, his eyes fixed on Ishta's trail.

Garander latched the barn door, trying to decide what to do. He didn't *know* that Ishta had gone to see Tesk, but it seemed likely. Would her tracks still be clear enough to follow in the woods, where the ground was less even and the branches overhead caught some of the snow?

Yes, he decided, they would. And their father might not realize what Tesk was until it was too late; if he thought the *shatra* was an ordinary man bent on debauching his daughter, he might do something that would force Tesk to defend himself.

The possibility that Grondar would catch Tesk off-guard and kill or seriously injure him occurred to Garander, but he quickly dismissed it. Tesk was *shatra*, and Garander had seen a little of what he could do. It was their father, not Ishta's playmate, who was in danger.

Garander glanced at the house, but decided not to take the time to alert his mother or his other sister. What could he say that would be any use? Instead he turned and set out after his father.

Grondar's footsteps were plain in the fresh snow, and for that matter, Ishta's were still visible as small oval depressions, even though she had been gone almost an hour and the snow was still falling steadily. Garander hurried.

He could see his father perhaps a hundred feet ahead, beyond the barn, looping around the woodshed; that was the route Ishta used to slip into the woods unseen from the house. Muttering curses under his breath, Garander followed as quickly as he could. He considered shouting, asking Grondar to come back, but what could he say to convince him?

"Ishta!" Grondar called, and Garander heard the anger in his voice. He guessed that his father had seen Ishta's tracks going into the forest, where she was forbidden to venture. Garander struggled to pick up his pace.

The snow was getting heavier; Grondar's earlier prediction that it would end by noon seemed less and less likely every minute. Garander could scarcely see his father through the swirling white. The footsteps were still clear, though. Garander followed as swiftly as he could, north around the barn, past the woodshed, across the ditch, around the oak, and into the forest.

It was late morning, but the heavy clouds blocked the sun and the snow obscured everything; Garander was not sure just where he was going. The snow clinging to every branch and sticking in patches to the trunks distorted the trees and made it hard to recognize landmarks.

"Father!" he called, though he was unsure what he would say if Grondar called back. He could his father's coat, the shoulders white with snow, moving through the woods ahead.

And beyond, deeper in the forest, just barely visible through the snow, he saw two figures that he thought must be Ishta and Tesk huddled beneath an improvised shelter, a broad length of white fabric stretched between two sturdy branches somewhat above head level. Garander could not hear them—the snow muffled all sounds—but they appeared to be chatting amiably, untroubled by Grondar's approach.

Tesk must have detected his approach, though; he was *shatra*, with supernatural senses.

Even as Garander thought that, he saw Tesk look up, suddenly alert. Then he moved, with that strange, smooth speed, leaping out from under his shelter to grab a tree limb, then swinging himself upward. He seemed to not so much jump as *flow* from branch to branch and tree to tree, moving higher and farther away with every transfer. It should have looked absurd, a man jumping around in the trees, but it didn't; it looked graceful and terrifying.

Then he was gone, lost amid the snow-covered trees, and Grondar was bellowing, "Ishta! Who was that with you?"

Ishta started. She was still sitting under the improvised shelter; she did not seem to have absorbed yet what was happening. She looked up, trying to see where Tesk had gone, but it was far too late for that.

"Ishta!" Grondar repeated.

"Father!" Garander called.

Then Grondar was at the shelter, where he reached beneath the fabric and grabbed Ishta's arm, dragging her out into the snow. "Who *was* that?" he demanded. "What is this thing?" He turned his attention to the cloth.

Garander could not see his father's face, but he had the impression that Grondar was staring. As he watched, Grondar released Ishta's arm and stretched out a hand to tentatively touch the shelter. "What *is* this?" he asked.

Then Garander was finally able to catch up to Grondar. "Father," he said, "are you all right?"

Grondar turned, startled. "What are *you* doing here?" he asked. "I told you to go inside!"

"I thought you might want my help," Garander said, realizing even as he spoke how ridiculous that was. He quickly improvised, "In case Ishta was stuck up in a tree or something."

"What would she be doing in a tree? For that matter, what is she doing *here*? Who was that? How did he…how did he *do* that? What's this thing made of?"

"I don't know," Garander said. "Father, it's snowing awfully hard now; I think we should all be getting back."

"In a moment," he said. "Your sister has a few things to explain first. Ishta?"

Ishta had finally gathered her wits enough to answer, "Yes, Father?"

"What *is* this thing?" He pointed at the shelter. "How did it get here?"

Ishta turned up an empty palm. "I don't know, Father. It was here when I got here."

"And you've been sitting under it?"

"Yes, Father."

"Did you notice that it's *warm*? And dry? The snow isn't sticking to it. At all. It should be cold and wet and covered in snow, and it isn't."

"It isn't?" Ishta seemed genuinely surprised. She turned to look at the shelter. So did Garander, coming up beside their father. Ishta was not tall enough to reach it easily, but Garander was. He raised a hand and cautiously touched his fingers to the white cloth.

The fabric was indeed warm and dry.

"That's *magic*," Grondar said, feeling the cloth with the palm of his hand. "Wizardry, maybe."

"I don't..." Garander began; then he caught himself. "Maybe."

"So, Ishta," Grondar said, glowering at his daughter. "Who was that you were talking to? How did he jump like that?"

Ishta looked at Garander, but he was not offering any help with this; he shook his head very slightly, hoping his father wouldn't notice the movement.

She decided there was no point feigning ignorance. "He said his name was Tesk... I mean, Kelder of Tesk," Ishta said.

"Where's Tesk?" Grondar asked.

Ishta turned up a hand. "How should I know?"

Grondar frowned. He glanced at Garander. "I never heard of it," Garander said. "But I'm not very good with geography."

"Did you see the way he bounded up into the trees, and leapt from branch to branch?" Grondar demanded. "He didn't look human!"

"He looked human to *me*," Ishta said defensively.

"Where did you find him? Did you *know* he was out here?"

Ishta hesitated. "I found him right here, sitting under the cloth," she said.

"Did you know he was there? Did you come here looking for him?"

"I never saw the cloth before!" Ishta said.

"Did you ever see *him* before?"

Ishta looked to her brother again, but once again, no help was forthcoming. "I might have," she admitted.

"So you've been sneaking into the woods?"

"Father," Garander interrupted, hoping to distract Grondar before he could work up serious anger, "shouldn't we be getting in out of the snow? It's coming down pretty hard."

Grondar looked up. The sky overhead was solid gray, and largely hidden by swirling snow. Then he looked at the shelter again. "We'll take this with us," he said. He grabbed the edge of the fabric and tugged.

It stayed where it was. It flexed in his hand, and the branches it was draped on bent slightly, but the cloth stayed firmly attached to the wood, though Garander could not see any pins or cords or other attachments.

Grondar's eyes widened, and he pulled harder. The fabric still didn't yield. He reached over and grasped the edge right next to one of the tree limbs, and yanked at it.

The limb beneath the fabric bent, but the cloth remained solidly attached.

"I don't see any nails," Garander offered. "Maybe it's glued."

"Maybe it's more magic," Ishta said. "It's Tes…Kelder's; maybe it won't let anyone else move it."

Grondar looked up into the trees where Tesk had vanished. "Do you think he might come back for it?"

"Why would he?" Garander asked, hoping to discourage his father from staying out in the snow.

"If it's magic, it must be valuable," Grondar said. "He wouldn't just abandon it. He'll come back eventually. So if we wait here—"

"Father," Garander said, trying not to sound desperate, "if he wanted to talk to us, he wouldn't have run off in the first place—and if he *does* come back, he might bring help. If he's got a magic cloth like this, he might have magic weaponry, too, or magic to summon allies. Or he might be a magician himself. I really think we should just leave it and go home."

Grondar glared at the cloth. "Maybe we could break off the branches and take the whole thing with us."

"Father, if he's a magician, or even if he just has magical allies, do we really want to steal from him?"

Grondar hesitated. "If he has allies or weapons, what's to stop him from killing us all in our beds?"

"Common sense, Father. Why would he want to kill us? If he meant us harm, he could have come any time—why would he come now, in the snow, when he would leave tracks?"

"He didn't leave any tracks when he ran away."

"There aren't a hundred trees around our house to hide in; he'd leave tracks *there*."

"Not if he has the right magic. Maybe he can fly, or tunnel through the earth."

"Or poof, just appear! But why would he *want* to?"

"Why was he sitting out here in the snow, talking to your sister?" Grondar shouted. "Who is he?"

Garander flinched. "Can we talk about this at home, please? It's cold, and the snow is covering our tracks, and I don't want to get lost in the woods, and Mother's waiting."

Grondar took one last look eastward into the depths of the forest, then turned and said, "Fine. We'll go. But we *will* talk about this when we get home, Ishta, and I expect a good explanation!"

"Yes, Father," Ishta said in the scared-little-girl voice she used when she was trying to appease her parents. Garander was amazed that that still appeared to work. It didn't work on *him*, and hadn't for years; it just annoyed him. Their parents, however, seemed more susceptible.

Together, the three of them turned and began trudging back toward the family farm, leaving the miraculously warm and dry shelter where it was. The tracks that Garander and his father had left were still fairly clear, despite the heavy snowfall, so there was no immediate danger of losing their way.

They had gone perhaps a hundred feet when Grondar paused for a few seconds to look back at the abandoned shelter, allowing Ishta and Garander to get a few yards ahead of him. That gave Garander a chance to lean over and whisper, "You idiot! What were you doing out here in this storm?"

"I wanted to be sure Tesk was all right!" Ishta whispered back.

"He looked fine to *me*, the way he went jumping through the trees. Why didn't he see Father coming and get away sooner, before he was spotted?"

"He thought it was *you*," Ishta said. "He said it was you. With the snow and everything, *I* thought it was you, too—you're more like Father than you think. I didn't know it was him until he started shouting."

Garander was not sure what to make of that. He asked, "So why did you stay out here once you knew he was safe?"

"We were talking!"

"You shouldn't have been! Not when you'd left tracks."

"*I* didn't know anyone was going to come looking for me! Why *did* he, anyway?"

"Mother wanted you for a fitting; she's cutting down one of Shella's dresses for you."

Grondar's voice interrupted. "What are you two whispering about?"

Garander looked back to see their father catching up. "Ishta was wondering why you were looking for her. I told her Mother wanted her for a fitting."

"That's right, she does! I'd almost forgotten about that; she's going to be annoyed it took this long to fetch you."

"Then I'll hurry!" Ishta broke into a run.

Garander ran after her. Grondar, he noticed, did not; their father was not as young and energetic as they were.

That was fine with him. That would give them another chance to talk.

The two burst out of the woods into the farmyard, leaped across the snow-filled ditch, and veered leftward around the woodshed. Beside the barn Ishta abruptly slowed, looking back to be sure they were out of their father's sight, and ahead to see that no one had come out of the house to see what was taking so long.

Garander came up beside her, and matched her pace.

"Ishta!" he said. "Maybe we should tell them the truth."

She glared at him. "Are you *crazy*?"

"He saw that cloth! He knows that's magic. You think he's going to believe you went into the woods in the snow for no reason, and just happened to find a mysterious stranger sitting under a magic tent?"

"It's not a tent."

"Well, whatever it is, that's not the point! The point is that he won't believe it if you say that's what happened."

"All right, fine, but we don't need to tell them he's *shatra*, do we? Can't we just say he's a magician?"

Garander hesitated.

"I mean, how would *we* know anything about *shatra*?" Ishta said.

"Because Father *told* us about them, silly! You think he won't remember that?"

"Maybe he won't!"

"You're being ridiculous."

"Well, you...you...you're right." She sighed. "But I'm not going to say the word until someone else does."

Garander glanced back to see Grondar rounding the bushes. "Fair enough," he said. "Now, come on, let's get inside where it's warm."

Together, brother and sister trotted toward the house.

CHAPTER EIGHT

Once inside, there was a brief dispute over priorities.

"Ah, there you are! Get over here and try on this dress," their mother said, looking up from a jumble of green fabric.

"There's something I need to discuss with these two," their father answered.

"It can wait," the elder Shella said, raising a needle and thread. "I want to get this done, so we can eat lunch!"

"I think—"

"You can talk while we're working. Ishta, put it on!"

Ishta threw her father a quick glance, then began taking off her coat. She didn't hurry.

Grondar fumed while his children removed coats, scarves, gloves, and boots, and put them all neatly away; he rushed to strip off his own outerwear, and stood waiting as Ishta ducked into the room she shared with her sister and changed into the green dress.

Garander, once he had his own gear put away, looked out a window. The snow was still coming down; the overcast so thick it was hard to believe it was midday. Quite aside from delaying any discussions of Tesk, he was glad to be safely inside; this snowfall was turning into a far worse storm than any of them had anticipated, worse than it had any right to be so early in the season.

He hoped the *shatra* would be all right, out there in the snow—but Tesk had lived alone in the wilderness for twenty years; he must have survived worse storms than this. And he could safely retrieve that magical cloth, now that Ishta and her family had gone.

That cloth had been a surprise; Garander had never seen anything like it. His father had guessed it was wizardry, but from everything he knew, Garander thought it must be sorcery—all of Tesk's equipment appeared to be sorcerous, not wizardly in nature.

Then Ishta emerged, the green dress hanging loosely on her. She stepped up on the stool as her mother approached with a mouthful of pins.

"Now," Grondar demanded, "how did you meet this Kelder of Tesk?"

Ishta glanced at Garander, then said, "I met him in the forest."

Her mother had been pinching in the fabric under Ishta's left arm; now she held that with one hand, took the pins from her mouth with the other, and asked, "Who's Kelder of Tesk?"

"Someone our daughter has been meeting in the woods."

"A boy?"

"A grown man, from what I saw of him," Grondar replied. "Not that I got a good look."

Ishta saw the stricken look on her mother's face and said, "It's nothing like that! We just talked. He never touched me."

"You'll swear to that?" Grondar asked.

"Of course I will! He didn't, I swear by all the gods!"

"Then why was he talking to you at all?"

"He was lonely, I guess."

"All right, then I'll ask again—how did you meet him?"

"I...I was wandering in the woods, and there he was, sitting on a branch."

"What were you doing in the woods?"

"Getting out of the sun. I knew if I went in the house Mother would find something for me to do, and if I went in the barn you would, and besides, I liked being outside in the fresh air. It's nice in the woods."

Grondar frowned. "Out of the sun? When was this?"

"A couple of months ago."

"Months?"

Ishta nodded.

"You're forbidden to go into the woods!"

"I know."

"And you went anyway."

She nodded again.

"And you've...all right, so you met this Kelder of Tesk in the forest, and you talked to him?"

"Yes."

"What did you talk to him about?"

Ishta turned up an empty palm, which tugged at the fold her mother was pinning. "How the trees grow, and what colors the leaves were, and what animals lived in the trees. Things like that."

"Did you ask him where he was *from*, and what he was doing in the woods?"

"He wouldn't tell me."

"You did ask?"

She nodded again.

"You didn't think that was *suspicious*?"

"I like him!"

Grondar growled. "Of course. So you met him in the woods, and you talked, and then what?"

"Then I went home for supper."

"And what did *he* do?"

"*I* don't know."

"But you saw him again?"

"Yes."

"How often?"

Ishta looked decidedly uncomfortable. "A few times."

"Every day?"

"No!" She hesitated. "Maybe once or twice a sixnight." Garander thought it had probably been more often than that, especially before they had realized he was *shatra*, but he didn't say anything.

"How did you know where to find him?"

"I didn't always; sometimes *he'd* find *me*. Sometimes he'd mark a trail for me, though."

"But he was always out there somewhere?"

"I guess so."

"Where does he *live*?" Ishta's mother asked, as she tugged at a seam.

"In the woods, he says."

Her mother glanced up at her. "He has a cabin somewhere?""

"I don't think so," Ishta said. "I think he sleeps in the trees, on the branches."

"Blood and death, why would he do *that*?" Grondar asked.

Ishta turned up a palm.

Grondar frowned again, and said, "From what I saw just now, he dresses strangely."

Ishta nodded.

"All in black."

She nodded again.

"Does he always dress like that, or was it because of the snow?"

"He always does."

Ishta's mother had finished pinning one side, and transferred her attention to the other.

"It looked like he was carrying some things."

"He has a pack, and he carries stuff on his back," Ishta said. "He doesn't have a home, so I guess he carries everything with him."

"So he doesn't have a home, but he does have belongings."

Ishta nodded.

"Like that magical cloth."

Ishta's mother looked at her husband, startled. Her elder daughter said, "Magic cloth?"

"A sort of tent," Grondar said. "It stayed warm and dry even in the snow." He met Ishta's eyes. "That was in his pack?"

"I guess," Ishta said. "I never saw it before today, and he already had it hung in the tree when I got there." She hesitated, and then added, "I didn't know he had it. I went out there to make sure he was all right—since he doesn't have a home to go to, I thought the snow might make things hard for him."

"But he had his magic."

She nodded again.

"Did you *know* he was a magician?"

Ishta glanced at Garander, then nodded. "I knew he has magic stuff."

"What *kind* of a magician is he? A wizard?"

Ishta shook her head. "He's not a wizard."

"A witch, then? Some of them like to wear black."

"No."

"Ishta, tell me what kind of a magician he is. Because the only other kind *I* know of that usually wears black is demonologists…"

"No! He's not a demonologist, Father. He's a sorcerer."

Garander grimaced, glad that the others were all too focused on Ishta to pay any attention to him. He knew, and he thought Ishta knew, that Tesk was not a sorcerer in the usual sense. He was something much worse.

"Ah." Grondar leaned back against the wall and crossed his arms over his chest as he considered his youngest child. "A sorcerer. Who lives in the woods, with no home to go to. Who talks to children, but runs away at the sight of an adult."

"Yes, Father."

"Do you know how ridiculous that sounds?"

"If I were making up a story, Father, I'd do a better job of it." Ishta looked insulted. "I'm telling the truth."

Grondar considered that for a moment, then abruptly turned his attention to Garander. "And you," he said. "Why did you follow me out there? Did you know she was meeting this mysterious friend of hers?"

"I…thought she might be," Garander admitted.

"So you knew he existed?"

"Yes, sir."

"Did you meet him the same time your sister did?"

"No, sir." Garander shook his head. "I only found out a couple of sixnights ago."

"And you didn't think to tell *me* about it? Or your mother?"

"I…I felt I owed Ishta a favor for letting the baron keep her talisman, sir, so I agreed not to say anything. He seemed harmless."

"Harmless? She says he's a *sorcerer*!"

"Well, but...she's been meeting him for months, and he hasn't done anything. He's just lonely."

"*Why* is this sorcerer so blasted lonely? Why is he lurking out there in the woods instead of coming out in the opening and earning an honest living?"

Ishta and Garander exchanged glances. "I...I don't know, sir," Garander said.

That was his first outright lie. He had shaded the truth, and answered vaguely or selectively, but this time he was simply lying.

Grondar stared at him. Garander could almost see his father thinking.

He knew his father was not a stupid man, so he was not surprised to see Grondar's mouth open slightly.

"Oh," he said, staring at his son. "A sorcerer. Sorcerers don't generally go leaping about like that. Not *ordinary* sorcerers, anyway. Not *our* sorcerers. But this man—is his name really Kelder?"

"No," Garander admitted.

"Did he *tell* you his real name?"

"Yes."

"Well?"

"I...I can't pronounce it. We call him Tesk."

"A sorcerer dressed all in black, with a name that isn't Ethsharitic, hiding in the woods, afraid to let anyone but children see him—he's a Northerner, isn't he?"

Garander nodded. "Yes, sir."

"He's been hiding in the wilderness for *twenty years*?"

"Yes, sir."

"You *knew* he was a Northerner?"

"Yes, sir." For a moment silence fell; Garander could almost feel Grondar's glare, and finally he said, "The war's been over since before we were *born*, Father. He knows it's over, and his side lost; he doesn't want any trouble. If he meant us any harm he could have killed us all in our sleep, but instead he's just talked to Ishta and kept her company."

"If he killed us, that would alert the baron that there was something dangerous in the area."

Garander didn't have a good answer for that. In truth, he had not thought of it.

"It's been twenty years," Grondar said thoughtfully. "How much magic can he have left?"

"I don't know," Garander said.

Grondar turned to Ishta.

"I don't know, either," she said. "He won't talk about things like that."

"Grondar," her mother said, "are you seriously telling me there's a Northern sorcerer still alive in the forest near here?"

"Oh, yes," Grondar said. "And he definitely still has *some* magic—there's that magic cloth, and you should have seen the way he moved! He didn't even look hum…"

He stopped in the middle of a word, staring at his wife.

"What is it?" she asked, frightened.

"He's not just a sorcerer, is he?" Grondar asked, turning back to Garander.

"I don't know what you mean," Garander said—lying again.

"He *isn't* entirely human, is he?"

"What *else* would he be?" Shella the Younger asked.

"*Shatra,*" Grondar said.

"I don't—"

"It's a *shatra*, isn't it?" Grondar interrupted, straightening up and glaring at his son. "That's how it could survive alone in the woods for twenty years. That's how it can move like that. That's why it doesn't dare let anyone who remembers the war see it—it *knows* that we might let an ordinary Northerner live, but *shatra* are just too dangerous. It'll be hunted down and destroyed if the barons or the overlords find out it's there."

Garander didn't say anything, but Ishta wailed, "He's my friend! I don't *want* him to be destroyed!"

"But it really *is* a *shatra*?" their mother asked, looking up from her pins.

"Yes," Garander said. "He is. But he's been there for twenty years and never hurt anyone! We didn't even know he was *there* until he got so bored and lonely he let Ishta find him!"

"But it's a *shatra*!" Grondar replied. "It probably killed *hundreds* of good people during the war!"

"And our people *wiped his out*! He says there wasn't a single survivor when he went back to his home village."

"Is that supposed to make me *trust* it?"

"No, I'm just saying the war was different! Both sides did things no one would do now."

Grondar stared at his son for a moment. "I wouldn't be too sure of that," he said. "The same people who ran things during the war are still running things now, pretty much. General Gor and Admiral Azrad call themselves overlords now, but they have as much power as ever. General Anaran may be dead, but from what I hear, his son Edaran isn't very different. The barons who meet at Sardiron are mostly the same men who tracked down and slaughtered the surviving Northerners. The wizards and theurgists say they aren't ever going to use their magic for war again, but I haven't heard anything like that about sorcerers or demonologists, and the wizards could change their minds. You three don't know what the World is like, growing up out here; people are still the same as ever. And *shatra* are still half-demon monsters. Maybe this Tesk really does want to live in peace, but that doesn't mean it *can*."

Garander stared back at his father for a moment, then said, "You know, there are other Northern monsters in the woods."

Grondar blinked. "What are you talking about?"

"There are mizagars."

It was Grondar's turn to stare. "How do you know?" he asked.

"Tesk told us."

"And you believe him?"

"Yes!" Ishta shouted. "Yes, we believe him. He's my friend. He never lied to us about being *shatra*; why would he lie about the mizagars? They obey him. He told them to stay away from us."

"It didn't lie about being a *shatra* because that's obvious!" Grondar replied. "I saw it for maybe half a minute at most, from a distance, in the snow, and *I* figured out what it was. It knew it couldn't fool you about that. But mizagars? Did it show you any evidence?"

Ishta looked at Garander, who turned up an empty palm. "No," he admitted. "But wasn't this Northern land during the war? *Shouldn't* there be mizagars? You always warned us about them."

Grondar frowned. "Maybe the gods and wizards killed them all."

"Or maybe surviving *shatra* who don't want to restart the war are holding them back."

"And maybe they all flew away to the third moon. *We* don't know what happened to them, and I'm not going to take a *shatra*'s word for it."

"So what are you going to do about Tesk?"

Grondar hesitated, then looked out the window at the snow piling up on the barn roof.

"Nothing," he said. "At least for now. I don't know how to catch it, and if I tried it would probably kill me. Even if it didn't want to—it's not human, and it probably can't always control its own actions. According to the stories I heard during the war, sometimes the demon takes over when it needs to fight; that's part of why we needed wizards or dragons to fight them, the demon part is more ferocious than anything that belongs in the World. So I'm not about to go after it, and with this snow I'll know if either of *you* goes into the woods after it, so you won't go warn it, either. When the weather lets up and we've all had time to think about it, maybe I'll send word to the baron. Or maybe I'll decide it's best left alone. I don't know. And neither do you—I don't care how much fun you had playing with it, it's *dangerous*, and you need to stay away from it!"

"That's right," their mother said, clearly upset. "You stay away from that thing! And Ishta, hold still, unless you want me to stab you with this pin."

Ishta stamped her foot, then straightened up and froze into position.

Garander looked at her for a moment, then at his father, then at the kitchen. "I'm going to get lunch," he said.

"You'll stay out of the woods?"

"Yes, sir."

"Then let me give you a hand with the food."

Father and son headed for the kitchen.

CHAPTER NINE

The snow stopped around mid-afternoon, leaving about a foot on the ground. Grondar and Garander slogged through it to the barn, where they checked on the livestock, then found shovels and began clearing paths between the various outbuildings. By suppertime they were both chilled to the bone and thoroughly exhausted.

As they worked Garander saw his father staring at the snow-covered woods, and studying the snow for tracks. He was obviously not convinced Tesk would remain safely hidden away. For his own part Garander thought the *shatra* was probably just fine where he was, out in the forest somewhere, and would not intrude where he wasn't wanted. He wondered whether Tesk even felt the cold; demons were supposed to be immune to heat and cold, weren't they?

By the time they finally went inside for supper and peeled off their sodden coats Garander was too tired to care what Tesk was doing. He was much more interested in eating the stew his mother had prepared, and then collapsing into bed.

The next day was mostly sunny, but cold; not much of the snow melted, and the glare off the white surface made any outdoor activity unpleasant. Accordingly, Grondar and his wife and children mostly stayed inside, huddled around the hearth, once the necessary chores were done.

At first they were largely silent, talking only about the minutia of their lives—how much firewood was stocked in the shed, what vegetables were in the bins, whether they had enough thread to do all the sewing Shella of the Green Eyes had planned, and so on. Shella the Younger asked Garander a few questions about what he had seen women wearing in Varag.

But then, out of nowhere, Grondar asked Ishta, "What did the *shatra* tell you about mizagars?"

"What?" She looked at her father, startled.

"You said the *shatra* told you things, and that there are mizagars in the forest. What did it tell you about mizagars?"

"Oh." Ishta thought for a second, then answered, "Well, he said they had been created by Northern sorcery three or four hundred years ago to watch border areas where the Empire didn't want to bother putting soldiers..."

Garander listened with interest. Now that Ishta was no longer trying to keep anything secret, and seemed to be over her anger at the loss of her talisman, she seemed eager to talk about Tesk, and to repeat everything he had told her over the past few months—not just about mizagars, but about trees and moss and squirrels and birds' nests and spiders and leaf mold and a hundred other things.

It occurred to him, as he listened, that Tesk knew as much about the forest as Grondar knew about farming, and Ishta had been far more interested in learning it than she ever had been in what her father had tried to teach her.

But then, she had always loved the woods, even before she knew anyone was living out there. Garander wondered whether there was some way she might make a living in the forest when she grew up; he had heard old stories that mentioned woodcutters and hunters, but he did not know of any such people in the present day. Despite the frequent parental warnings of danger, he had never seen any game bigger than a rabbit in the woods. He didn't really see how anyone could make a full-time job out of hunting rabbits. If anyone wanted that many rabbits it was easy enough to raise them on a farm, as old Elkan did.

Perhaps there was some other occupation that would suit her interest in the wilderness.

After supper, as the family gathered around the hearth again, Ishta was tired of talking, but now Grondar was the one who seemed eager to speak. Instead of talking about the farm as he usually did, though, he talked about his days in the Ethsharitic army during the Great War. He had served seven years in the Central Command under General Anaran, but he had never actually met the legendary war leader. He had never seen any *shatra*, or any mizagars, either. He had seen dragons, but only from a safe distance—a mile or two. He had seen three wizards, but had never spoken to any of them. His company had had a witch to look after their health, but he had never seen her do any magic other than healing. He knew there were wonderful stories about the war, about gods and heroes and monsters, battles and magic, stratagems and surprises, but most of what he remembered was mud and cold and hunger, and never knowing where the enemy was or what was going on. He had been in four small battles and two or three skirmishes too small to qualify, and had seen perhaps thirty of his fellow soldiers die—mostly from arrows or sorcery, not the sort of close-in sword fight that the stories talked about. Sometimes he didn't know how men had died; he saw them lying on the ground, covered in mud and blood, and didn't have time to worry about it. He had never been stuck with the unpleasant duty of hauling the bodies to the pyres, though he had helped build the pyres a few times.

He described the smell of a battlefield after the fighting was over, the stink of the dead. He talked about the smell of the pyres, and the smoke staining the sky.

Over the years Garander had heard his father tell a few war stories, but never like this.

Finally, during a brief pause in the flood of memories, Garander's mother asked, "Why are you telling us this all of a sudden?"

"The *shatra*," Grondar replied. "It's brought the war back."

"No, he hasn't," Ishta said. "The war's still over. Tesk doesn't want it back."

Grondar shook his head. "It's not like that. It's…" He took a deep breath and held it for a moment, then let it out. "My life is in two parts," he said. "There's the war, and there's after the war. They're two different lives, in two different worlds. *Shatra* are from the war. If there are still *shatra* out there, then there might be other things I thought were gone—officers and orders and marching and killing, wizards and dragons, magic and monsters, all those things I never want to see again. And the things I thought I would keep forever, maybe I don't get to keep them—the farm, and my family, and my friends. During the war I never got to stay in one place for very long; we would have to move because the front was moving, or because we were needed somewhere, or because it wasn't safe anymore where we had been. Whole villages would grow up in a month when an army camped somewhere, when everyone came to support the army, and whole villages would disappear overnight when the Northerners showed up."

"Father, he's just one left-over *shatra*," Garander said.

"But what's it doing there?" Grondar asked angrily.

"Nothing! He's just living in the woods," Ishta said.

"Why?"

"He doesn't have anywhere else to go!" Garander said. "He can't go home; his home is gone. The whole Northern Empire is gone. And he can't come live anywhere with ordinary people, because he's *shatra*!"

Grondar stared silently at his son for a moment.

"I'm sorry he's brought back all these bad memories, Father," Garander said, "but he didn't do it on purpose. He doesn't mean any harm."

"How do you *know*?"

"Because he's had twenty years to do whatever terrible evil thing he might be planning, and he hasn't done it. Listen to what Ishta said—he didn't talk to her about war or killing. They talked about trees and sunlight and field mice."

Garander was surprised at the vehemence in his own words. He had never intended to defend Tesk; he had had his own doubts about the Northerner. Something about his father's stories, though, had brought this out—he had needed to convince both his father and himself that Tesk was not part of those long-ago horrors, not anymore.

"*You* stopped being a soldier," Ishta said. "So did Tesk."

"It's not just a soldier," Grondar said. "It's a *shatra*. It *can't* stop being that."

"But he stopped fighting, just as you did," Garander said.

"It's late," Shella of the Green Eyes said, speaking for the first time since asking what had brought on her husband's stories. She got to her feet. "I'm going to bed. Ishta, you should be in bed, too."

With that, the family gathering broke up. Garander banked the fire for the night and made sure the doors and shutters were secure while the others retired to their bedrooms, and then climbed the stairs to his own bed in the attic.

He huddled in his bed, waiting until his body had warmed it enough to sleep comfortably, and thought over the evening's conversation. He had expected his father to think Tesk was dangerous, but he had not expected the *shatra*'s presence to trigger all those wartime memories. He hoped there would be no other surprises. His worries gradually blended into dreams as he fell asleep, and that seemed to sap them of any urgency.

The next day it snowed again, and they were all busy tending to the farm, making sure the stores were full and secure and that the livestock were safe from the weather, but the several days following were clear and cold.

A sixnight after his first sight of Tesk, around midday, Grondar came in from the barn, stamped the snow from his boots, and announced, "I'm going to go see Felder."

Startled, Garander asked, "Why? Are we short on something?"

Grondar glared at him. "No. Do I need my son's permission to visit our neighbor?"

Garander glanced around at his mother and sisters, but they were obviously not eager to get involved. "No, of course not, Father," he said.

Grondar relented slightly. "I want to make sure he's all right, that he was ready for the snow."

"Oh."

"And I'm going to warn him that we've seen a *shatra* in the woods."

This time it was Garander's mother who spoke. "He'll think you've gone mad."

Grondar turned up an empty palm. "Let him." Then he grabbed his hat and marched out the door.

Over the course of the next sixnight Grondar visited Kolar down by the ford, and old Elkan, and Rulura the Witch, and finally he went into the village of Ezval to spread the news more widely.

Garander also visited some of their neighbors, not to spread any news, but to see how his father's reports had been received. He talked to Kolar's son Karn, and Elkan's granddaughters, and a woman he met at the smith's forge whose name he didn't know.

No one actually seemed to be convinced there was really a *shatra* in the forest, but they didn't seem to think that Grondar was mad, merely that he had seen *something* in the woods and had misinterpreted what he saw. He had presented his story in rational terms, and had admitted the possibility he was wrong, while saying he didn't think he was.

And he had apparently not mentioned that two of his children had befriended the monster. Garander was grateful for that, anyway.

Karn asked him, "So have *you* seen this half-demon thing?"

Garander turned up a palm. "I did see *something* in the woods. It looked like a man to me, but I couldn't be sure."

"So your father isn't completely imagining it?"

"No, there was *something* there. I thought maybe it was a ghost, but I saw it."

"Huh. I *thought* it was awfully early in the winter to be going hearth-crazy. If you both saw it, I guess there was something to see."

"Ishta saw it, too," Garander said.

"What about Shella?"

Garander shook his head. "She doesn't go out near the woods if she can help it. My mother wasn't there, either." He noticed the look in Karn's eyes when he said Shella's name; it might not be that long before Karn would be his brother-in-law, unappealing though that prospect might be.

After the visit to Ezval Grondar seemed to feel he had done his duty, and stopped his expeditions. Two days later the first real blizzard struck, and the question of any further visiting was moot. As the snow piled up and the wind howled in the eaves just keeping the family and livestock alive and healthy was enough to occupy everyone's time.

It appeared they were in for a hard winter, as this blizzard was a bad one, bad enough that the elder Shella wondered if they had somehow offended the gods, while Grondar suggested there might be magic involved.

Whatever the reasons for the storm's ferocity, there was nothing they could do but wait it out.

As the storm continued Ishta worried about Tesk, but Garander assured her they had experienced worse in previous years, even if she didn't remember it, and Tesk had presumably survived those winters well enough.

Ishta did not seem entirely convinced, but she was not stupid or desperate enough to go out in the storm looking for her demonic friend; she knew how easy it was to get disoriented in all that whiteness and howling wind, and how quickly a person—or at least the goat they had lost during a storm two years earlier—could freeze to death. They used tethers and guide-ropes just to get from the house to the barn; venturing into the woods was out of the question.

After a day and a half the storm eased, and when Garander returned from watering the cattle he found Ishta leaning out the door, staring toward the forest.

"He's fine," Garander told her as he reached the house. He pulled her inside and slammed the door. "Don't let out all the warmth."

"We don't *know* he's fine," Ishta said. "I know you said he's survived worse, when I was little, but we don't *know* that. He might have been hiding in a cave up in the hills or something back then, and maybe *this* time he was caught off-guard."

"Well, there's nothing we can do about it," Garander replied.

"We should check on him!"

"In this weather? We can't."

"When the snow stops, I mean."

Garander sighed. "Ishta, if he *is* in trouble, it'll be too late by then, even if we could find him."

"We should look, though! He's part demon; maybe he…oh, I don't know."

"Neither do I," Garander admitted. "But if you're really that worried, I'll help you take a look when the weather lets up. You can't go out there alone in all this snow. And we'll have to tell Father—he'd see the tracks, in any case."

"But he told us to stay away from Tesk!"

Garander had momentarily forgotten that; doing his chores in the blizzard had distracted him. He frowned.

Just then their sister Shella opened the door and stepped in, carrying an armful of firewood. Ishta glanced up at Garander.

"We'll talk later," he said. Shella threw him a curious glance, but said nothing.

The snow stopped completely that evening, and by morning the clouds had blown away, leaving a white world ablaze with light, sun reflecting from every snow-covered surface. Grondar put the children and himself to work, shoveling out paths and clearing snow from windows and doors; it was tiring, but the effort kept them warm.

Around noon Garander was up in the loft, clearing the loft door and making sure the weight of the snow had not cracked any rafters, when he glanced out across the north field, toward the forest.

A thin line of smoke was rising from the trees.

He blinked, then smiled. There was only one way there could be a fire out there in these conditions. Tesk had survived the storm.

He took one more look around, gave the loft door a final swing to make sure no snow blocked its movement, then latched it and headed downstairs to tell Ishta that the *shatra* was alive.

He found her clearing snow from the chicken run, where she received the news with less delight than Garander had expected.

"He built a fire?"

"Well, someone did, and who else could it be?"

"But *anyone* could see it!"

Annoyed, Garander asked, "Who else *is* there around here?"

"The neighbors! Felder can probably see it."

Garander had to stop and think a moment, then said, "From his house it probably looks like it's ours."

Ishta opened her mouth to argue, then stopped. "Oh," she said.

"Tesk isn't stupid," Garander pointed out.

"What about from Kolar's farm?"

"I'm not sure he could see it at all; he's on the other side of the south ridge."

"What about Shessin…no, I guess not." Ishta frowned. "Let me see it."

The two climbed back up to the loft, where Garander opened the door and pointed out the thin trail of pale smoke.

Ishta squinted out into the glare. "I can hardly see it," she said. "It's *white* smoke. You didn't say that."

"I told you he wasn't stupid."

Garander had thought that would settle the matter, but that evening Ishta pulled him aside and made it clear that she still wanted to check on Tesk when she got a chance, and she expected Garander to help her.

"But you'll leave tracks!" Garander protested.

"Maybe we can hide them somehow."

Garander had no idea how they could hide tracks in snow this deep—the blizzard had deposited about a foot and a half of snow, with drifts as much as ten feet high. Of course, the wind that made those drifts had also scoured some areas down to a mere inch or two, and there was a long arc across the north field where that had happened. He wondered whether they could use that somehow.

It was four days later, though, that Ishta came up with her own solution—hide *behind* the drifts, where their tracks would not be visible from the house or barn. That would not take them all the way, but it might be enough to keep their father from noticing their trail.

It was obvious that she was not going to be deterred, so Garander accompanied her, crouching behind the drifts as they wound their way around the barn, past the bushes, across the north field, and into the woods.

They had scarcely stepped into the shadow of the first few trees when Tesk called to them.

"*Hsst!*" he said, and both of them looked up to see him crouched on a tree limb, about fifteen feet up. Garander immediately looked at the snow beneath it; there were no footprints.

There were mounds of snow fallen from branches, though, which could have been normal, but was probably Tesk's doing. He must have made his way through the treetops.

"Tesk!" Ishta shouted.

Tesk immediately placed a finger to his lips. "Sound travels well in this weather," he said.

"I'm so glad to see you!" Ishta exclaimed, a little more quietly.

"And I am pleased to see you."

"I was afraid you'd freeze out here, in that storm!"

Tesk smiled. "I have my magic," he said. "I am fine."

"We saw the smoke from your fire," Garander said. "Four days ago."

"I intended you to," Tesk said. "That was a signal to let you know I was safe."

"So that's why I never saw smoke in the forest before?"

Tesk nodded. "I do not need fire often. When I do, I have ways of hiding it. I let you see that one deliberately."

"I was worried," Ishta said. "Especially when we saw the smoke right after the storm, but then it was gone again later."

"It was intended to reassure you. White smoke will always mean I am safe. If I am not, the smoke will be dark."

Ishta nodded understanding.

"I am glad you and your family were safe."

"Why wouldn't we be?" Garander said. "We have a house, we aren't out in the woods!"

"Still, a storm can be dangerous. I came to see you were safe that night."

"You did?"

Tesk nodded.

"I didn't see footprints," Garander said.

Tesk smiled at that. "I have magic."

Garander smiled back, then turned serious. "Father has told the neighbors you're here," he said.

"Did they believe him?"

"I don't know," Garander admitted. "Probably not."

"Then I will not worry about it, but I thank you for the warning." Then his head jerked up slightly. "I think you should go. Your father is moving this way."

Ishta turned to stare back toward the farm, but Garander hesitated. "Would you be willing to talk with him sometime?" he asked.

Tesk stared at Garander for a moment before answering, "I would. But not now." Then he turned and slid up the tree, disappearing quickly among the snow-covered branches.

When the two of them got back to the barn they found Grondar standing by the well, staring out across the north field. He saw them arrive, and for a moment the three of them just stared at one another.

It was Grondar who broke the silence. "He's still out there?"

"Yes," Garander said, expecting a speech about how dangerous Tesk was, and how they should stop disobeying orders and stay away from the *shatra*, but instead Grondar just nodded.

"Be careful," he said.

CHAPTER TEN

The winter was indeed a harsh one, but Grondar had seen to it that his family was prepared for it. Meals got smaller and less interesting as the sixnights passed, and the pile in the woodshed shrank to a tiny fraction of its original size, but they were never in serious danger of either starving or freezing.

There were four blizzards in all, and a fifth storm that came close to qualifying, and after each one Garander peered out the loft door to see a thin streak of white smoke on the northeastern sky. He had no idea how Tesk was surviving out there in the forest, with no real shelter and no obvious food supply, but apparently he was doing just fine.

Finally, though, the days grew longer, the sun rose higher, and the snow began to melt. The cattle and chickens began to thrust their heads out out of their pens, enjoying the fresh air and sunlight. Grondar set Garander to sharpening the plow blade and checking the harness while he himself inspected the fences and marked the boundaries.

Ishta was given various tasks around the house and yard, but Garander was not surprised to see more than once that she had done a quick and sloppy job, and then slipped away. He was fairly certain she was sneaking into the forest to see Tesk, and not just playing in the irrigation ditches.

The two Shellas, mother and daughter, were airing out the house and the linens, and cleaning the accumulated grime from the floors.

For his own part, Garander did not feel any great urgency about visiting Tesk. He was curious about what the *shatra* was up to, and how he had survived the winter, but getting the farm ready for spring planting was far more urgent. He wanted to have fresh vegetables again, something more than dried beans and withered carrots; he wanted to see the grain bins full again. Once that was taken care of, he could spare the time to take a stroll in the woods and chat with the Northerner.

The snow had diminished to scattered islands where the bigger drifts had once stood, and the paths were starting to dry out and pack hard again, when a stranger's voice called from across the west field.

"*Hai*, the house! Is this the home of Grondar of Lullen?"

Garander looked up from his work and saw a man standing near the boundary stone, waving an arm over his head. There were at least two other figures behind the waver.

Garander got to his feet and hung the leather strap he had been inspecting on a peg by the barn door; then he looked around for his family.

His mother and Shella the Younger were in the house, and probably had not heard the hail. Ishta was not in sight; he had last seen her feeding the chickens that morning. His father was at the far end of the south field, a distant speck on the landscape, wielding a hoe or shovel on something. He probably had not heard the call, either.

The only strangers who Garander had ever seen come calling were tax collectors; so much, he thought, for the baron's promised payment for Ishta's talisman.

There was no point in putting it off, though. He stepped away from the barn and called back, "Who asks?"

"Lord Dakkar, Baron of Varag, sent us to speak to Grondar," came the answer. The stranger waved at his companions.

Garander did not remember the tax collectors traveling in groups. He glanced at his father's distant silhouette, then began marching westward; he didn't want to interrupt whatever Grondar was doing down there by the south fence if this was something that Garander could deal with himself. As he went he beckoned for the strangers to approach; there was no reason he should have to do *all* the walking.

The field was muddy, so Garander did not follow a straight line, but looked for the driest ground. When they met in mid-field, and he looked up from his feet, he was astonished to realize he recognized two of the visitors.

There were four of them in all, and each carried a good-sized pack on one shoulder. Two were soldiers in the same uniforms the baron's guards in Varag wore, while the other two were the wizard Azlia and the sorcerer Sammel. They clearly recognized him, as well.

"I'm Garander Grondar's son," he said. "Grondar of Lullen is my father. What's your business with him?" It almost certainly had something to do with Ishta's talisman, he thought.

The lead soldier glanced at the others, and appeared about to speak, when Azlia interrupted. "Hargal, we know this young man. Let me handle this." She stepped forward.

The soldier turned up a palm and moved aside.

"Wizard," Garander said. "Why are *you* here?"

"There have been reports," she said, "that your father claims to have seen *shatra* in the woods beyond his farm."

Garander's mouth opened, then closed again. He had not expected that. "Oh?" he said.

"Yes. Do you know anything about that?"

"I'm not sure what you mean."

"*Did* your father see *shatra* in the forest?"

Ordinarily, Garander would have said that they would have to ask his father, but in this case he did not want them to do that. He just looked blank.

"Do you know what a *shatra* is, boy?" asked the soldier Azlia had called Hargal.

"I've heard my father talk about them," Garander said. "They were a Northern thing in the war, weren't they?"

Hargal gave the magicians a disgusted glance.

"Ordinarily," Sammel said, "we wouldn't take reported sightings of leftover *shatra* very seriously, but in *this* case we recognized your father's name and remembered the talisman your little sister found, so we knew there had been Northern activity near here during the war. If a real *shatra* survived anywhere, this is as likely a place as any."

"I wouldn't know," Garander replied.

"Where's your father, boy?" Hargal demanded. He was obviously not inclined toward patience with this farmboy, regardless of what the magicians said.

"I'm not sure," Garander said, carefully not looking toward the south field. "We're getting ready for the spring planting; he could be anywhere."

"Then we'll wait until he comes home for supper. Come on." Hargal started marching past Garander, toward the house.

"Wait a minute!" Garander protested. "This is our land; you can't just come bursting in here!"

Hargal stopped, and turned to stare at Garander. His hand dropped to the hilt of his sword, and slowly, deliberately, he drew his blade and brought it around, then raised the point and pressed it to Garander's throat.

Garander tried to step back, but found the other soldier was behind him, his own weapon unsheathed and held ready. The youth turned to see that Azlia had drawn her own dagger, and her other hand was groping for something in her pack. Sammel had unslung *his* pack, and was holding it ready.

"I think," Hargal said, "that we can go wherever we please. Did you not understand that we are here on the baron's business?"

"But...but it's our land!"

"It's within the baron's domain, and you are the baron's subjects," Hargal answered. "Do you deny that?"

Garander looked down at the steel blade at his throat, and said nothing.

"We mean you no harm," Hargal said, "but you will *not* interfere with us. Is that clear?"

"I don't understand what this is about," Garander said. He glanced toward the house, and saw his sister Shella watching from the window.

"It's about the *shatra*," Hargal said. "What do you know about it?"

"Nothing!"

Hargal glanced at the two magicians.

"The talisman isn't ready," Sammel said. "I can't tell whether he's lying."

"I don't sense any magic," Azlia added.

"I don't understand!" Garander repeated.

He was stalling for time, but he was unsure why; he did not have any plans that would be helped by a delay. All he could really hope for was that a few more minutes would give him a chance to think of something.

He was not even sure why he did not simply admit that yes, he knew there was a *shatra* living in the forest beyond the north field. It was not as if he thought these two soldiers would be any threat to Tesk.

But the magicians were an unknown element. His father's superiors, during the war, had said that if anyone encountered a *shatra* they should call for magicians, but were these two what those officers had had in mind? Garander had always assumed that all the *powerful* wizards and sorcerers lived far away, in one of the Ethshars—Azrad's Ethshar, or Ethshar of the Sands, or Ethshar of the Rocks, or Old Ethshar. Azlia was probably a real wizard, but Garander had not actually seen her perform any magic when he had first met her in Varag; Sammel had seemed knowledgeable about sorcery, but he, too, had not really done anything magical. Tesk, on the other hand, was loaded down with sorcery. He could burn a tree down by pointing a stick at it; he could stay warm and dry in a blizzard. Was there anything Azlia and Sammel could do to him?

Perhaps, Garander thought, he *should* tell them about Tesk…

But no. The real danger was not so much that they would harm Tesk, but that Tesk would kill them, and the baron would blame Garander and his family.

"We have come here," Hargal said, "to determine whether or not a *shatra* has somehow survived, and is living in this area. There is nothing very complicated about that, is there?"

"But…aren't *shatra* extremely dangerous?" Garander asked. "When my father told me about them he said his orders during the war, if he saw a *shatra*, were to get away from it as fast as he could and call for a dragon. He said a *shatra* and a full-grown dragon were a pretty even match. What would you do if you found one?"

"You let us worry about that!"

Garander glanced at the magicians, who were listening with interest—and perhaps some concern. "But look, sir, if a *shatra* kills the four of you, the baron might take it out on my family. I don't want that!"

"So there *are shatra* around here?"

"I told you, I don't know!"

"Garander," Azlia said, "we aren't here to fight whatever it was your father saw. We just want to know what it *is*. As you say, *shatra* are dangerous. It's important for Lord Dakkar to know about anything that threatens his people, and that includes any leftover Northern monsters."

"If it was really a *shatra*," Sammel said, "we'll go back and tell Lord Dakkar. We aren't going to get killed, and no one is going to blame your family for anything."

"You won't try to put a spell on it?"

"I wasn't *planning* to," Azlia replied.

"I don't think you *could*," Sammel said.

Azlia threw him an irritated glance, then turned her attention back to Garander. "So, let's start at the beginning. Your father saw something in the forest?" She gestured toward the trees visible beyond the farm. "Over there?"

Garander decided that sooner or later, at least some of the truth would come out. "Yes," he said. "It looked like a man dressed all in black, carrying a big pack."

"Did *you* see it?"

Reluctantly, Garander nodded.

"When?"

"Around the time of the first snowfall."

"Not since then?" Hargal demanded.

"No," Garander said. He was giving an almost honest answer to that one—he had seen the smoke from Tesk's signal fires, but he had not seen Tesk himself in months, not since the brief meeting after the second snow.

"Have you seen any tracks in the snow?" Sammel asked. "Since then, I mean?"

"What kind of tracks?"

"The kind a man might leave."

Garander shook his head. "Just my family's. And some birds and small animals."

The magicians exchanged glances. "If it *was* a *shatra*, it's probably long gone," Sammel said.

Hargal finally lowered his sword. "So we've come here for nothing?"

"Not necessarily," Sammel said. "We might be able to pick up its trail." He hefted his pack. "I have some sorcery that might help."

"And I have spells that might, as well," Azlia said.

"Assuming there's anything to find," Hargal said. "I'm not convinced these people really saw anything."

"Neither am I," Garander said, startling the soldier. "We saw a dark shape in the snow, but it could have been almost anything, really."

"You said it was a man," Azlia said.

"I said it *looked* like a man," Garander said. "It was snowing, and it's easy to get fooled by trees and shadows in the forest."

"Hmph." Hargal sheathed his weapon, and said, "We still need to talk to your father. You don't know where he is?"

Garander shook his head.

"Then we'll wait at the farm. Come on." Without waiting for Garander or the others he marched past him, headed for the house.

Garander could not think of any way to further deter the invaders, and instead turned and hurried to keep pace with Hargal. As he turned he glimpsed Shella dropping the window-curtain back into place; he hoped Hargal had not seen it. Perhaps his mother and sisters would stay quiet, and not let the big man know anyone was there. He struggled to keep up with Hargal's long strides.

The magicians and the other soldier followed, not quite as briskly.

When Garander and Hargal were perhaps three-fourths of the way across the west field when the farmhouse door opened and a small shape dashed out, headed away from them—Ishta.

For a moment Garander thought she was headed for the forest to warn Tesk, but at the corner of the house she turned south, rather than continuing to the east, and Garander realized she was going to fetch their father, not to warn the *shatra*. He relaxed slightly, and only then noticed that he had been tensed, his shoulders hunched, ready to run or fight.

That was stupid, he tried to tell himself; he wouldn't stand a chance in a fight with a trained soldier like Hargal, and probably couldn't outrun him, either.

Even if he *did* outrun him, what good would it do? What would he do? Where would he go? He didn't know how to find Tesk, and finding him would probably only make matters worse.

He glanced to the south and saw Ishta running across the field; Grondar looked up from his work as his daughter approached.

Hargal apparently did not notice; he marched on toward the house.

A moment later the soldier's gloved fist pounded on the door, and Garander heard his mother's voice call, "Who is it?"

"We've come on the baron's business!" Hargal shouted, as Garander came up beside him.

"Why should I believe you?" Shella asked. The door remained firmly shut.

Hargal's disgust was obvious. "I'm wearing Lord Dakkar's uniform, and who else would it be? Does it even *matter*? I'm the man with a sword. Open the door!"

"My husband will be here soon!"

"Good! That's who I came to see."

"What do you want with my Grondar?"

Hargal sighed. "That's none of your business—it's *his*."

"What have you done with my son?"

"Nothing! He's right here!" He turned and jabbed Garander with a finger. "Calm your mother down, boy."

"Mother, it's all right!" Garander called. "They've come about those stories Father told the neighbors!"

"What stories?"

"About seeing a monster in the woods!"

There were a few seconds of silence, and then the latch lifted and the door opened. Shella of the Green Eyes peered out. "What monster?"

"Your husband claimed he saw a *shatra*," Hargal replied.

"He did?"

"Yes!"

The magicians and the other soldiers finally caught up, gathering at the door. "*Hai*," Azlia called. "I'm the wizard your son met in Varag."

"She is, Mother," Garander confirmed.

"The baron's wizard?"

"Yes."

Shella considered that for a moment, then said, "My husband will be here soon." Then she closed the door.

CHAPTER ELEVEN

Grondar came around the corner of the house with a hoe in his hand and Ishta at his heel. "What's this?" he demanded.

"Are you Grondar of Lullen?" Hargal demanded in reply.

"I am," Grondar said, stopping a few feet away and raising the hoe. "Who are you?"

"Hargal of Varag, in the service of Lord Dakkar," Hargal replied. "The baron sent us to talk to you."

"The baron?" He looked past Hargal's shoulder at Garander, who nodded. "What does he want with me?"

"You reported seeing a *shatra* in this area, did you not?"

Again, Grondar looked at his son, but this time Garander kept his face as blank as he could. He saw Ishta, standing behind their father, look frightened, and hoped none of the baron's representatives noticed—or if they did, that they misinterpreted her concern.

Grondar considered for a second or two, then lowered the hoe and said, "Yes, I did."

"The baron takes an interest in potential threats to the safety of his people," Hargal said. "A *shatra* would qualify, don't you think?"

"Of course I think it's dangerous!" Grondar replied, thumping the hoe on the ground. "That's why I warned my neighbors. But I didn't think the *baron* would concern himself with it! I'm not even sure we *are* his people, and not Lord Edaran's."

Hargal smiled an unpleasant smile. "Well, Lord Dakkar certainly thinks this is part of his own domain, and he's sent us to investigate."

"Very well," Grondar said. Then he looked expectantly at the soldier.

Hargal barely hesitated before asking his first question. "You saw a *shatra*?"

"I did," Grondar said firmly.

"You're *sure*?"

Grondar hesitated. "Fairly certain," he said.

From Hargal's reaction, Garander did not think that was the answer he had expected. "Tell me about it," the soldier said. "Where did you see it? When? What did it look like?"

Grondar looked at his son again, but then turned up a palm. He pointed to the northeast. "In the woods, over that direction, around the time of the first snowfall—maybe the end of Leafcolor?"

"Not since then?"

"No."

"What did it look like?"

"Like a man dressed all in black, with a strange black helmet—*all* his clothes were strange. He had a big pack on his back, with several carved sticks tied to it."

Hargal glanced at Sammel, who nodded. This evidently did not satisfy the soldier, who asked Grondar, "Why did you think it was a *shatra*?"

"Because it fit the description my lieutenant gave us back during the war perfectly!"

"But the war is long over and the Northern Empire is gone. What made you think it wasn't just a strangely-dressed man? Perhaps someone who found some old Northern gear?"

"Because nothing human ever moved like that! It ran up a tree and then jumped from branch to branch as if it was swimming through the air, faster than any fish ever swam in water. Just the way the lieutenant said *shatra* moved."

Garander saw the two magicians exchange glances. Sammel adjusted his pack, then asked, "Where did you see it, exactly?"

Grondar pointed again. "Over there. In the forest."

"How far inside the forest?" Sammel asked, as he fished in his pack.

Grondar hesitated, and turned to the direction he had been pointing, considering the question. "Fifty or sixty yards, perhaps?"

"What were you doing that deep in the woods in the snow?"

Grondar blinked. "Gathering mushrooms," he said.

"In the *snow*?" Hargal demanded. Meanwhile, Sammel had apparently found what he had been looking for; he pulled an object from his pack that Garander could only describe as a big golden egg with a handle. He began fiddling with it, squeezing the handle.

"Well, if we'd waited, they'd be buried, wouldn't they?"

"They were good mushrooms," Garander volunteered, before anyone could argue. "The orangey-brown ones. They're all gone now."

Sammel turned, the egg-thing in his hand. "You were with him?"

"Sort of. I was looking a little ways away. I told you I saw something, but I wasn't as close as my father was."

"Anyone else?"

Garander was careful not to look at Ishta. "No."

Hargal asked Grondar, "Did anyone see it besides you two?"

"Not that I know of."

Garander was pleasantly surprised to hear his father tell this out-right lie—but then, he was protecting his daughter. Garander knew that however unhappy his father might be about Tesk's presence, however displeased he might be with his children's actions, he still loved them and wanted to keep them safe.

"Do you have any evidence?" Hargal asked. "Any way to prove the two of you didn't just make it up?"

"No," Grondar replied, "but why would we make anything up?"

"To keep people away, perhaps? You might have something in the woods you don't want anyone else to find?"

Grondar looked genuinely puzzled. "Like what?"

Sammel was pointing the egg-thing at Grondar; Garander guessed it was a talisman of some sort. "You really saw a *shatra*, as you de-scribed?" he asked.

"Yes, I did," Grondar answered.

Sammel looked at his talisman and said, "He's telling the truth."

"So there really is a *shatra*?" Hargal asked.

"Well, there *was*," Sammel replied. "That was months ago, accord-ing to these two."

"Show us where," Hargal ordered.

Grondar looked from Garander to Ishta, then spread both hands. "This way," he said.

Garander and Ishta followed along as their father led the four outsid-ers past the barn, around the woodshed, across the north field, and into the woods. As they walked, Sammel put his golden egg-talisman back in his pack and dug out a boxlike blue thing with two handles and four shiny inset squares.

Snow still covered parts of the forest floor; the springtime sun had not penetrated to melt it as much as in more open areas. Last year's leaves made a sodden layer beneath and between the snowy patches, providing a soft surface that gave uncomfortably beneath their feet. Still, the party of seven trudged on until they came to the tree where Tesk had set up his magical shelter. There was no sign of the cloth there, but Garander remembered the shape of the branches, and was sure his father had found the right tree.

"Here," Grondar said, pointing. "That's the tree it ran up."

Hargal looked at Garander.

"This is it," Garander said.

"You're sure?"

Father and son nodded, and Hargal looked to the baron's sorcerer.

Sammel raised his blue device and waved it around slowly, watch-ing the shiny insets as he did. One of them seemed to flash, Garander thought, but it might have just been catching the sun through the branches overhead.

"There's been sorcery here," Sammel said. "Probably not recently, though."

"Could it be left from the war?" the other soldier asked.

Sammel shook his head. "It's not *that* old."

"It's consistent with Grondar's story?" Azlia asked.

"I'd say so, yes." The sorcerer frowned at the blue talisman. "But I think the *shatra*, if that's what it was, may have come back once or twice since then. There are traces that might be from only a few sixnights back, not Leafcolor."

Garander did not like the sound of that. He had been starting to relax, thinking that Tesk could easily avoid these people, but their magic might be enough to track the *shatra* down.

"If you can give me an exact time," Azlia said, startling everyone, "I can see if it was really a *shatra*. It might just be some sorcerer pretending to be one, to scare people."

Sammel turned to look at her. "How exact?"

"Within a quarter of an hour."

Sammel snorted. "I can't do *that*!"

Azlia turned to Grondar. "Can you?"

"Uh…it was the day of the first snowfall. In the morning." He glanced at Garander. "Perhaps an hour before noon?" He turned up an empty palm. "You understand, we are farmers—we have no clocks, we live by the sun, and the clouds hid it from us that day."

"What day was that?"

Both Grondar's palms turned up, and he shook his head.

"The first snowfall in Varag was on the twenty-third of Leafcolor," the soldier whose name Garander did not know volunteered. "It was probably the same here."

"How do you remember that?" Hargal asked, startled.

"My sister was born on the twenty-fourth of Leafcolor in 4999," the soldier said. "She celebrates her birthday with a big dinner every year, and this year I missed the feast because of the snow."

"We can try that," Azlia said. She set down her pack, knelt beside it, and began rummaging through it.

"What are you doing?" Garander asked, staring at her.

"The Spell of Omniscient Vision," she replied. "Or at least, I'm seeing whether I brought the ingredients."

"The Spell of…what? What's that?"

She pulled out a small black box, then looked thoughtfully up at the sky. "It will allow me to see this place as it was on the morning of the twenty-third of Leafcolor. But it doesn't work in sunlight; we'll need to find someplace dark." She set the box aside, then reached back in the pack and brought out a handful of strange gray cones, each one tagged with a colored ribbon that had been pinned to the base. The cones varied from the size of a baby's thumb to the size of Shella's spindle; Azlia selected a medium-sized one with a blue-green ribbon and set that atop the black box. "It also takes about an hour to prepare, maybe a little more, and then the vision lasts no more than a quarter-hour." She looked up at Grondar. "Is there somewhere I can work undisturbed for an hour, where the sun cannot reach? A cave, perhaps, or a root cellar?"

"I don't…" Grondar began.

"We have a root cellar!" Ishta volunteered excitedly.

"That should work," the wizard said. She dropped the other cones back in her pack, and buttoned a flap over them.

Garander was torn, unsure whether to be angry with Ishta for her outburst; he was afraid of what the magicians might discover, but at the same time, a chance to actually *see* their magic in action was hard to resist.

Besides, who ever heard of a farm that *didn't* have a root cellar? And this time of year it would of course be mostly empty, since the family and livestock had been eating its contents all winter.

"I'll show you the way," Grondar said resignedly.

"Will you let us watch?" Ishta asked.

Azlia looked at the girl and smiled. "If you like," she said. "But you must *promise*, swear by any gods you know, not to interrupt the spell! It could do terrible damage if anything goes wrong."

"I'll keep an eye on her," Garander said. He did not admit, even to himself, that this was really just an excuse to watch the magic himself.

"And I'll watch over all of you," Hargal said.

"Is there *room* for all of you in this root cellar?" Sammel asked.

Garander had not thought about that. "How much space do you need?" he asked Azlia.

"Not much," she said as she closed up her pack, leaving the black box and the gray cone to one side. "Room to raise both elbows on either side, and an arm's length in front." She looked around, still kneeling, then drew a knife from her belt. She looked at the tree where Tesk had sheltered from the snow, then used the knife to cut a glyph into the matted leaves by her left knee. Garander had no idea what the glyph meant, since he could not read much. He stared at the knife, which seemed to gleam unnaturally bright; it was clearly not an ordinary steel blade.

Grondar noticed where his son's gaze was focused. "I think it's silver," he whispered.

Azlia looked up. "Yes, it's silver," she said. "Or silver-plated, anyway; I'm not sure pure silver would be strong enough." She sheathed her knife, then hoisted her pack onto her shoulder. She picked up the black box and gray cone and got to her feet. "Let's see this root cellar."

Grondar looked around at the others, and decided nothing more need be said. He turned and led the way back to the farm.

As they walked, Garander leaned over and whispered to Ishta, "You don't want to help them find...uh...anything, do you?" As he spoke he watched Azlia, three or four paces ahead; the wizard had already demonstrated that she had keen ears, and Garander did not want her overhearing.

Ishta looked up at him, startled. "They won't find him if he doesn't want them to." Her whisper was not quite as quiet as Garander might have hoped.

"Ishta, she's a *wizard*. Remember what Father said he had orders to do if he saw a *shatra*?"

"Send for a dragon!"

"A dragon *or a wizard*."

"Oh. Oh, yeah." She glanced at Azlia's back. "I guess I forgot. But what could she do?"

"I don't know, and that's why I'm worried."

Just then Azlia glanced back over her shoulder at them, and Garander decided not to risk further conversation.

A few minutes later they were back at the farm, where Grondar led the way down through the barn's lower level to the root cellar. He opened the door and stood aside, letting the wizard peer in.

The room was dark and cool, the walls of rough stone and the floor of hard-packed earth. Wooden bins lined both sides, leaving a narrow path down the middle. On a shelf just inside the door stood a small lantern holding a stub of candle.

Azlia seemed more concerned with the heavy wooden ceiling than anything else; she leaned in, studying it for any signs of sunlight. Finding none, she turned to Grondar and said, "This should do." She set her box and cone on the shelf beside the lantern, then drew the silver knife from her belt. She transferred it to her left hand and then, to Garander's astonishment, stabbed her own right index finger, drawing a bead of blood. Then she began speaking, but her voice had changed—it had dropped almost an octave in pitch, and the tone had altered so that it barely sounded human as she recited something incomprehensible. Then she curled the fingers of her right hand into a fist except for the index, which she held out, straight and rigid.

The drop of blood burst into flame, bright and yellow. Azlia used it to light the candle stub, then curled her finger; the magical flame instantly went out.

Garander stared, and realized his mouth was hanging open. He snapped it shut, then glanced at Ishta.

Her mouth was open, too.

"She's just showing off," Sammel muttered behind them. "I could have lit it more quickly."

Azlia turned. "I heard that. I'm also getting the sense of the magic in this environment."

"I thought you said you needed darkness," Grondar said.

"It's really just sunlight that's a problem," Azlia said. "In fact, I need light to work, and the candle's easier than a spell."

"But you *lit* it with a spell!" Ishta said.

Azlia smiled at her. "Just a little one. It's called the Finger of Flame. A proper light spell that would last long enough would be much more difficult."

"Oh." Ishta continued to stare as the wizard picked up the lantern and marched down the three steps into the root cellar. She took up a position in the center of the chamber, then held the lantern high as she looked around.

"This should do." She unslung her pack and dropped it to the earthen floor, then looked back at the others. "Anyone who wants to watch, get in here. Anyone who doesn't, go away. And close the door behind you."

Garander and Ishta almost collided with one another as they hurried down into the cellar; behind them, Hargal moved onto the steps and closed the heavy wooden door behind himself. The chamber was plunged into near-darkness, with the lantern's dull glow the only illumination.

Garander hesitated for a moment, wondering what he was getting himself into, trapping himself in here with a wizard and a soldier and his silly little sister. But then he remembered he was about to see a demonstration of *real magic*, of wizardry.

But he didn't want to stand here for an entire hour, with Hargal right behind him. He turned and clambered into one of the bins, kicking aside a few scattered onions that still lingered in the bottom.

Ishta followed his example, climbing into a bin on the opposite side. Then both of them settled down to watch Azlia perform her spell.

CHAPTER TWELVE

Garander had never imagined magic could be so dull. For over an hour Azlia had stood, or knelt, or sat, waving her silver dagger around and chanting unintelligible nonsense. The black box had turned out to hold nothing but a smooth pebble the size of a sparrow's egg, and the gray cone was some sort of incense that burned with a faintly salty smell; Azlia moved the pebble about, sometimes holding it in one hand while her dagger was in the other, sometimes setting it on the ground, and the gray cone smoldered and burned on the floor in front of her, filling the root cellar's air with smoke that made Garander's eyes itch. There was also an occasional odd tingling sensation that he supposed was magic, but it was not especially powerful.

The candle-stub in the lantern flared and flickered in unnatural ways, and Azlia's knife sometimes seemed to be glowing with its own blue light, but even that lost all interest after awhile. Ishta had fallen asleep after perhaps half an hour, and there were times when it took an effort for Garander to remain awake himself, but he held out, hoping something exciting would happen eventually.

And then the wizard picked up the little gray stone and held it out in front of her, and it began to glow a color Garander had never seen before. She released it, but instead of falling it hung there, suspended in the smoky air directly above the stump of the cone of incense.

"The spot I marked with the rune of location, at one hour before noon on the twenty-third of Leafcolor, in the five thousand and eighteenth year of human speech," Azlia said in clear Ethsharitic, in her own natural voice.

Garander jerked upright and stared. "Ishta!" he hissed.

"Hm?" The girl stirred. Garander could not reach her to shake her awake, but Hargal took pity on her, leaned over the side of the bin, and patted her shoulder. Then he straightened up to watch the spell.

Ishta yawned and sat up; then she caught sight of what was happening a few feet away and stared, her mouth open.

The pebble was spreading, as if it was not a stone but a drop of oil upon a surface—and the surface was vertical and invisible. It became something like a pool or a window, hanging in the air of the root cellar before the wizard Azlia, an arm's length from her face. Through it, Garander could see the forest—not as they had seen it today, on the eighteenth of Thaw, but as it had been on the twenty-third of Leafcolor, with snow falling steadily and blanketing the ground.

And there at the base of a tree, sitting side by side under that magical cloth, were Ishta and Tesk. There was no sound—or rather, no sound but the breathing of the four people in the root cellar, and the heavy tread of Hargal's boots as he moved closer to the floating image. The long-ago Tesk said something, and the Ishta image laughed. Then she reached out to scoop up some snow and tried to fling it at the *shatra*, but he somehow managed to dodge it without rising, letting it splat against the trunk by his shoulder.

"Oh, no," the present-day Ishta murmured. Garander saw Hargal turn to look at her before returning his attention to the conjured image. The soldier leaned forward, studying the vision.

"Can you make it show that part again?" Hargal asked. "Where he dodges the snow?"

Azlia shook her head.

Garander realized that the image was still expanding; that wintry forest now filled the entire far end of the root cellar. It was almost as if Tesk and the second Ishta were here in the storeroom with them.

The two had settled back against the tree again, talking silently and watching the snow fall. Garander watched in fascinated horror, expecting to see his father and himself appear at any moment.

But they did not. Tesk alerted at something, said something to Ishta—and then the image vanished, an effect midway between a bubble popping and smoke dispersing, and the entire root cellar was plunged into darkness. The candle-stub had finally burned out, and the incense had burned down to a small pile of ash.

For a moment the blackness seemed absolute. Garander heard his companions breathing, and heard a small plop, but he saw nothing at all—until his eyes adjusted enough to make out the faintest of blue glows where the wizard's dagger gleamed.

"I'll get the door," Hargal said, and Garander heard the rustle of cloth and the creak of leather as the guardsman marched back up.

Then the latch rattled, the hinges squealed, and daylight spilled into the room, forcing everyone within to blink and squint.

"I'm sorry I couldn't show you more detail, or repeat anything," Azlia said. "The spell doesn't work that way; you get maybe ten to fifteen minutes, just the way it happened, and then you're done. I'd need to do the entire spell over to show you anything a second time, and there's no way to change the angle or distance."

"I think we saw enough," Hargal said. "I'd say yes, that was a *shatra*." He turned to glare down at Ishta, who crouched in the vegetable bin. "And I'd say that someone besides father and son most certainly *did* see it."

"I didn't…I mean, I didn't know…" Ishta began.

"Leave her alone!" Garander said. "She's just a girl!"

Hargal turned to face him. "I'd say *you* didn't seem very surprised by what we saw. I think you knew more than you said."

"He wasn't in the image," Azlia said.

"No," Hargal agreed. "But…"

"But I would have been, in another moment," Garander said, interrupting the soldier. There was no point in trying to hide anything anymore; these two really were magicians, and could find out all the secrets. Instead, he intended to tell the truth and hope he could convince them to leave Tesk alone. "My father and I found Ishta there, talking to the *shatra*. We didn't tell you because she's just a girl, and we didn't want her involved."

"Hmph." Hargal frowned at him, and then at Ishta. "You *befriended* that thing?" he asked her.

"He's not a *thing*!" Ishta protested. "He's nice! Nicer than *you*, anyway!"

"The baron doesn't pay me to be nice."

Just then Sammel leaned in the door. "I heard the latch, and the voices," he said. "Did the spell work?"

"It worked," Azlia said, as Grondar and the other soldier appeared on either side of the sorcerer. "It seems that the young lady here made friends with our Northern abomination."

Garander could see that his father looked miserable. "He's not an abomination," Garander said. "He's a *shatra*, but he knows the war's over. He won't hurt anyone."

"He's nice!" Ishta insisted.

"If it's really a *shatra*, it's half-demon," Sammel pointed out.

"You've spoken with it," Hargal said to Ishta. "I saw that." Then he turned to Garander. "Have *you* spoken with it?"

Garander nodded.

"And you?" The soldier looked at Grondar.

"No," Grondar said. "I saw it with my children, but it fled at the sight of me, leaping up into the tree, just as I told you."

"You saw it with your children."

"Yes."

"And how did that happen?"

"Ishta slipped away, and Garander and I followed her tracks in the snow."

"She slipped away." He turned back to the girl. "Why did you do that?"

"I wanted to be sure Tesk was all right. I didn't think he had anywhere to go to get out of the snow."

"Tesk. Tesk?"

"That's what we call him," Garander volunteered. "We can't pronounce his real name correctly."

"It's Northern," Ishta added. "It doesn't sound like anything Ethsharitic."

"You knew it was there? And that it was a Northerner?"

Ishta threw Garander a look, but he turned up an empty palm to indicate he didn't know how to help her. Then he decided that yes, he *did* know, and he spoke before she could. "We knew," Garander said. "We had met him before, and we figured out he was a *shatra*. But by then we *liked* him."

"I've never, ever heard of anyone *talking* with a *shatra* before," Azlia said.

"They usually didn't get a chance," Sammel said. "Most people who met *shatra* didn't get a chance to do anything but die."

"That was during the war!" Ishta protested. "It's different now!"

"But it's still a *shatra*," Hargal said. "It's still a half-demon monster."

"Sort of," Garander said. "He doesn't seem like a monster."

"But it's still half demon?"

"Yes," Garander reluctantly admitted. "But the man part is completely in control of the demon part."

"How do you know?" Sammel asked.

"Tesk said so!" Ishta exclaimed.

"And you believe it?"

Garander and Ishta exchanged glances. "Yes, we do," Garander said.

"*I* didn't," Grondar said. "That was why I warned the neighbors."

Sammel paid him no attention as he focused on Garander and Ishta. "You do understand that demons lie, don't you?"

"So do ordinary people," Ishta pointed out.

"I don't think he was lying," Garander said.

"He might just be wrong," Azlia suggested. "Maybe he *thinks* he has the demon under control, but it could take over if the circumstances call for it."

"Excuse me," Grondar said, "but what does it matter? What can you do about it, in any case?"

Sammel and Azlia exchanged glances as Hargal replied, "Lord Dakkar sent us to determine whether you really saw something dangerous in the woods, and to deal with it appropriately."

"We didn't think it was really a *shatra*," Sammel added, "but we thought it might be a monster of some sort, and we were authorized to kill it if we thought it posed a threat to anyone."

"You think you can kill a *shatra*? The four of you?" Grondar asked.

"We don't know," Azlia admitted. "We don't have the sort of high-order destructive spells that the old combat wizards had during the war, and we don't have any dragons handy, but I'm a wizard, and Sammel is a sorcerer. I think we might have a decent chance."

"I don't," Grondar said.

"Can you even *find* him?" Garander asked.

"Now that we know what we're looking for, I believe we can," Sammel said. "I have talismans that can track anyone if I can find a trace to start with, and there are probably still traces around that tree."

Ishta threw Garander a worried look at that.

"We haven't seen Tesk all winter," Garander said. "He may not even be in the area anymore."

"Well, we'll see," Sammel said.

Azlia was staring at Ishta. "You really do like it, don't you?"

"Yes!" the girl replied. "He's nice! And he keeps the mizagars away."

"He…what?" Azlia looked to Sammel for an explanation.

"Mizagars," Sammel said. "Another Northern monster. They weren't remotely like people, though; they were crawling horrors, about the size of steer but with much shorter legs, a little like giant lizards. And they had plenty of teeth and claws—they ate people, if they could get them."

"You're saying 'had,' not 'have,'" Grondar said. "Why?"

"So far as I know, they're extinct," Sammel replied.

Grondar looked unconvinced. "There's a lot of unexplored country out there."

"Tesk says there are still mizagars in the hills," Garander said. "We don't see them because he ordered them to stay away."

"Is that possible?" Hargal demanded.

"I don't know," Sammel said. "I don't know if *anyone* knows. We don't know much about Northerners or their creations, not really."

"Tesk says mizagars were trained to obey Northern officers, and *shatra* were all officers," Garander said. "He showed us his rank talisman."

"It glowed," Ishta added.

"It *could* be true," Sammel acknowledged. "We just don't know."

"If it is, and you kill Tesk, you'll be letting dozens of mizagars come down from the hills and attack us."

Sammel glared at Garander.

"That's right!" Ishta said. "You can't hurt Tesk, or the mizagars will get you!"

Garander suppressed a sigh. Ishta was not helping her own cause. "Listen," he said, "Tesk has been out there in the woods for twenty years and he's never hurt anyone. Why is he suddenly a problem just because a couple of us saw him?"

"Because the baron says it is," Hargal answered.

"But what if we could show you that he really is harmless?"

Hargal snorted. "A *shatra* is not harmless."

Garander could hardly deny that. "All right, not harmless, but what if we could prove he doesn't want to hurt anyone? I mean, if you're right, and he's dangerous, and you try to kill him, you might just make him angry. You don't know whether you can kill him—you said so yourself." He gestured toward Azlia. "You might get *yourselves* killed, instead."

"How would you prove he's not dangerous?" Azlia asked.

"I...I would just..." Garander stopped. He had not thought this out yet.

"You could talk to him, and see for yourselves!" Ishta exclaimed. "You'd see that he's nice and doesn't want to hurt anyone."

"We might just see that it wants us to *think* it's harmless," Hargal said.

"We might see that the *man* means us no harm," Sammel said, "but what of the demon?"

"He *controls* the demon!" Ishta insisted.

"You don't *know* that!"

"What if we could prove he *does* control the demon?" Garander asked.

"How would you prove that?" Hargal asked.

"I don't know yet," Garander admitted.

"Well, you think of a way to prove it, and we can discuss it further," Hargal said. "Right now, I see our duty as determining whether the *shatra* is still in the area, and if it is, we need to either kill it or drive it away." He looked at Azlia, deep in the root cellar. "Have you got the magic to do that?"

"I can find it," Sammel said from beyond the cellar door. "I'm not sure I can destroy it."

"I don't know what I can do," Azlia said. "I have things I can try, but whether they'll work on something that's half-demon, I don't know. Other kinds of magic sometimes interfere with wizardry."

"You've never fought a demon?" Garander asked.

"Of course not," the wizard said. "I've never *seen* a demon. Since the end of the war the only demons in the World are the ones demonologists summon."

"And left-over *shatra*," Hargal added.

"And left-over *shatra*," Azlia acknowledged. "Anyway, there aren't any demonologists around here. I've never met one, or a *shatra*, so I've never seen a demon."

"Are there other *shatra* nearby?" Ishta asked.

Azlia shook her head. "Until your father warned your neighbors," she said, "we didn't think there were any *shatra* left anywhere. Now, can we get out of this cellar and get on with our business?" She gathered up her black box and other belongings and started toward the door.

"Of course," Hargal said, stepping aside into the barn.

Garander watched the soldier and the wizard leave, joining his father and the others in the main part of the barn; then he clambered out of the vegetable bin.

On the far side of the cellar Ishta was climbing out of her bin, as well, and the two of them met in the central passage. There they both paused, looking out the open door at the adults.

"We need to warn Tesk," Ishta said.

Garander nodded. "We need to find out what *he* thinks about all this," he said.

"If we warn him, he can go hide up in the hills."

"I hope so," Garander said.

He did not say anything to Ishta of what might happen if Tesk was unwilling or unable to hide, but he was thinking about it. Tesk might think he was in control, and he might know the war was over, but when it came down to the facts, *shatra* were created to kill people. Could Tesk really overcome his own nature if these magicians and soldiers attacked him, or would he fight back and slaughter them all?

"We need to find him before they do," Garander said.

"I can do that," Ishta said.

Startled by her confidence, Garander turned to look at his sister. "You can? You're sure?"

"I'm sure."

"Any time you want?"

Ishta hesitated, then said, "I think so."

Garander started to ask how, then caught himself. If she wanted him to know, she would have already told him. He looked out at the adults again. They did not look as if they were going to take immediate action, and the day was wearing on.

"If they haven't done anything by bedtime," he said, "I think we should slip out and find Tesk. If we try to get away now, though, they'll notice."

Ishta nodded. "All right."

"I'll wake you. When I do, be very quiet—we don't want to wake Shella."

Ishta nodded again.

"Now, let's get out of here before they realize we're up to something."

Ishta nodded again, and hurried up the three steps to the barn. Garander followed close behind, trying to look innocent.

CHAPTER THIRTEEN

Garander did not need to worry about rousing Ishta without waking Shella; Ishta was still wide awake and waiting for him when he slipped into the girls' room.

Fortunately, the baron's agents were sleeping in the barn; at first Garander had feared one or more might have been stationed in the house, but they had arranged otherwise. Slipping out of his own room in the attic would have been difficult if Hargal or the other soldier, whose name appeared to be Burz, were sleeping on his floor.

He was grateful that their father had taken pains to lay the floorboards straight and tight throughout the house; there were no creaks or pops that might have wakened Shella or his parents as he walked.

"Come on," he whispered.

Ishta did not hesitate or argue, but slid out of her bed. She hissed, "Turn around," and Garander obeyed. He heard a rustling, and when he turned back she had doffed her nightgown and put on a thick red woolen tunic.

Garander had simply gone to bed in his clothes, and pulled on his boots before coming to fetch Ishta, but he did not share his attic, while Shella would have noticed if Ishta did not change. He nodded approvingly, then pointed at her feet.

She pulled on slippers; her boots were by the front door. Garander frowned, then turned up a palm and gestured for her to follow him as he headed out into the main room.

Ishta shook her head vigorously, and grabbed his hand. Startled, Garander stopped and stared at her.

She pointed to the window.

"Why?" he asked, with a wary glance at Shella.

"You can see the door from the barn," Ishta said. "They might be watching."

Garander paused, considering. He had not thought about that, but she might be right. The baron's people might well have a guard posted. "Then how do…" he began.

Ishta raised a silencing finger, then pointed at the window. Garander had doubts about whether he would fit through the opening, and what they would find outside it, but Ishta seemed very sure of herself, and definitely had a more successful history of sneaking out than he did, so he followed as she cleared hairbrushes and nail files from the top of the heavy chest of drawers she and Shella shared, then pulled out a drawer of the wooden chest and used it as a step to climb onto the top, where she silently opened the shutter and casement and slid out into the night beyond.

Garander was much heavier than his sister, and held the window frame firmly with both hands as he clambered up onto the chest of drawers, so as not to tip it over. He gained the top without incident, and squeezed through the narrow window.

The drop to the ground was only a few feet, but it was longer than he had expected. He had been unable to see anything clearly and had not noticed that the ground outside the window was still snowy, so he landed badly, his feet sliding out from under him and his shoulders slamming back against the wall. His head struck as well, but not as hard.

"*Shhh*!" Ishta hissed angrily.

Garander sat up, rubbing his head, and was suddenly aware that he was sitting in muddy snow in his breeches and tunic; his coat was still hanging on its hook by the front door. Suppressing a growl he jumped up, brushing himself off.

"Come on," Ishta said, and he followed her bright tunic around the corner of the house, down the ditch behind the kitchen, and past the washhouse.

A moment later they were in the woods. It was becoming very obvious that Ishta had done this many times before, and Garander wondered just how much of her activities Ishta had hidden from the rest of the family.

The lesser moon was bright in the eastern sky and a sliver of the greater moon shone in the west, so the darkness was not complete, but Garander still marveled at how his sister could find her way so readily in the dark. Even she surely could not see Tesk's usual markers in this gloom, though—how did she hope to find the *shatra*?

And then a hiss from above brought brother and sister to an abrupt halt. Garander stopped in his tracks and looked up into the branches of a big oak, unsure whether he expected to see a bird, or a snake, or some other creature—did mizagars climb trees?

But instead he saw Tesk, squatting on a limb perhaps twenty feet off the ground, his body almost invisible in his black clothing, but his face somehow lit as if it were in full daylight. Something glowed green on one wrist.

"Tesk!" Ishta called happily. "We were looking for you!"

The Northerner seemed to slide sideways. The light vanished from his face and wrist for a moment, and Garander could see nothing but a faint outline, black on black, as the *shatra* moved down the trunk of the tree, to reappear standing before them. His face was once again illuminated, though Garander still could not see where the light was coming from, and again, a talisman glowed green on his wrist.

"I conclude there is a problem," he said.

Garander looked at Ishta, but she was looking expectantly at him. He turned back to Tesk. "The baron," he said.

Tesk seemed to take a second longer than usual before responding. "A local administrator?"

"Lord Dakkar, Baron of Varag," Garander explained. "He claims this land as his."

Tesk cocked his head slightly. "Which land?"

"All of it," Garander said, waving an arm. "The forest, our farm—he says it's all part of his domain."

"Ah," Tesk said. "*Lord* Dakkar. I had not understood your government to operate in this fashion. I thought your father owned the farm."

"He *does*," Ishta said. "He cleared the land himself!" She glanced uncertainly at her brother. "At least, that's what he says."

"Our father owns the farm," Garander confirmed. "He *did* clear it himself. But the baron collects taxes once a year, and protects the land from…well, from anything dangerous."

"My mother says that we shouldn't be paying his taxes," Ishta said. "*She* says Lord Edaran of Ethshar is our real overlord."

"Well…" Garander hesitated, as Tesk, clearly not yet understanding the situation, waited patiently for further explanation. The youth took a deep breath. "That part doesn't matter. The point is, Lord Dakkar claims to be our ruler, and he heard there was a *shatra* here, so he sent some of his people to investigate."

"How did he hear this?"

"Our father told the neighbors about you. The story got to Varag, and the baron heard it."

Tesk frowned. "This is unfortunate."

"Yes."

"This baron sent soldiers?"

"Two soldiers," Garander agreed. "And a wizard, and a sorcerer."

"Two?" Tesk held up two fingers. "Only two?"

"They didn't think there was really a *shatra* here," Garander said, almost apologetic. "And he did send his two best magicians." And quite possibly, Garander thought, his *only* magicians.

"Yes," Tesk said. He appeared thoughtful.

"I...we thought you should know."

"Yes," Tesk said again. "Thank you."

For a moment no one spoke; then Ishta asked, "What are you going to do? Will you kill them all?"

Tesk shook his head. "I have no desire to kill anyone." He seemed to shake himself, like a dog shedding water, then continued, "I was aware there were strangers, but I did not understand their nature. That was why I remained near your home, so that I might intervene if it appeared necessary. But now it appears that perhaps I would do better to go far away. If they are not certain that a *shatra* is here, then we do not want them to find one. I can retreat to the hills until they abandon their search."

"No," Garander said unhappily. "They *do* know you're here. They know we spoke with you. The wizard cast a spell that showed them. And the sorcerer says he can find you."

"An Ethsharitic sorcerer says this? He boasts. But the wizard—I do not know what the wizard can do."

"Can't you just tell them you're nice now?" Ishta asked.

Tesk smiled. "I do not think they would believe me."

"They wouldn't," Garander agreed. "There are too many stories from the war. Now they know you're here, I don't think they'll ever give up on finding you."

"This wizard—is he very powerful?"

"She," Garander said. "Her name is Azlia. I don't know how powerful she is. I don't think she's *really* strong, or she'd be living somewhere like Azrad's Ethshar, not in a town like Varag."

"Perhaps," Tesk acknowledged.

"You could kill them all!" Ishta exclaimed.

Appalled by his sister's bloodthirsty suggestion, it took a few seconds before Garander could say, "That would just make it worse! Then they'd *know* he's dangerous!"

"And they would stay away!" Ishta insisted. "They'd be too afraid to bother you!"

"No," Tesk said. "They would not."

"They'd keep sending more and more powerful magic until they killed him," Garander said. "Wizards, dragons, whatever it takes. They might even be able to get the theurgists to send gods after him."

"That is correct," Tesk agreed. "If I killed the baron's representatives, the baron could not permit me to live. I would be a threat to his authority."

For a moment none of them spoke; then Garander asked, "Do you really think the sorcerer is wrong when he says he can track you?"

Tesk gave an odd little snort. "I am certain. I was *designed* to avoid such things! But my creators did not understand wizardry, and I do not know what wizards can do."

"I don't know, either," Garander said, "but maybe you could get away if you went far enough up into the mountains."

"My homeland lay *beyond* the mountains. I could return. But it is a wasteland now; I would be alone."

"You'd be alive."

"As would the baron's representatives. Perhaps, if no one is harmed, they will not pursue me."

Garander, remembering what Hargal had said—"we need to either kill it or drive it away"—nodded. "I don't know about Lord Dakkar, but his man said he would be satisfied if you were gone, even if you were still alive somewhere out in the wilderness."

"But I'd never see you again!" Ishta wailed. "You can't do that!"

"I do not want to," Tesk said, "but I see no better choice."

"They might find you anyway! And what about the mizagars?"

"Yes, in time the mizagars would be free to attack your people. My orders can only restrain them for a few months. But if your baron has magicians who can kill me, those magicians can kill mizagars."

"I'm not sure he *does*," Garander said. "But somebody does."

"No!" Ishta insisted. "You need to stay here and *show* them you're nice!"

"I would like to, Ishta," the *shatra* said, "but I do not know how."

"Just…just *show* them. Talk to them. Be nice to them!"

"I do not know how," Tesk repeated.

Garander remembered more of his conversation with Lord Dakkar's agents. "They don't think you can control your demon side," he said.

Tesk had been looking down at Ishta. Now he met Garander's gaze. "Yes?"

"They said that if we could *prove* you can always control it, we could discuss…well, discuss things further."

"I control the demon," Tesk said. "If I had orders and attempted to defy them, perhaps then the demon could not be restrained, but I have no orders. I have had no orders for twenty years, and the demon sleeps. It will not wake unless I allow it."

"You… What if…" Garander was struggling to express thoughts he had not fully formed.

"Yes?"

"What if we could *prove* that?"

"How?"

"Suppose someone tried to kill you, and you didn't kill *him*?"

"Please explain further."

"Well," Garander said, "suppose someone attacks you. They think you would defend yourself by killing your attacker. They probably think the demon wouldn't *let* you do anything else. I mean, if there was ever a time the demon would take over, wouldn't that be it?"

"I can defend myself without killing."

"Can you…" Garander was still struggling with his own idea. "Can you not even defend yourself?"

Tesk stared at him. "Then I would be killed, would I not? This does not seem useful."

"No, but—you're *so* fast. Could you just…defend yourself, but not fight back?"

"Ah." Tesk blinked.

"I mean, if anything would show that the demon is under control, and that you don't have to be dangerous, wouldn't that do it?"

"Yes!" Ishta shrieked. "We'll show them he's safe!"

Tesk's eyes met Garander's, and they shared a moment of amusement.

"I do not know if this plan will succeed," Tesk said. "I think it is worth trying."

"If it doesn't work, you can still flee into the mountains," Garander said. "If you haven't hurt anyone, they may not think it's worth chasing you."

"This is true."

"Then you don't have anything to lose!" Ishta said.

"Indeed," Tesk agreed. "It would appear I do not."

"Then we'll arrange a meeting," Garander said. "Tomorrow afternoon, in the north field?"

Tesk nodded. "I will watch for your arrival," he said. "Signal me with a raised arm when you are ready to proceed."

Garander nodded. "I'll wave," he said. "And if something goes wrong, I'll do this, instead." He patted his thigh. "That will mean you should get away while you can."

"Understood."

For a moment the three of them stood, unsure what else needed to be said; then a cold breeze reminded Garander that they were standing out in the woods in the middle of the night, with no coats, and he was *freezing*.

"I'll see you tomorrow, then," he said.

"Tomorrow." The glow of Tesk's face abruptly vanished, and a second later the green light on his wrist went out, as well; he was just one more shadow among the many that filled the forest's darkness. Then, without as much as a rustle, he was gone, and Garander and his sister were standing alone among the trees. Garander shivered.

He liked Tesk, but he had to admit there was something creepy about him—and besides, it was cold. Ishta's feet must be half frozen in those thin slippers.

"Come on," he said. "Let's get back indoors."

Ishta nodded, and the two of them turned and headed for home.

Clouds had moved across the lesser moon, and the night was even darker than before; Garander found himself stumbling across roots and fallen branches, while he could hear mud sucking at Ishta's slippers. He wondered how she would hide or explain the inevitable stains once they were safely back in the house.

For that matter, he was sure his own breeches must be stained, and he *knew* they were wet—the cold was thoroughly uncomfortable.

Then they emerged from the trees behind the washhouse and stepped down into the ditch. A moment later they were below the bedroom window.

For the first time, Garander realized they had left it open. The room must be freezing, with all that cold night air getting in! What if the chill had woken Shella up?

"Give me a boost in," Ishta said.

Startled, Garander obeyed, but even as he did he wondered how she got back in when he wasn't with her.

Once Ishta was safely inside he grabbed the window frame and pulled himself up—which was more difficult than he had expected.

"Brace your feet against the wall," Ishta called down.

"I am!" he whispered back.

A moment later he sprawled awkwardly across the top of the chest of drawers, and barely caught himself before toppling heavily onto the floor. He peered over at the dark lump that was Shella; she did not stir.

"She never wakes up," Ishta said. "I don't know why she sleeps so soundly, since she hardly does any work, but she does."

Garander could not be sure in the darkness, but he thought he saw Shella move, as she had not when he made his clumsy entrance; she seemed to hunch her shoulders. She might, he thought, not be as sound a sleeper as Ishta thought.

But that did not matter. Moving as quietly as he could he closed the casement and the shutter, then slipped out the bedroom door and headed for the attic stair.

Tomorrow was going to be an exciting day, he told himself as he climbed. Once in his room he sat on the edge of his bed and pulled off his muddy boots, hoping he would be able to sleep in such a state of nervous anticipation.

He need not have worried; he had scarcely settled back on his pillow when his eyes closed and slumber overtook him.

CHAPTER FOURTEEN

Guests or not, there were chores to be done in the morning—livestock to feed, water to fetch, and any number of other mundane tasks to be performed. Garander was startled to find Azlia helping him with the chickens; she offered no explanation beyond a cheerful "Good morning!" and he decided not to ask.

As they finished up, she said, "Tell me about the *shatra*."

Garander suddenly realized why she had been helping him; she wanted to know more about her quarry. She had gotten him alone, ingratiated herself...

But he had nothing to hide. In fact, he *wanted* to tell her. As he hung up the feed bucket he said, "We call him Tesk because we can't pronounce his name; it's long and strange. He speaks Ethsharitic, but he pronounces his words strangely and sometimes gets things a little wrong."

"Where does he live? Do you know?"

"He lives in the forest—he doesn't need a house. His magic keeps him warm and dry. I'm not sure how he finds enough to eat."

"You're sure he doesn't have a cave or some other hiding place somewhere?"

Garander turned up an empty palm. "How could I be sure? But I don't know anything of one, and I've seen him sit in a snowstorm as comfortable as an ordinary man at his own hearth."

Azlia nodded. "How long has he been out there?"

"He says he's been alone in the woods since the end of the Great War—he was out there watching the borders when the gods destroyed the Empire. I suppose they overlooked him."

"He's been alone out there for twenty years?"

"That's what he says."

"Why didn't anyone know about it until now?"

"He didn't want them to. He can hide really well when he wants to."

"But then how did *you* find him?"

"Ishta led me to him." Before Azlia could ask the obvious next question, he continued, "And *she* found him because he wanted her to. He got lonely, and thought that a child wouldn't know any better than to talk to him."

"Don't parents around here tell their children not to talk to strangers?"

The empty palm came up again. "Do children in Varag do everything their parents tell them?"

Azlia smiled at that. "I suppose not."

"He didn't come looking for her, after all; he just stayed in the woods and let *her* find *him*. I think he may have known she wasn't allowed there, and if she was already breaking one rule, why not another?"

"I see."

"He didn't want to just stay out in the forest forever. He may be part demon, but he's part man, and men get lonely."

"He waited twenty years, though."

"He knew what would happen if the overlords of Ethshar found out a *shatra* had survived. He hoped that by now we'd all have forgotten what *shatra* were."

"That's not the sort of thing people forget."

"I guess not," Garander acknowledged, turning up a hand. "But remember, he doesn't know much about us. His people were different from ours."

"People are people," the wizard said.

Garander's mouth twisted wryly. "So you're saying Northerners were just like us?"

Azlia paused. They had left the barn and were standing in the yard, halfway to the house. "Well, no," she said. "Some things were different, some were the same."

Garander nodded. "So he *hoped* that *shatra* were forgotten. But he wasn't surprised when we figured out what he is."

"So you did know?"

"Not at first. But our father told us some things about the war, and we figured it out."

"And you still talked to the *shatra*?"

"By then we knew him, and we knew he didn't mean us any harm. After all, if he wanted to kill us, he'd had twenty years to do it."

"If he *was* really here all along."

"Where else could he have come from?" Garander asked.

Azlia took a second to think, then said, "So you really don't think he wants to hurt anyone?"

"The war's over. He knows that."

"What about the demon?"

Garander hesitated, then said, "He says that the demon can't control him unless he tries to disobey his orders—and for twenty years now, he hasn't *had* any orders, so the demon's harmless."

Azlia considered this for a moment. Garander glanced around, and saw Hargal and Grondar walking through the west field. No one else was in sight; Shella and their mother were probably in the house, but where Ishta, Sammel, and Burz might be he did not know.

"You don't want us to hurt him, do you?" Azlia asked.

"No, we don't," Garander confirmed. "Ishta and I, I mean. I don't know about anyone else. We *like* him."

"How do you know he hasn't gone off where we can't find him?"

Garander took a deep breath. "Because I talked to him," he said. "Last night."

Azlia smiled. "Ah," she said.

"He'd be willing to talk to you all, to *show* you he's safe."

"Oh?"

"If he does, if he can convince you he won't hurt anyone, will you go away? Go back to the baron and tell him there's no need to kill the *shatra*?"

Azlia hesitated. "I don't know," she said. "It'll take more than words to convince us."

"I think we can show you more than words."

"You have something planned?"

"Maybe." Garander frowned. "I'm glad I had a chance to talk to you; I don't think Sammel really listens to me, and that Hargal scares me. I don't know if I could have told them what I just told you."

"You don't think it's an accident that *I'm* the one who helped you this morning, do you?"

Garander had not given the matter any conscious thought, but now that it had been pointed out, it seemed obvious. He grimaced; these people weren't stupid. At least, the magicians weren't, and Hargal didn't seem to be; he really couldn't say about Burz. They must have noticed that he found Azlia easier to talk to than the others. "I guess not," he said. "But could *you* talk to the others, then? Sammel and the soldiers?"

"That's what I plan to do, yes. So, when did you have in mind for this demonstration?"

"After lunch."

"Today?" She sounded surprised.

Garander nodded.

"I thought you would need a few days to arrange it."

"No," Garander said. "This afternoon."

"Then I have some preparations to make."

Startled, Garander said, "You do?"

"I do." She looked around, and spotted Hargal. "Excuse me." Then she turned and marched off, headed directly toward the soldier and Garander's father.

This abrupt departure caught Garander by surprise; for a moment he simply stood and watched her go. Then, gathering his wits, he headed into the house.

Burz was standing just inside the door, watching Garander's mother and sister as they worked in the kitchen. The soldier turned as the youth came in, and asked, "Where's the wizard?"

"She went to talk to Hargal," Garander said, pointing.

Burz frowned. "Excuse me." He brushed past Garander and stepped out the door. Garander let him go, then greeted his mother and settled on a chair by the hearth.

A moment later the door opened again, and Ishta entered. "They're all talking over there," she said, pointing to the west.

"All of them?" Garander asked.

She nodded. "The sorcerer was following me around while I did my chores, but when he saw the others talking he went over there, too."

"Did he talk to you?"

"He tried to. I wouldn't talk to him. They want to kill Tesk, so I'm not going to talk to any of them."

"Oh." That was typical of Ishta, Garander thought—though he wondered whether she might have talked more than she wanted to admit. Sometimes she couldn't keep quiet, especially when she was excited or angry. But Sammel didn't know her; he wouldn't have known how to get her started.

"Would you two like to make yourselves useful?" their mother called.

Garander resisted the temptation to answer her question honestly, and instead got up and headed for the kitchen.

He had expected the baron's people to be impatient to get on with meeting Tesk, but they did not seem to be. When Grondar came in he reported that they had been talking quietly and not letting him hear, and had then all gone into the barn and closed the door. He clearly did not appreciate being shut out of his own barn, but he was not inclined to argue with soldiers and magicians.

The family went about their business, not saying much about their uninvited visitors. When the time came to make lunch, Garander asked his mother, "Should I tell the...our guests?"

His mother snorted. "Let them feed themselves!"

Accordingly, the five of them ate a quiet meal, leaving the baron's agents to their own devices. Garander did not think any of them would starve.

When everyone had eaten, the table had been cleared, and Shella the Younger was washing the dishes, Garander rose. "I need to talk to the wizard," he said.

"I'll come along," Ishta immediately announced, springing to her feet. Garander repressed a sigh; Ishta could be distressingly obvious, and indeed, the rest of the family plainly saw that something was up.

"Fine," he said, with a glance at their father. "But be quiet."

Ishta nodded.

"Son," Grondar said.

"Yes?" Garander answered, dreading what his father might say.

"I assume you are not simply looking for the wizard in hopes she might show you a few spells."

"No, Father."

"I hope you aren't planning to do anything that might bring the baron's wrath down upon us. Remember, while he may not have a great deal of power in his own right, he is one of the Council of Barons. If Ishta's friend angers Lord Dakkar, it may bring not just the soldiers of Varag, but the armies and magicians of Sardiron and all its allies down upon us. Don't judge them all by the two out in the barn, either; there are wizards in the World who can move mountains. And the dragons who fought for Ethshar in the Great War are not all dead; I don't know what became of them, but I'm sure there are those in the baronies who *do* know, and who can call some of them back if the need arises."

"I'm not trying to anger anyone, Father. I just want to convince the baron's people that Tesk is harmless and should be left alone."

For a moment the two men, father and son, looked at one another, assessing each other. Then Grondar said, "You do have a plan, then?"

Garander nodded.

"Is there anything I can do to help?"

Garander started to say that there was not, but then a thought struck him. He glanced at Ishta, but she was leaving it all to him. "You know, if you could bring some of the neighbors, so *they* can see that Tesk won't hurt them, that might be helpful."

Grondar raised his chin, considering, then asked. "How long do I have?"

Garander turned up an empty palm. "I'm not sure. Perhaps an hour? Perhaps two? No later than mid-afternoon."

Grondar nodded. He turned and called, "Shella, leave the rest of the dishes for later, and get over to Kolar's place. Bring anyone there who can spare the time—tell them it's about the *shatra*."

Startled, Shella dropped a dishrag. "What?"

"I said, go fetch Kolar and his family. Tell them we have the baron's magicians here to deal with the *shatra*, and they're invited to watch." He turned back to Garander. "Do you know where?"

"The north field."

"Good. Wife, can you see to Elkan? I'll tell Felder myself, and the village if I have time."

Startled by this sudden helpfulness, Garander stood, mouth agape, for a moment, as his parents and sister found their coats and prepared to go.

Grondar saw him. "Well?" he demanded. "Don't you have something to do?"

"I don't…I mean, yes, but now it…maybe I should wait…"

"Get on with it, whatever it is," Grondar said with a wave.

"Come on," Ishta said, tugging at his sleeve.

Garander started toward the door again, and had lifted the latch when his father's voice stopped him again. "Son?"

"Yes, Father?"

"Be careful."

"Yes, Father."

With that parental concern in his ear, Garander stepped out into the chill of early spring and headed for the barn, with Ishta close on his heels.

Azlia and the others were waiting for him, and at least some of their preparations were obvious—the two soldiers wore breastplates and helmets, while the sorcerer had assorted talismans slung about his body on straps and cords. The wizard had doffed her traveling cloak and was wearing a blue gown and velvet cap; a black ribbon was tied around her right wrist, securing a small metal object with a complex and unfamiliar rune painted on its face, and several pouches and vials were strung on her belt. Garander guessed that the four of them were ready for combat.

"There you are," Hargal said. "What's this demonstration you have planned for us?"

"Well, it's…it's not so much a demonstration as a chance to talk to the *shatra* yourselves, so you can see that he doesn't mean any harm."

"Tesk wouldn't hurt anyone!" Ishta burst out.

"It's a *shatra*," Hargal said. "They were made to kill people."

"He's a person!"

Azlia interrupted. "We can talk to him?"

"You said that if we could prove he can control the demon, you wouldn't kill him, right?"

The soldiers and magicians exchanged glances. "All right," Hargal said. "I guess we can agree to that."

"Well, that's what we plan to do."

"How?" Sammel asked.

Garander hesitated, and then decided not to explain. He had *intended* to tell them, but now he thought that would be a mistake. *He* trusted Tesk to keep his demon half leashed, but these four did not, and they were not likely to agree to something that might get them all killed if it turned out Tesk could *not* restrain the demon. "You'll just have to come and see."

"Come where?" Hargal asked. "Can't it come here?"

"Just out to the field," Garander said. "I don't…there isn't enough room in here."

Again, the four looked at one another; then Azlia said, "Come on."

Garander and Ishta led the way out of the barn and around to the north field. Although the snow was almost gone from the field, the ground was unpleasantly soft underfoot; no one wanted to rush across it, for fear a foot might sink into the mud, so the six of them made a slow parade out to the center.

The sky was overcast, the sun hidden behind clouds, but it did not look likely to rain.

When Garander reached what seemed like a good spot—near the center of the field, clear of snow, and on ground that was not *too* soft—he stopped. He waited for the others to gather around him.

They did, but he noticed Sammel watching the forest suspiciously, and both soldiers had their hands on the hilts of their swords. Azlia's hand was on the hilt of her silver dagger.

"Well?" Hargal demanded. "Now what? Where is it?"

"It's not far away," Garander said. "But first—Sammel, you said your sorcery could track a *shatra*. Tesk says it can't."

Sammel frowned. "Your *shatra* is correct. I could follow its path for a few yards, no more."

"So if Tesk goes into hiding, you can't find him."

Sammel did not bother to answer; he just looked at Azlia. "*I* can find him," the wizard said. "I know he's less than half a mile from here."

"Do you really think you can kill him?"

"I don't know," Azlia answered. "I think I could give it a good try."

"What about you two?" Garander asked, gesturing at Hargal and Burz.

"Depends how much truth there is in the stories," Hargal said. "If they're all true, then no, I can't, but if they're the exaggerations some of us think they are, then maybe I can."

"All right," Garander said. "You're about to get a chance to try." He raised his arm above his head.

A weird ululating wail shattered the afternoon calm; the baron's agents all whirled, looking for the source.

Garander turned more slowly. He had never heard the sound before, and had not expected it, but after an initial start he was not terribly surprised. He supposed Tesk wanted to make a dramatic entrance.

And sure enough, under the trees to the north stood a black-garbed figure, scarcely visible in the shadows.

The others spotted him soon enough; Sammel pointed, in case anyone had missed the mysterious figure.

Then Tesk ran out to them, moving with that supernatural speed and inhuman smoothness—not in a straight line, but zigzagging across the field.

He stopped about twenty feet away.

"I am Tezhiskar Deralt aya Shatra Ad'n Chitir Shess Chitir," he said. "I understand you wanted to speak with me."

CHAPTER FIFTEEN

For a moment no one spoke; then Burz exclaimed, "It's real!" His hand fell to the hilt of his sword, but he did not draw the blade.

"We knew that," Hargal snapped, not looking at his subordinate. His eyes were locked on the *shatra*. He did not touch his own weapon.

"I am real," Tesk said. "I am *shatra*." He stood calmly, hands at his sides.

"What are you *doing* here?" Burz asked.

Tesk glanced at Garander and Ishta, then said to the others, "I have come to persuade you to leave me alone."

"But…you're a *shatra*," Sammel said.

"Yes. I have already confirmed that." Garander doubted that anyone who didn't know Tesk would have noticed it, but he thought the *shatra* sounded amused.

"*Shatra* are inhuman monsters created for the sole purpose of killing people."

"That is false," Tesk replied. "We had *several* military purposes."

Azlia cleared her throat. "I notice you don't deny being an inhuman monster."

Tesk made that odd shoulder movement. "I do not deny my nature. The cause I was created to serve is no more, however, and now I am content to live quietly and do not wish to harm anyone. I have come here today in the hope that I can convince you of this truth."

Azlia glanced at Garander and his sister.

"You wouldn't take *my* word for it," Garander said, not so much to Azlia as to the others, "so I thought maybe *he* can convince you."

"I have lived in these woods for twenty years," Tesk said. "When the war ended I had no home to return to, so I remained in this area, where I had been positioned during the final campaign. I have not harmed anyone. I have not interfered with the clearing of land or the building of structures in what was Imperial territory. I acknowledge that the war is over, and my nation was defeated and destroyed; I have nothing left to fight for except myself." He paused, blinked as if startled, and then added, "And my friends." He gestured at Ishta and Garander, then continued, "I believe your baron sent you to kill me, to protect his people from me. It is not necessary. I will not hurt them."

"How can we be sure of that?" Hargal asked warily.

"I have been here for twenty years and harmed no one."

"So you say."

"You say you know what I am. You cannot believe that anyone would still live within a mile of this place if I did not wish them to."

"We know *what* you are," Sammel said, "but we don't know *why* you're here. For all we know an outpost of the Northern Empire has survived somewhere beyond the mountains, and has sent you to test our resolve."

"If such an outpost survives, I am unaware of it."

The conversation was not going the way Garander had anticipated, and he spoke up, trying to force it back on the intended path. "Look, he's been here for months, at the very least, probably years, and he hasn't hurt anyone, and he's not *going* to hurt anyone. You can go back to Varag and tell Lord Dakkar that!"

"But we don't *know* he won't!" Azlia protested. "What if the demon is just waiting until the time is right?"

"I control the demon," Tesk replied calmly.

"*Do* you?" the wizard demanded.

"I do," Tesk answered.

This was the moment Garander had hoped for. "We can prove it!" he said.

"How?" Sammel asked. "That's the thing, boy—even if everything the *shatra* says is true, how can you know that he can really keep the demon in check?"

"Test it!" Garander said. "Do something the demon wouldn't allow." He gestured at Burz's hand, the one clutching his sword. "Take a swing at him—he won't hurt you."

"He'd kill me!" Burz said, stepping back and raising his hands.

"No, he won't!"

"Well, I'm not about to find out!" The soldier retreated three steps.

Garander turned to Hargal, but he shook his head. "I am not about to fight a *shatra*, boy. Maybe *you* think he can control the demon half, but *I* don't."

Garander had not expected this reaction, and for a moment he hesitated. He *should* have expected it. He trusted Tesk, but of course these people didn't. That was the whole *point* of this.

He straightened up and threw back his shoulders. "Fine!" he said. "Then give me your sword, and *I'll* try to kill him!"

"What?" Ishta cried. "No, Garander! He's our friend!"

Garander ignored his sister. "Give me your sword," he said, looking at Hargal and holding out his hand.

Hargal looked at the youth, then at the *shatra*, and then at the magicians, considering. Then he said, "Why not?" He drew his sword, watching Tesk as he did so, then reversed it and passed it to Garander hilt-first.

Garander accepted it warily. He had never held a sword before.

The grip was not so very different from some of the farmyard tools he had used, and the weapon was lighter than he had expected, with less weight in the blade than he had thought it would have. He hefted it in his right hand, then ran his left along the back of the blade, feeling the metal.

It was fine steel, not the ordinary iron used in most farm implements—smooth and strong, not as cold or heavy as iron, but heavier than any knife blade he had ever wielded. It was stiffer than the two-handed scraper, but with more give than the posthole drill.

"Stabbing gives you more reach and power than slashing," Hargal offered helpfully. "It's easier to miss with a thrust, though."

"That will not be a concern," Tesk said. "You will not strike me." He made no move to retreat, though.

Garander took a step toward the *shatra* and swung the blade at Tesk's chest much as he swung a scythe when harvesting wheat.

Tesk moved in an odd twisting motion that was not what Garander would ordinarily have called ducking, but that somehow let the sword pass harmlessly over his head. Then he was upright again—or rather, more nearly upright; he remained in a half-crouch.

Garander remembered Hargal's advice, and tried jabbing the point at Tesk.

The *shatra* moved sideways in a quick, snakelike motion and the blade once again passed by harmlessly.

Garander frowned. Tesk was making this look too easy. He had to show these people that Tesk could control his demon even when threatened, and so far, Garander's attacks did not look like a real threat at all. He glanced around at the baron's agents, and saw Ishta covering her mouth with her hands—*she*, at least, thought Tesk was in danger.

And he noticed other figures standing at the edge of the field—his mother, and old Elkan, and as he watched his sister and Kolar walked up.

He had to show them all that Tesk could be trusted not to hurt anyone. Garander pursed his lips, tightened his grip on the sword, and attacked again.

This time he did not stop with a single blow; instead he swung the sword wildly back and forth, whipping it through the air, changing height and angle as he struck repeatedly at the *shatra*.

Tesk did not even retreat, let alone defend himself or strike back; he was simply never in the blade's path. Garander had no idea how he was doing it, but sometimes the blade passed over his head, sometimes to one side or the other, and once under his feet as the *shatra* jumped up to let a low swing go beneath him.

Angered despite himself, Garander drew the sword back and charged at Tesk, intending to strike him down, or at least to threaten him sufficiently to force some sort of direct response. Instead he found himself stumbling awkwardly past as Tesk sidestepped out of his path.

He whirled as quickly as he could, sword slashing, trying to go after the *shatra* before he could react, but there was nothing a mere human could do that was faster than the *shatra*'s reactions. His blade once again passed through empty air, and Tesk was still standing in almost the same spot, unsmiling, but untroubled by this ongoing assault.

Garander glanced at his audience and saw Hargal whispering to Burz while keeping an eye on the combatants—or rather, on the boy and the *shatra*, because what was happening here could scarcely be called combat. Embarrassed, Garander redoubled his efforts, charging, jumping, slashing, and stabbing, but all to no effect; Tesk dodged every blow without any apparent effort.

And then suddenly Tesk moved in a new and unexpected way, and Garander saw *another* sword-blade miss the *shatra*. Shifting his attention, Garander saw that Burz had drawn his sword and joined the fray.

"Come on, boy," Burz called. "He can't dodge us both."

Garander raised his weapon and did his best, while Burz attacked from the other side.

Tesk demonstrated that Burz was wrong; he *could* dodge them both, though now one blade or the other sometimes passed very close to those tight black clothes.

Tesk did not move out from between his two attackers, though. He just avoided their blows as he maintained his position.

"Boy!" Hargal called. Garander ignored him; he was determined to get Tesk. For a moment he completely forgot that this whole demonstration was intended to *help* his friend; right now his blood was racing, and he wanted only to *hit* his elusive foe, to strike something other than air with his borrowed blade.

"*Boy!*" Hargal bellowed, so loud that Garander started and almost dropped his sword. He stopped his attack. Did this mean the big soldier was convinced? He turned.

"Give me that thing," Hargal said, holding out his hand. "You're no swordsman. You're more likely to hit Burz, or your own foot, than the *shatra*."

Reluctantly, Garander stepped over to the baron's man and handed him the weapon. As he did, he heard a gasp. He turned.

Burz had not stopped *his* attack. He had paused, yes, but then he had launched a sudden jab at Tesk's back, hoping to catch the *shatra* by surprise.

The gasp had come from the observers as the soldier's blade passed no more than three inches from Tesk's side, under the *shatra*'s arm—but it had not touched him, any more than any of the earlier attempts.

Then Hargal charged in, sword raised.

Garander watched helplessly as the two soldiers tried to hit Tesk. For the first few moments they fought silently; then Hargal called, "We aren't going to kill you, Northerner! We just want to see whether you bleed human red or demon black."

"My blood is red," Tesk replied. "But I will not permit you to see for yourself."

As the struggle continued, Garander reluctantly admitted to himself that Hargal was right—he was no swordsman. The two soldiers were able to actually force Tesk back a few steps, though their blades still never touched him.

Someone threw a rock, but Tesk ducked it easily, even though he had not been looking in that direction.

"How does he *do* that?" someone asked; Garander turned to find one of the villagers at his elbow. His father had arrived without his noticing, bringing more of their neighbors. The audience had grown to perhaps two dozen people of various ages and sexes, including Garander's entire family.

"He's a *shatra*," Ishta said proudly.

"It's sorcery," Sammel said. "Or maybe demonology."

"Can't you tell which?" Garander asked him.

Sammel shook his head. "Not from here. Not without doing some tests."

"You could do the tests."

"I'd need to lower my defenses to do that."

"What defenses?"

Sammel lifted one arm, revealing a glowing red disc strapped to his wrist. It had previously been hidden by his sleeve. "I came prepared," he said. "In case this didn't go well. So did Azlia."

"So lower your defenses! You can *see* he won't hurt you!" Garander hoped the sorcerer didn't hear his frustration, but the entire purpose of this demonstration had been to show that they did not need to fear Tesk.

Just then Burz and Hargal launched a coordinated attack, Burz striking at Tesk's head while Hargal tried a sweep at his legs, and the *shatra*'s mid-air somersault that avoided both blows drew gasps and applause from the crowd.

"I don't think I care enough which sort of magic it is to expose myself to something that can do *that*," Sammel replied.

"But he's not a threat! Don't you see? Three of us have been doing everything we can to try to kill him, and he hasn't even drawn a weapon!"

"He *is* a weapon," Sammel answered.

At that, Garander almost despaired. He looked for Azlia, to see if the wizard might be more amenable to reason.

She was standing back a little apart from the crowd, her silver dagger in her hand. She was gesturing in the air and muttering, as she had when she summoned the vision in the root cellar.

"She's casting a spell," he said, and only realized he had said it aloud when Sammel and Ishta turned to look at her.

"That's cheating!" Ishta said.

"We don't know what *kind* of spell," Garander said, even as he felt a sinking in his belly.

"It's nothing terrible," Sammel told them. "We talked about this beforehand—she's just testing whether her magic can affect the *shatra*. If she were seriously trying to harm him, she wouldn't do it out here in the open."

He sounded sincere, but Garander was not entirely convinced, and he didn't think Ishta was, either. There was not much they could do about it, though, so they merely watched as the fight continued.

It really wasn't much of a fight, though. Tesk continued to dodge everything the two soldiers did. There was a brief moment of excitement when blue sparks burst from Azlia's dagger, momentarily distracting everyone but Tesk and Hargal, but other than that the demonstration had become repetitive, more tedious than thrilling. It dragged on, and on, until finally Burz staggered back, exhausted.

"I give up," he said. "I can't touch him."

The crowd watching burst into applause.

"You haven't even made him angry!" Garander called. "You see? He isn't a threat to anyone."

Hargal, panting, stopped fighting and lifted his blade to point skyward. "*We* certainly aren't a threat to *him*," he said.

"So there's no need to fight!" Garander exclaimed. "There's nothing to worry about. If he wanted to hurt anyone, he'd have done it already."

Reluctantly, Hargal nodded. "We certainly couldn't stop him." He glanced at the wizard, but Azlia sheathed her dagger with one hand and turned up an empty palm with the other.

"We did kill some *shatra* during the war," Grondar said. "It must be *possible*."

Tesk looked at Azlia, much as Hargal had a moment before. "It is possible," he said. Unlike Burz and Hargal, he did not sound tired or short of breath. Then he turned to Grondar. "But there is no need to kill me. Your children trust me, and I have not harmed them. The war is over. I want peace."

"Maybe he *can't* hurt anyone anymore," someone called from the crowd. "Maybe there's a spell on him!"

"Maybe the gods did something to him!" another voice suggested.

Garander was about to shout out a denial, then caught himself; if the neighbors wanted to believe that, then so much the better! He could see Tesk considering the matter, and he, too, apparently decided not to insist on the truth.

Assuming that it *was* the truth; Garander realized that he did not actually know. Maybe Tesk *had* been magically defanged somehow, whether he knew it or not, and that was why he had been allowed to survive the end of the war.

Other voices spoke up, and in a moment the field was loud with chatter and argument.

Garander listened, but did not follow the discussion very closely; as far as he was concerned, the most important thing was what was *not* said: No one was calling for Tesk's death. There were no cries of "Kill the monster!"

And then Ishta suddenly ran out onto the field and threw her arms around Tesk's waist. "You're safe!" she said. "You convinced them!"

The conversation died as everyone stared, and then Hargal spoke, slowly and deliberately.

"You're right," he said. "I'm convinced. The *shatra* doesn't mean us any harm—and if he did, there isn't anything we could do about it."

"So you'll tell Lord Dakkar that?" Grondar asked.

Hargal nodded. "Of course, he may not believe me," he said.

"Well, we'll support you," Sammel said, gesturing at Azlia and himself.

Ishta was still hugging Tesk; Garander noticed that the *shatra* had not hugged her back, but was smiling happily. Now she released him, and turned to the crowd. "Tesk," she said, "I'd like you to meet my mother, Shella of the Green Eyes, and my father, Grondar of Lullen. And these are some of our neighbors…"

The neighbors stepped forward to be introduced; some even shook Tesk's hand. Any fear they might have had of the Northern monster had been banished by the display of dodging and Ishta's obvious affection for him.

Garander did not participate; instead he watched the baron's four representatives. They did not join in the camaraderie, but gathered to one side and spoke quietly amongst themselves. They did not seem happy or excited, as most of the others were; they seemed disappointed and worried.

Ishta seemed to think that all the trouble was past, and that she and her special friend could now go on as before, meeting in the forest to talk without worrying about secrecy or danger.

Watching the visitors conferring, Garander did not think the danger was over.

CHAPTER SIXTEEN

The baron's party left the next morning, heading back to Varag to bring Lord Dakkar their conclusions. Garander, both his sisters, and his parents gave them a friendly send-off, watching and waving as the foursome trudged off to the west.

Tesk was not there; he had retreated to the forest shortly after the introductions, saying that he had been alone too long to be comfortable among so many people. Several of the neighbors had seemed disappointed that they had not had a chance to talk at length with the mysterious Northern monster, but they had all gone home peacefully.

After the four were gone, and after their daily chores were done, Garander and Ishta slipped away for a brief visit with Tesk. They found him sitting in a tree, perhaps six feet off the ground, waiting for them; Garander hoisted Ishta up to sit beside him, then climbed up and found a seat on another limb. The *shatra* seemed his usual calm self, and after some polite discussion Ishta asked, "Aren't you glad they'll leave you alone?"

"They may not leave me alone," Tesk replied. "They will report to their superior—the baron. He will determine what will be done."

"Well, yes, but you heard them say they'll tell him you don't want any trouble," Garander said.

"We do not know whether they spoke the truth. They may change their minds after taking time to consider. And we do not know how influential they really are."

This matched some of Garander's own unspoken concerns, but Ishta insisted, "No one's going to bother you!"

"I hope you are correct," Tesk answered.

The next few sixnights went well; the weather stayed relatively dry, allowing Grondar and his family to get much of the plowing and planting done. Ishta was able to slip away and visit with Tesk a few times, but Garander was generally kept too busy.

His mother suggested to Ishta she could invite Tesk for supper one night, which surprised the girl; what surprised Garander was when Ishta actually made the offer, and Tesk accepted.

Both Shellas went all out to make the best meal they could; the elder Shella had Garander slaughter one of the hogs, and presented her family and Tesk with a spectacular rib roast, mushroom soup, boiled apples, fresh bread, and herb butter.

The conversation was dominated by Grondar and Tesk exchanging war stories; Shella the Younger said little but seemed fascinated with the *shatra*, and Garander worried that she might be getting foolish romantic notions. When he got a chance he whispered to her, "Remember, he's at least twenty years older than you, *and* he isn't entirely human."

"Shut up!" Shella hissed in reply, and Garander thought she blushed. She did a better job of hiding her interest afterwards, though.

After the meal they gathered around the hearth with a bottle of wine; Garander wondered whether Tesk realized what an extravagance this was. No one in the area had succeeded in growing decent grapes, which meant that wine had to be bought from merchants in Varag, with cash money; the family rarely drank any except at Festival, and even then they were limited to a bottle or two. The conversation continued, but became more general; Garander's mother asked Tesk about his family, and only realized too late that not only were they were all dead, but that most of them had been killed by the gods of Ethshar in the campaign of extermination that ended the Great War.

When the wine was gone Shella invited Tesk to stay the night, but the *shatra* politely declined. Garander was relieved by that; although everyone seemed determined to treat Tesk as just another neighbor now, he was not. He was still a monster, even if a friendly one. Garander had risked his own life to prove that Tesk would not kill anyone, but that did not mean he was entirely comfortable with having the Northerner around while he slept.

Besides, the house was small, and crowded enough with just the five of them.

"I'll fetch a lantern to light you home, then," Grondar offered.

Tesk smiled slightly at that. "It is not necessary," he said. "I can see well in the dark."

"Oh," Grondar said, looking at the *shatra*'s eyes. "Of course you can."

Tesk had set his pack by the door; now he gathered it up and left. Garander went to the door, intending to watch their guest safely out of sight, but Tesk had already vanished.

He was pleasant company, but he really was not human.

It was mid-afternoon about ten days later, while Garander was hoeing weeds from the west field under scattered clouds on a cool spring day, that he heard an unfamiliar voice call, "*Hai!*"

He looked around, startled, but did not see anyone at first. Then he noticed a shadow, and looked up.

A red and brown carpet was hanging in mid-air, about fifteen feet off the ground, and a man in a blue robe and pointed hat was standing on it.

"I'm looking for Grondar of Lullen," the stranger shouted.

"He's my father," Garander replied. "What do you want with him?"

"I understand he's captured a *shatra*."

Garander blinked. "Ah…no."

"No?"

"He hasn't captured anyone."

"But there *is* a *shatra* in the area?"

Garander did not appreciate strangers coming around making demands, especially since it probably meant someone else wanted to kill Tesk—or perhaps that Lord Dakkar had hired new, more powerful magicians to carry out the execution. "Who wants to know?" he called back.

"Lord Edaran of Ethshar," the stranger said.

Startled, Garander frowned. "The overlord of Ethshar of the Sands?"

"Exactly."

Apparently the news of Tesk's existence had spread farther than Garander had expected. "Are you claiming to be Lord Edaran?" he asked.

The stranger let out a bark of laughter. "Gods, no!" he said. "He just hired me to find the farm with the tame *shatra*. I'm called Zendalir the Mage. And you are…?"

"Garander Grondar's son. And there's no such thing as a tame *shatra*."

Zendalir looked down his nose at Garander. "Well, I wouldn't have thought so, but we've gotten pretty definite reports of one."

"There's one in the area, but he isn't tame."

"But it *is* a *shatra*? You're certain?"

Garander had to think how he could phrase his response to give away as little as possible. He did not like this arrogant fellow, but he did not want to antagonize Edaran of Ethshar, who was one of the three most powerful non-magicians in the World. In the end he kept it simple. "Yes, I'm certain."

"Excellent! I'd like to see it, if I may; is there someone here who can arrange that?"

"Just see him?"

"Yes. I'm not going to kill it, if that's what you're worried about."

It was. *Seeing* Tesk was not so terrible, and was definitely preferable to killing him, but Garander was still wary. He said, "He may not want to see you, and we can't *make* him do anything."

"Can't you? I understood your family rendered it unable to harm people."

For a moment Garander wondered what the magician was talking about, but he quickly realized this was a bizarre misinterpretation of the demonstration they had staged, showing that Tesk could control his demon. "No," he said. "He *chose* not to hurt anyone."

"A *shatra* chose not to kill Ethsharites?" The mage cocked his head. "We had assumed you had it under some sort of geas."

"No." Garander shook his head. "He's not stupid. He knows the war is over. He just wants to be left in peace."

"Well, *that* isn't going to happen!" Zendalir said with a broad smile. "Is there some way you can arrange for me to speak to it, or whoever is in charge of it, on Lord Edaran's behalf?"

"No one is in charge of him," Garander said.

"Its representative, then?"

Puzzled, Garander said, "Representative?"

"Someone who can deliver the overlord's offer."

"I'm his friend," Garander said, smacking the hoe's head on the dirt by his feet. "I can tell him what you want."

"A *shatra* has friends?"

"This one does."

"Oh, very good! Tell it…"

"Him," Garander corrected.

"Of course. Tell *him*, then, that Lord Edaran wishes to engage his services, and will pay a generous stipend."

It took a moment for Garander to make sense of this; he knew the words, but did not see how they could apply to Tesk. Finally, though, he said, "The overlord wants to *hire* him?"

"Yes."

"To do what?"

"You understand, boy, that we had thought we would be hiring your father—that he controlled this *shatra* somehow. You tell me that isn't the case, so it seems Edaran needs to employ the *shatra* directly. Very well; that removes an unnecessary layer of administration. Yes, we want to hire him."

"To do *what*?" Garander repeated. "He'll want to know."

"I should think it would be obvious. We want to study his magic, so that we can use it for the good of the Hegemony of the Three Ethshars."

This had not been obvious to Garander at all. It did make a certain amount of sense, though. "I can tell him," he said. "But I don't know if he'll be interested."

"Well, I hope we can at least open negotiations."

Garander turned up an empty palm.

Zendalir looked around, tapping his chin through his beard. "I can provide him with transportation to Ethshar," he said. "Or I can bring Lady Shasha here, to conduct the overlord's business."

"Who's Lady Shasha?" Garander did not keep up with politics, or try to remember all the names, but he was fairly certain he had never heard of a Lady Shasha.

"Oh, she's one of Edaran's advisors," Zendalir said. "He's appointed her to handle this matter. She's actually the one who hired *me*, though I did get my instructions from the overlord himself."

That did little to convince Garander of her intelligence; the flying carpet was impressive, but Zendalir did not seem very diplomatic, and his grotesque misunderstanding of the situation was somewhat worrisome.

"I think it might be best if this Lady Shasha came here," he said.

"Would tomorrow afternoon, around this time, be agreeable?"

"It sounds fine to *me*," Garander said, "but I don't know what Tesk will think."

"Tesk? I thought your father's name was Grondar."

"It is. We call the *shatra* Tesk. His real name is too hard to pronounce."

Zendalir looked startled. "It has a *name*?"

"Of course he has a name!"

"All right, all right!" He held up both hands. "I'll be back tomorrow with Lady Shasha to discuss terms, then." He paused, staring at Garander. His tone was harsher as he added, "And I certainly hope, boy, that you haven't been playing some sort of trick on me. It will not go well for you if it turns out you are *not* the *shatra*'s friend. If you have misled me in any way, now is the time to admit it—I will accept it as harmless youthful foolishness today, but tomorrow I will be far less forgiving."

"I certainly haven't *intentionally* misled you," Garander said, resisting the urge to say more and make it clear just what he thought of the magician's wits. Insulting a magician to his face was at least as stupid as anything Zendalir had done.

"Very well, then," Zendalir said. "I shall see you tomorrow." He raised a hand.

"Wait!" Garander called.

Zendalir paused in mid-gesture. "Yes? You have a confession after all?"

"No, of course not. In case Tesk asks, though—what kind of magician are you?"

Zendalir drew himself up to his full height, clapped a hand on his chest, and announced, "I am a *wizard*, boy! What else could I be? Did I not tell you I am a mage? Do you not see this magnificent carpet?"

"Oh—does mage mean wizard? I didn't know."

"A mage is a *master* wizard, you...lad! It denotes one who has attained a certain status in the Wizards' Guild! And this carpet could be nothing but wizardry!"

"All right. We don't see much magic out here."

"Then how did—ah, but you claim the *shatra* is not enchanted." He waved a hand. "It's not my concern how you did it. I will see you tomorrow." With that, the carpet rose, rotated a half-turn, and sailed off to the south.

Garander leaned on his hoe and watched it go. It had scarcely reached the horizon when both his sisters came running toward him.

"What was *that*?" Shella called.

"A wizard," Garander replied. "On a flying carpet. He wants to talk to Tesk."

Shella clapped her hands. "A real wizard?"

"You've met a wizard before," Garander pointed out. "Azlia was a wizard."

"But she didn't have a flying carpet!"

"What does he want with Tesk?" Ishta asked. She sounded worried.

Garander could not help smiling at the absurdity. "He says Lord Edaran wants to *hire* him."

Shella's hand flew to her mouth. "Lord *Edaran*? Of *Ethshar*?"

Garander nodded.

"Hire him to do what?" Ishta demanded.

"To teach him Northern magic, I guess," Garander said, turning up an empty palm.

Both girls fell silent at that; Garander nodded.

"Can he *do* that?" Shella asked.

"I have no idea," Garander replied.

"If he wants to hire Tesk, why did he leave?" Ishta asked.

"He'll be back tomorrow," Garander said. "I promised I'd tell Tesk about the offer, and if he's interested, he can meet the overlord and talk it over."

"Lord Edaran is coming *here*?" Shella squeaked. "I need to wash my hair!"

"No, no," Garander said. "The wizard is coming back tomorrow with the overlord's advisor, Lady Shasha. If Tesk wants to talk to Lord Edaran he'll have to go back to Ethshar with them." Only after he had said this did the oddness of Shella's comment strike him. "Wash your hair?"

Shella blushed, and turned away, saying, "I'm going to tell Mother."

"I'll tell Tesk," Ishta said.

"I'll come with you," Garander told her. "I told the wizard *I* would talk to Tesk." Then he raised his voice to call after Shella, "Tell Father, too! Ishta and I are going into the forest!"

Shella waved a hand in acknowledgment. Garander stared after her.

He had just realized why she had wanted to wash her hair before meeting Lord Edaran. She had listened to too many old stories about farm girls marrying princes. Lord Edaran was only seventeen or eighteen, and Shella was sixteen, so the idea wasn't *completely* absurd, but the overlord was already married and the father of a son. None of the overlords had ever married more than one woman at a time, so far as Garander knew, and somehow he doubted anyone was going to break that tradition by marrying Shella.

No wonder she had blushed when she realized how silly she was being.

"Come on!" Ishta said. "Let's go find Tesk!"

Garander insisted on stopping in the barn to put the hoe away, but then let Ishta lead the way into the woods.

Tesk had apparently not been expecting them; they wandered among the trees for perhaps half an hour before he finally came ambling toward them. Garander wondered where he had been, and why, but then reminded himself that it wasn't really any of his business; despite what Zendalir might think, Tesk was free to do as he pleased and did not need to answer to anyone.

"Tesk!" Ishta called, the instant she spotted the *shatra*. "There's a wizard looking for you, from Lord Edaran!" She ran toward him as she spoke.

Tesk caught her up and swung her around in a circle before setting her back on her feet. Garander remembered when their father used to do that; he had stopped a couple of years ago, apparently thinking Ishta was too old for such things. Ishta apparently didn't agree—or perhaps it was different when it was an adult friend, rather than her father. Once she was standing on her own, Tesk asked, "Who is Lord Edaran?"

Ishta was too shocked by this ignorance to respond immediately, so it was Garander who said, "He's the overlord of Ethshar of the Sands—a big city fifty leagues south of here. His father was General Anaran."

"Anaran. Ah, yes. His son rules this city, this Ethshar of the Sands?"

"Yes." It occurred to Garander that Tesk probably knew nothing of history after the fall of the Northern Empire, so he explained, "Admiral Azrad, General Gor, and General Anaran set up a new government after the war, with themselves as overlords, and their homes became cities called Ethshar. General Anaran died a few years ago, though, and Edaran took over as the new overlord of Ethshar of the Sands when he was just a boy, no older than Ishta is now."

"A boy? Ruler of a city?"

"My father says they couldn't agree on anyone else. His advisers actually run everything. Or at least, they did; there are rumors that Edaran's trying to take charge."

"I see. There is a wizard looking for me?"

"Yes!" Ishta exclaimed.

"Not Azlia?"

Garander shook his head. "No, Azlia works for Lord Dakkar. This was a man who calls himself Zendalir the Mage. He says Lord Edaran sent him."

"How does Lord Dakkar relate to this?"

"He doesn't. This is Lord Edaran's doing—at least, that's what the wizard says."

"Does every lord have a wizard working for him?"

Garander turned up an empty palm. "I guess so. I don't really know."

"You call Edaran an overlord—is Lord Dakkar one of his underlings?"

"No, Lord Dakkar is one of the Council of Barons."

Tesk stared at him for a moment, then said, "You said that Azrad, Gor, and Anaran set up a new government for Ethshar, ruled by three overlords."

"That's right."

"Then what is this Council of Barons?"

Garander realized he had neglected to explain that, and tried to put it as simply as he could. "Oh, well—not everyone accepted the new government. Some of the commanders on the northern front said they weren't going to take orders from anyone anymore, now that the war is over; those are the barons. Or at least, those were the first barons; some of their children have inherited their titles now. And they hold meetings at Sardiron of the Waters to discuss things, and settle any disagreements—that's the Council."

"Tell him more about the wizard!" Ishta burst out.

Tesk held out a hand to silence her. "I am trying to learn this. So after the Northern Empire fell, the Kingdom of Ethshar fell, as well?"

"Well…" Garander hesitated. He had never thought of it in those terms, but now that Tesk asked, he had to admit it was true. "Yes, I guess so. There's Old Ethshar in the south, and I don't know anything about it, and then the Hegemony of the Three Ethshars in the middle, and the barons and wilderness in the north. So the World is in three pieces now."

Tesk smiled a tight little smile at that. "So it's no more united now than it was during the war."

"Tell him about the wizard!"

Garander and Tesk ignored Ishta's outburst. "So Lord Dakkar of the Council of Barons sent his wizard to find me last month," Tesk said, "and now Lord Edaran of Ethshar sends *his* wizard to find me."

"That's right," Garander said.

"Lord Dakkar claimed to be protecting his people from the terrible Northerner," Tesk said, "and you said this is his land. Why, then, is Lord Edaran seeking me?"

"Tell him, tell him!" Ishta said, bouncing up and down with excitement.

"He wants to hire you," Garander said.

Tesk looked almost stunned, an expression Garander had never before seen on the *shatra*'s face. "*Hire* me."

Garander nodded.

"To do what? Slaughter his enemies? Destroy the Council of Barons, so that he and Gor and Azrad can reclaim the north?"

Garander hesitated. Although he had not allowed himself to think about it, Tesk's guess sounded somehow more believable than Zendalir's story—but did Edaran really want to throw away twenty years of peace and start a new war? And a war that would be worse, because both sides would be Ethsharites, really, even if the barons no longer used the name.

"The wizard says they want to study your magic," he said. "I don't know if that's the truth."

"Then what *do* you know, Garander, my friend?"

"I know that the wizard says he'll be back tomorrow, with Lady Shasha, one of Lord Edaran's advisors, to talk to you about it."

"On a flying carpet!" Ishta said. "Zendalir was flying on a big red carpet!"

Tesk considered this, then asked, "And what if I do not choose to speak with them?"

"I don't know," Garander said. "But…well, the wizard did say that I would be sorry if I had lied to him."

Tesk's usual grim expression turned even grimmer. "He threatened you?"

"Only if I was lying."

"And how is he to determine whether you lied? Will he use his magic, or his assumptions, to determine the truth?"

"I don't know," Garander admitted.

"I will be there," Tesk said.

"Mid-afternoon in the west field?"

"I will be there," the *shatra* repeated.

It sounded to Garander just as much a threat as the wizard's.

CHAPTER SEVENTEEN

Late the next morning Garander and Ishta were in the barn, tending to the livestock, when Ishta said, "If Tesk goes to work for Lord Edaran, he'll go to Ethshar, won't he?"

"Probably," Garander said, as he dumped a bucket of offal in the pigs' trough.

"But then we won't see him anymore!"

"Probably," Garander agreed.

"But then I don't want him to go!"

"It's up to him," Garander said, as he watched the pigs eat.

"Maybe I could go to Ethshar *with* him!"

Garander started to say that was silly, that she had no business in Ethshar, but then he caught himself. Why *shouldn't* she? She had never shown any great interest in staying a farmer.

"I'd miss you," he said.

"You could come, too!"

He shook his head. "I'm a farmer," he said. "I like it here."

Ishta was clearly distressed at this. "It's *boring* here!"

"It's home."

"You're being silly."

He smiled. "*I'm* being silly? *You're* the one who wants to run off to the big city!"

"What's silly about that?"

Garander did not have a good answer for that, so he didn't say anything more. They finished their chores in silence, and emerged from the barn into bright daylight.

The days were growing warm quickly now. The spring rains had been a little sparse, the weather dry enough to worry their father, but it certainly made it pleasant to spend time outdoors. Garander paused to look around at the fields.

Something was moving, off to the west, on Felder's land. He stared. There were people approaching—a *lot* of people.

"Ishta, go get Father," he said.

"What?" Ishta turned to see where her brother was staring, and spotted the advancing crowd. "Who are *they*?"

"I don't know," Garander said. "Go get Father." There were at least a dozen people in that group, and they were definitely heading directly toward the house. They were still too far away to make out details, but several of them could have been wearing Lord Dakkar's livery.

Ishta finally obeyed, dashing for the house—she and Garander both knew Grondar probably wasn't there at this time of day, but their mother almost certainly was, and should know where her husband was working.

For his part, Garander began marching forward to meet the approaching throng—not hurrying, but walking with a steady pace. He intended to meet them at the property line.

He had misjudged the distance, however, and the group was already on his family's land before Garander could reach the boundary.

He recognized them well before that, though. Hargal and Burz and Azlia and Sammel were all near the front of the party. Behind them were at least a score of soldiers—Lord Dakkar must have sent almost his entire company of guards.

Then Garander saw the sedan chair, and realized the baron had probably not *sent* them; he had *brought* them. He also realized not all of the soldiers wore the same colors, and some of the people who weren't wearing breastplates and kilts were in colorful robes and fancy hats—more magicians.

The approaching people saw him, of course; a soldier pulled aside one of the curtains on the sedan chair and spoke to the passenger. Garander could not hear what was said, but a response was relayed through the company, and the four men holding the chair lowered it to the ground.

The entire party came to a stop a few feet from Garander, and Hargal stepped forward. "Hello," he said.

"Hello, Hargal," Garander replied. "What's going on?"

Hargal glanced back at the sedan chair. "You'll recall I told you I couldn't promise the baron would agree with us that your *shatra* was best left alone."

"I remember."

"He didn't."

"Is this mob here to kill Tesk, then?"

Hargal smiled humorlessly. "No, not at all. We're here to *recruit* him."

Garander smiled back. "That's interesting."

"Isn't it?"

"Recruit him to do what?"

"I am not entirely clear on that, to be honest. To serve as a military advisor to the Council of Barons, I think."

Garander considered that for a moment, then said, "Did you know this isn't his only offer?"

"What?" Hargal's jaw dropped.

"Lord Edaran's representative will be here this afternoon to present *his* offer of employment."

"Lord Edaran? Of Ethshar?"

Garander nodded. "One of his wizards was here yesterday, to arrange a meeting."

"*Was* he." It was not a question.

"It's quite a coincidence, isn't it?"

"It might be," Hargal said. "Or it might be that I have not been kept fully informed, and this explains the haste with which this expedition was launched." He threw a glance over his shoulder.

"I wouldn't know about that," Garander said, turning up an empty palm. He, too, glanced at the gathered company. "Who *are* all these people? Is this the baron's entire court?"

Hargal's wry smile reappeared. "Oh, more than that. It seems the Council of Barons has been discussing your friend's survival. You see here not just four-fifths of the guardsmen of Varag, and all three of the town's magicians, but representatives of several other baronies, and half the magicians of Sardiron of the Waters. Lord Dakkar is not acting alone this time."

"Oh," Garander said.

"You said Lord Edaran is sending a representative; what about the other two overlords?"

"No one's mentioned them."

Hargal nodded. "Interesting." His gaze rose slightly, looking past Garander. "Your father is coming," he said.

Garander turned, and saw that the soldier was correct—Grondar and Ishta were hurrying toward them. Garander waved in what he hoped was a reassuring fashion, to let his father know that there was no immediate threat.

A moment later Grondar marched up and demanded, "Who's in charge here?"

"That would be Lord Dakkar," Hargal said, gesturing at the sedan chair. Garander noticed that a man in an embroidered tunic was standing by the chair, leaning down to speak with its occupant.

"Lord Dakkar?" Grondar said, in a far less assured tone than his initial question. "The baron?"

"That's right."

Grondar gathered himself, and some of the assurance was back when he said, "I want to know what all you people are doing on my land."

"We've come to negotiate with the *shatra*," Hargal said. "We mean no harm to you, or him, or anyone else here, and the baron intends to compensate you for any inconvenience this unexpected visit may cause."

"Compensate how?"

"That remains to be seen—but rest assured, Grondar of Lullen, Lord Dakkar does not want to antagonize you. He is aware of your friendship with the *shatra*."

"Then this is meant to be a *friendly* negotiation?"

"Oh, absolutely! Now that we know it's *possible* to negotiate with a *shatra*, Lord Dakkar has every intention of keeping this amicable. Surely you realize the *shatra* could be a great asset to the barony?"

Grondar glanced at Garander, who turned up a hand. "I had not given the matter much thought," the elder man said.

"Well," Hargal said, "they sent me to talk to you first because we already know one another somewhat, but perhaps I should turn matters over to Velnira, the baron's chamberlain." He beckoned to someone in the crowd behind him, and a woman in a fine green gown with a heavy golden chain around her neck stepped forward.

"Garander," Grondar said, "go tell your mother what's happening."

"And perhaps Ishta could go fetch the *shatra*?" Hargal suggested. "I recall she was his closest friend."

"There's no hurry," Grondar said.

"Besides," Garander said, "he's already supposed to meet Lord Edaran's representative right here in a few hours. All you need to do is wait."

Grondar looked annoyed. "Go tell your mother," he said. "Ishta can stay here with me, so she can see that I'm not promising anything Tesk wouldn't like."

Garander guessed that their father was more concerned with keeping Ishta out of trouble than keeping Tesk happy, but either way, it was not an unreasonable suggestion. "Yes, sir," he said. He turned and trotted toward the house.

He doubted that it was a coincidence that both lords had sent delegations so close together; probably one of them was spying on the other. Or *both* of them were spying on each other. He wondered just what they wanted to do with Tesk—and whether they even *knew* what they wanted. He knew, from dealing with his sisters, that sometimes people wanted something just because a rival wanted it. That wasn't just a girl thing, either—there had been plenty of times when he was little when he would want a particular toy or food entirely because Shella wanted it. At the time he would never have admitted it, would have insisted that he had good, solid, sensible reasons for wanting whatever it was, but now, looking back, he knew that much of the time he had really just wanted to keep it away from his sister.

He had tried to outgrow it, and had more or less managed it where Shella was concerned, but he knew the urge was still there, and he suspected that something very similar was driving at least one of the delegations.

When he reached the house he found his mother and sister cleaning the mattresses, and quickly explained the situation. He had expected them both to rush out to see the baron's people, but instead his mother said, "Are they going to be there for long?"

"Well…until Tesk comes to meet them," Garander said.

"You're sure he's coming?"

"Well, he said he would meet the *other* group, the ones from Ethshar, so I expect he'll come."

"And when are *they* due?"

"Mid-afternoon."

"Then we have time, and I want to get this done. Grab that end and lift." She gestured.

Garander desperately wanted to see what was going on in the west field, but he obeyed; he had to admit that getting the winter dirt out of the bedding and fluffing it up would make sleeping more comfortable, especially when the weather turned warm.

They had arranged everything around the fire, where the heat would dry the straw and fabric and the smoke might drive out some of the bedbugs, and were admiring their handiwork, when his mother asked, "They aren't expecting us to feed them, are they?"

It was about lunchtime, and she had not seen the size of the baron's company, so it was not an unreasonable question. "I certainly hope not," Garander answered. "There are dozens of them; there's no *way* we could feed so many."

Shella of the Green Eyes nodded. "Your father will want his lunch, though. And your sister."

"I suppose so, yes."

"I'll make something you can take for them. And tell them we'll be out once I've cleaned up the dishes."

Garander nodded.

He ate in the house with his mother and sister—salt pork and turnips, washed down with small beer. When he was done his mother handed him a bag of fried sausages and yesterday's bread, and a jug of strong beer from last year's brewing. Garander frowned. "What about Ishta?" he asked. "You don't want her drinking that, do you?"

"She can come fetch her own water."

Garander didn't argue; he accepted the bag and jug and headed out while the two Shellas cleared away the plates and pans.

The scene in the west field was rather different now; the baron's party had made camp. That field was planted in wheat; Garander hoped they would not chew the soil up enough to ruin the crop.

Grondar was sitting on a camp chair, talking with the woman in the green gown—Velnira, Lord Dakkar's...something. Garander did not remember her title. Ishta was standing nearby, looking bored. Garander wondered whether the two adults were discussing the terms of the baron's offer to Tesk, or maybe what sort of compensation would be paid for the intrusion on the farm—or were they just chatting? He trotted toward them.

Velnira looked up at his approach, and Grondar turned. "Ah, son!" he called. "This is Velnira of Varag. Her uncle was my regiment's quartermaster, old Alden One-Eye."

Chatting, then. But perhaps they had already covered weightier matters. "I brought lunch for you and Ishta," he said, lifting the bag.

"Good!" Grondar clapped his hands. He turned back to Velnira. "I hope you don't mind if we eat; I trust you have your own supplies. While I would hardly deny a guest proper hospitality, I can't feed a host like this, and I'm sure the baron wouldn't expect me to."

"No, of course not!" Velnira said. She had a very nice voice, Garander thought, even if her face was not particularly appealing. "You go right ahead. I think we've covered everything important."

Grondar nodded and rose, then looked around for Ishta. He found her, put an arm around her shoulders, and then held out the other arm for the bag of food.

A moment later the three were seated cross-legged between two furrows, and between bites Grondar was explaining to his son the terms he had set.

"No more taxes, ever," he said. "A round of copper—a *round*, not a bit—for every night these people spend on our land. That's the fee for lodging here, regardless of how the negotiations turn out, and if Tesk agrees to serve Lord Dakkar, we'll have an additional silver bit apiece for our help."

"I don't think he'll agree," Garander said.

"No, you don't understand—the baron has *already* agreed..."

"No, Father, I mean I don't think *Tesk* will agree."

"Oh, well." Grondar turned up a temporarily-empty palm before grabbing the beer jug for another swig. "We'll have the copper all the same."

"I wouldn't trust the baron about the taxes."

"Oh, I don't. And even if I did, his heir won't be bound by it. But it might last a few years."

Garander nodded, and looked around. The baron's party seemed to be settling in for an extended stay; they had pitched tents and set out firepots. Folding chairs, like the one Grondar had been using when Garander returned, were everywhere, but were still insufficient for the throng, leaving most of the soldiers to sit on the fresh-turned earth. It did not look like a group that had come simply to offer a man a job. "Do you think they're really just here to recruit Tesk?"

"I don't know," Grondar admitted.

"What do you think they'll do if he says no?"

"*I* think he'd rather go to Ethshar!" Ishta said.

"He might," Garander said. "Or he might want to stay where he is. I mean, he didn't want to sleep in our barn or anything; I think he *likes* living in the forest."

"That's just not right," Grondar said. "For a man to live like that."

"He's *not* really a man," Garander said. "He's half demon."

Grondar grunted unhappily. "He'll be here today, won't he?"

"He said he would," Ishta said.

"He did," Garander confirmed. "And so far, he's always done what he said he would."

Grondar started to reply, but a shout interrupted him. He and his children turned to see what was going on.

The baron's people were getting to their feet, staring and pointing to the south. Garander turned in that direction.

He noticed from the corner of his eye that his mother and sister were approaching from the house, having presumably finished cleaning up, but that was not what had caused the excitement. No, what had the attention of Lord Dakkar's company was a flying carpet sailing toward them, perhaps a half-mile away and sixty feet off the ground.

And this time there was not just one figure on it, but half a dozen.

CHAPTER EIGHTEEN

Garander watched as the carpet glided down to a landing a few feet away. He recognized Zendalir, but the others were strangers—finely-dressed strangers. In fact, their clothes were not quite like anything Garander had seen before, even in the pictures in his mother's books, and he realized these must be the latest fashions from Ethshar. Shella was probably ecstatic about getting a good look at them; he glanced at his sister's face, and her expression told him he was right.

He guessed that the woman in the maroon velvet gown with the flared waist was Lady Shasha; she seemed to be in charge. The others were probably a mix of magicians and minor officials. Combined with the baron's party, Garander was sure this was by far the most people who had ever been on the family farm at one time.

Looking back, he saw that soldiers were leaning into Lord Dakkar's tent to tell him of this new development, and Velnira was marching across the black earth toward the newcomers.

The woman in the maroon dress stepped off the carpet, and seemed a bit startled by how much her slipper sank into the soft ground, but quickly recovered. She marched toward Grondar.

"I am Lady Shasha of Ethshar, advisor to Edaran, Overlord of Ethshar of the Sands, Triumvir of the Hegemony of the Three Ethshars, Commander of the Holy Armies and Defender of the Gods," she announced, looking up at Grondar. "May I ask to whom I am speaking?"

"I'm Grondar of Lullen," Garander's father replied. "This is my farm."

Lady Shasha curtsied. Garander had never before seen a woman do that seriously; until now, the only time he had seen anyone curtsey it had been his mother doing it as mockery. When his mother did it Garander had thought it was ridiculous and had laughed; when Lady Shasha curtsied, it was graceful and elegant and not laughable at all. "Thank you for your hospitality," she said.

"I didn't…" Grondar began, but then he stopped. After all, Garander thought, what could he possibly say? He had not invited the overlord's advisor or her companions, but he was hardly in a position to turn them away. He had known they were coming, and had done nothing to stop them. Instead he managed a crude bow and said, "You're welcome."

"I have come to speak with the person who presents himself as *shatra*, on behalf of Lord Edaran," she said. "Could you assist me?"

Grondar looked about helplessly, and Garander spoke up. "He should be here soon. He knew you were coming."

She curtsied again. "Thank you, sir. And you are…?"

"Garander Grondar's son."

"I am honored to meet you."

Garander did not believe that for an instant, but he bowed in acknowledgment. Then he gestured and said, "This is my sister Ishta. She was the one who first met the *shatra*."

Lady Shasha nodded, but apparently deemed another curtsy excessive. "That's my mother, Shella of the Green Eyes," Ishta said, pointing. "And my sister, Shella the Younger."

The noblewoman acknowledged the two new arrivals with another nod. "A pleasure," she said. She raised her head toward Lord Dakkar's company. "And those?"

"The household of Lord Dakkar, Baron of Varag, my lady," Velnira said, before anyone else could respond. She had joined the family during the introductions. "I am Velnira, chamberlain to Lord Dakkar."

"Ah. One of the men who meet at Sardiron of the Waters, this Dakkar?"

Even Garander recognized the deliberate insult in this phrasing, in the refusal to acknowledge any of the baron's titles or authority. He saw Velnira's expression harden. "Exactly," she replied. "The one in whose domain we are standing."

"It was my understanding that this family owns this land." She gestured at Grondar and the others.

Velnira did not reply immediately, and Lady Shasha turned back to Grondar. "You say the supposed *shatra* is expected soon?"

Grondar looked helplessly at Garander, who said, "Yes, my lady."

"Is there somewhere we might speak privately?"

"Well, I…" Grondar began.

"You will do no such thing!" Velnira snapped. "We will not tolerate foreign overlords conspiring in secret."

"I regret to say that none of the overlords are with us today," Lady Shasha answered calmly.

"But their representatives are—and you are not welcome."

"Oh?" She turned to Grondar again. "Are we unwelcome?"

"I…I don't…"

"It is not his decision!" Velnira shouted.

"Wait a minute," Grondar protested.

Before anyone could react, Ishta called, "Look!" She pointed.

Most of the people within earshot looked, and saw Tesk moving toward them in that inhumanly smooth way of his. Ishta had not been the only one to notice; several voices in Lord Dakkar's camp were raised as well, announcing the *shatra*'s approach. Hands fell to weapons, or were raised to point; Garander saw weapons being drawn, which he thought was a mistake.

And then Tesk was there, standing amid Garander's family, looking calmly at Velnira and Lady Shasha. "I understand you wanted to speak with me," he said. He glanced at the baron's camp. "There are more of you than I expected."

Lady Shasha immediately curtsied again, and asked, "You are the *shatra*?"

"I am." He did not look at her as he replied, but scanned his surroundings quickly.

"I am delighted to meet you, sir. How should I address you?"

"Ishta calls me Tesk," the *shatra* replied, returning his attention to the Ethsharite. "I do not find it objectionable."

"Very good," the noblewoman said. "I am Lady Shasha of Ethshar, advisor to Edaran, Overlord of Ethshar of the Sands, Triumvir of the Hegemony of the Three Ethshars, Commander of the Holy Armies and Defender of the Gods."

Tesk turned to the other woman. "Who are you?"

"Velnira, chamberlain to Lord Dakkar, baron of Varag."

Tesk nodded, then turned back to Lady Shasha. "You want to hire me?"

"Lord Edaran wishes to offer you a position in his court, yes."

"And you," Tesk said to Velnira. "What does Lord Dakkar want?"

"Why, he, too, wishes to employ you."

"Why?"

Velnira blinked in surprise. "He thinks you... He thinks he could..."

"He is in that tent?"

"Ah...yes, but..."

"He brought all those people?"

"Yes, he..."

"A job interview does not require soldiers and magicians."

Velnira opened her mouth, but before she could speak Tesk turned to Lady Shasha. "You brought magicians, too."

"We did," Lady Shasha acknowledged. "We wish to study your magic—so much Northern magic was lost forever when the empire fell! Zendalir was hired to provide transportation, while the others are here to evaluate your magical artifacts and abilities. And these two courtiers are here to answer any questions you might have about the overlord's government, and your prospective position in it."

That actually sounded quite reasonable to Garander; Lord Dakkar's actions were not as easily explained away.

"And Lord Dakkar brought his soldiers to protect you from these Ethsharite magicians!" Velnira burst out. "You can't trust these people. You live in the baron's territory, and he has come to protect you from these intruders."

Garander had been focused on this discussion, but a sound distracted him, and he turned to see a dozen of the baron's soldiers advancing toward Tesk, weapons ready in their hands. Behind them stood a man in a gaudy red-and-gold tunic, with a golden band around his head. At first Garander thought this must be another magician, but then he realized it was Lord Dakkar himself.

"You!" the lead soldier bellowed, pointing a sword at Lady Shasha. "Get away from him!"

Lady Shasha drew herself up to her full height—which was not very great; she barely came to Garander's shoulder. "I do not take orders from you!" she snapped.

Tesk stepped in front of her. "I am speaking with this person," he said.

"She's trespassing!"

"No, she isn't," Grondar said, startling Garander. "I invited her."

"The baron says she's trespassing!"

"The baron does not own this land," Grondar replied angrily. "I do!"

"The baron—"

"The baron did not clear this land with his own hands," Grondar interrupted. "*I* did. The baron did not plow and sow and reap these fields. The baron did not build this house or that barn. This is *my* land."

"This land is under the protection of Lord Dakkar, Baron of Varag," the soldier insisted.

"This is *my* land," Grondar repeated. "*I* say who comes and goes here."

Garander stared at his father in astonishment. He had never before heard Grondar say anything about the baron but acceptance and praise. It had always been his mother who expressed doubts about leaving the hegemony of Ethshar and siding with the barons of Sardiron.

But until now the baron had always been far away in Varag, not camping in the west field. Lord Dakkar had never before asserted any claim to Grondar's farm.

Something rustled, and Garander glanced over to see the flying carpet hovering a foot or so off the ground, apparently ready to take to the air. In the other direction, someone in the baron's camp shouted for archers.

He turned to Tesk, but the *shatra* was simply watching and listening, standing between the soldiers and Lady Shasha, but otherwise doing nothing to calm the situation. Ishta was staring wide-eyed at the approaching soldiers, while both Shellas, mother and daughter, were backing away.

"Stop it!" Garander shouted, surprising even himself. "Stop it! You're being stupid!"

"I am merely presenting Lord Edaran's offer," Lady Shasha protested.

"I didn't mean you," Garander said. "I meant them!" He pointed at the baron's men. "Don't you people realize there are *magicians* on that carpet? *Powerful* magicians? And that you're facing a *shatra*? I know you didn't see the demonstration last month, but you must have heard stories about *shatra*!"

"We have our own magicians," the lead soldier replied.

"Do you have your own *shatra*? Do you think you can recruit him by starting a stupid fight?"

"Sheathe your weapons!" the man in red and gold called. "The boy is right."

The soldiers hesitated, but obeyed, and cleared a path as Lord Dakkar marched up to where Tesk and Grondar's family stood.

"I am Lord Dakkar, Baron of Varag," he said. "I have come to discuss your future, *shatra*."

"As have I," Lady Shasha said.

"I do not think my future concerns either of you," Tesk replied.

"Of course it does!" the baron said.

"Lord Edaran hopes you will consider his offer," Lady Shasha added.

"What will happen if I do not?" Tesk asked, turning to look over his shoulder at the Ethsharite noblewoman.

Lady Shasha turned up an empty palm. "Who can say? But should you not *hear* his offer before rejecting it?"

"And my offer as well!" the baron snapped.

Lady Shasha nodded a polite acknowledgment, which the baron greeted with a glower.

"Then present your master's offer," Tesk said to Lady Shasha.

"Lord Edaran sends his greetings," Lady Shasha recited, "and assures you that he understands you owe him no loyalty and are not a subject of the Hegemony of the Three Ethshars. This offer is to you individually, from Lord Edaran personally, and is not from any government of Ethshar, past, present, or future. The other overlords of the Hegemony are not involved, nor are any other officials. In recognition of your unique situation, he does not ask or expect any oath of fealty or political concession.

"Lord Edaran offers you a home in Ethshar of the Sands, the exact details to be negotiated to suit your preferences. He offers his full pardon for any past offenses you may have committed against the people of Ethshar in the Great War, and in addition to your lodging a salary equal to that of his senior advisors, which would at present be the sum of thirty-six gold rounds annually. He does not rule out further compensation, to be negotiated upon your arrival within Ethshar's walls. These terms are offered for an indefinite period, to be terminated at *your* pleasure, not his own.

"In exchange, he asks full access to your magical devices, of whatever nature, and your instruction in their use. He asks that you permit other magicians in his employ to study you and all magic associated with you, and that you do no harm to any citizen of Ethshar of the Sands except in self-defense. He also asks that your services be exclusive to himself, and that you will not allow anyone other than Lord Edaran and his designated representatives any use of your magic or abilities.

"And inasmuch as he has been told that you do not wish to fight, he assures you that he has no intention of asking you to do so. You will not be asked to serve as an assassin, or in any military role whatsoever, but he hopes you will consider serving as his personal bodyguard on occasions when he feels it suitable. That is not a requirement, though—it is your magic, and not your personal service, he most desires to obtain."

Her message delivered, Lady Shasha took a deep breath, and smiled up at the *shatra*. "He hopes for a prompt and positive response," she added.

Garander found that deep breath distracting, so he did not see Tesk's immediate reaction; when he did look at the *shatra*'s face he could read nothing in the expression there.

Then Tesk turned to Lord Dakkar and asked, "What are *your* terms?"

The baron bit his lip, then said, "I can't match that salary. Perhaps if some of my fellow barons contribute, we could. I can give you a house in Varag, though, and servants to staff it, and the freedom to go wherever you please within the territory of the barons of the council at Sardiron— it sounded to me as if Lord Edaran would require you to stay in Ethshar of the Sands."

Tesk turned back to Lady Shasha.

"I don't know if he would *require* it," she replied, "but I believe he would indeed *expect* it."

Tesk nodded. He glanced at the baron, then at Velnira, then at Ishta, before turning back to Lady Shasha and replying, "If so, I cannot accept Lord Edaran's offer."

"Oh, but surely—" she began.

"*Cannot*," Tesk said. "Not *will* not. You seem to forget I am not a free man. I am *shatra*, bound to the service of the Northern Empire."

"But the Northern Empire is gone," Garander said. "Isn't it?"

"Of course it is!" Velnira exclaimed.

"It is," Tesk agreed. "That does not alter the magic that binds me."

"I don't understand," Garander said.

"I must obey the orders I was given by my commanders," Tesk said. "The destruction of the Empire and the end of the war does not change that—this is *magic*, not human choice."

"But what orders do you still have?" Garander demanded. "You said yourself you had no orders!"

"I did say that," Tesk acknowledged. "That was not accurate. I have had no *specific* orders for twenty years, but the *general* orders that I was given still hold. I cannot sleep in any permanent structure. I cannot sleep in the same spot twice within thirty-six hours. I cannot sleep within forty feet of anyone other than members of the Empire's military. Have you never wondered why I never built myself a house? Why I did not accept an invitation to stay the night in Grondar's home? Garander and Ishta, you have asked me why I chose to live alone in the woods for so long—this is why. I *cannot* live indoors; it is not permitted."

For a moment no one spoke; then Lady Shasha said, "Perhaps accommodations could be made. There is an area in Ethshar known as the Wall Street Field..."

Tesk shook his head. "No," he said. "I would be too exposed in an open field, and too enclosed by the city walls. Besides, you ask for my magic. That cannot work to your satisfaction."

"I don't..." Velnira began.

"I will show you," Tesk said, reaching up and pulling a long black wand from the pack on his back.

Garander heard several people gasp, and saw several, including Velnira and Lord Dakkar, step back, away from the *shatra*. For himself, he stared at the black rod, trying to decide whether it was the same one Tesk had demonstrated to Ishta and him in the forest months ago.

Then Tesk pointed the wand at one of the tents the baron's men had set up. "See where I press my thumb," he said, and Garander watched as he set his thumb into a flattened oval on the side of the wand.

The tent exploded into flame, much as that stump had in the *shatra*'s previous demonstration; bits of burning fabric scattered in all directions, and there was a moment of chaos as some people fled in terror from the explosion and debris while others ran to stamp out the flames.

When the shouting had subsided, and the fires had all been extinguished, Tesk tossed the rod to Lord Dakkar.

"Here," he said. "You try it."

CHAPTER NINETEEN

Lord Dakkar caught the wand, but then stood, shoulders hunched, staring at the *shatra*, the black weapon seemingly forgotten.

"Try it," Tesk repeated. "You wished to use my magic."

The baron's brows lowered and his mouth turned down. He turned and held the rod out to the leader of the band of soldiers behind him. "Try it," he said.

Startled, the soldier hesitated, but Lord Dakkar thrust the wand at him. "Take it!"

The man took it, then looked questioningly first at his lord and master, and then at the *shatra*.

"Point it at your target," Tesk said. "Then set your thumb on that oval." He indicated the relevant spot. "When you feel a faint warmth, press."

"I don't...my lord, where should I aim it?"

Lord Dakkar looked around, then pointed. "That fence."

"Wait..." Grondar began, but several hands flew up to warn him away, and he did not finish his protest.

The soldier aimed the wand as he had been directed, then hesitated. "Like this?"

"Yes!" Lord Dakkar snapped.

"Your thumb on the oval," Tesk said. "You should feel a faint warmth almost immediately."

"I don't feel anything," the soldier answered. "It just feels like a stick."

"Press anyway," Lord Dakkar growled.

The soldier jammed his thumb down on the oval, but nothing happened. He repeated the gesture, jabbing futilely, then turned, eyes wide and worried, to the baron. "It's not working, my lord."

"Should I try?" one of the other soldiers asked, stepping forward, and Garander recognized Burz.

"There's no point," Lord Dakkar said, waving the offer away. "It won't work, will it?" He glared at Tesk.

"It will not work," Tesk agreed. "None of my magic will work. Ask Grondar and his son about my shelter cloth."

Lord Dakkar looked at Grondar, and again dismissed the suggestion with a wave.

"*I* would like to hear about this shelter cloth," Lady Shasha said.

"It's…it's a piece of cloth that Tesk put in a tree over his head when it was snowing," Garander said. "It was warm and stayed dry no matter how much snow fell. It clung to the tree branches. When my father and I tried to move it, we couldn't. We didn't see any nails or anything holding it in place, and it just looked like ordinary cloth, but we couldn't pull it loose no matter what we did."

"But the *shatra* could?"

Garander nodded, and Tesk said, "It was created for my use, and no other person's. *All* my tools and weapons were. Even the talisman I dropped for Ishta to find, the one that Lord Dakkar claimed—it will not work properly for anyone but me."

"But it glowed," the baron said. "And showed us glyphs."

Tesk nodded. "Those say that it is the property of the Empire and should be returned to the nearest military people immediately. That is all it will do until it is in my hand again."

"You said it wasn't any use anymore!" Garander said.

"It is not. But if *I* hold it, the glyphs will say that I have no new orders."

"None of us read Shaslan," Lord Dakkar said. "It could be saying anything."

"You saw three sets of glyphs, no more," Tesk said. "Those are the three lines of the message asking the finder to return it to the military."

"So you say," Lord Dakkar growled, but Garander did not really think he disbelieved the *shatra*.

"Yes," Tesk answered.

"Perhaps you could tell us how to bypass these restrictions, or create *new* devices that don't include them," Lady Shasha suggested.

Garander tried to judge Tesk's reaction from his expression, but the *shatra*'s face had never been easy to read. He seemed more puzzled than anything else. "I am not a sorcerer," he said.

"But you have all these weapons!" Velnira protested.

Tesk pointed at the soldier who still held the black wand. "He has a sword," he said. "Does that mean he is a smith?"

"It's not…" Velnira stopped in mid-sentence, looking from Tesk to Lord Dakkar and back.

"I am not a sorcerer," Tesk repeated. "I know how to *use* my tools and weapons. I know nothing of how they are made or why they work."

"Weren't you taught to repair them if they were damaged?" Lady Shasha asked.

Tesk shook his head. "The demon portion of me could make certain small repairs, and I have a device that would summon a *fil drepessis*, a…a thing that would fix damaged talismans. I could not make any repairs without the help of either the demon or a *fil drepessis*."

"You still have the demon."

"The demon is asleep. You do not want it to wake."

Garander certainly agreed with that, but from what he saw on certain faces he did not think everyone else present did.

"Perhaps a demonologist could be useful in that," Lady Shasha suggested.

"Oh, blast the demon," Lord Dakkar said. "Just let a sorcerer at your talismans! He should be able to figure them out."

"I do not think so," Tesk said.

"And what if we try?" Lord Dakkar said.

"I would advise against it," Tesk said. "It has protections. If nothing else will convince you, though, I will not stop you."

Lord Dakkar stared at him for a moment, then turned to the soldier with the wand and said, "Take that thing to Sammel. See what he can do with it."

"This is not safe," Tesk said.

"Your lordship," Garander said, surprised at his own courage in addressing the baron directly, "Northern sorcery is dangerous! Someone could get hurt."

"Sammel knows something about Northern sorcery, boy."

"I know!" Garander said, a trifle desperately. "He's the one who told me how dangerous it is!"

"Then trust him to know how to handle it safely!" Lord Dakkar turned away. "Velnira," he called back, "*you* talk to him! See if we can't make *some* arrangement."

"Excuse me, Tesk," Lady Shasha said, before Velnira could react. "What will happen when this sorcerer tampers with your wand?"

"One of two things," Tesk replied. "Either nothing at all, if he cannot penetrate its protective magic, or it will kill him."

"Kill him *how*?"

Tesk did that odd shoulder bob that Garander knew was his equivalent of turning up an empty hand. "I do not know." He looked down at Ishta, and his face darkened. "Ishta should not see this," he said.

"I'm not a baby," Ishta protested.

"You are not a baby," Tesk agreed, "but you are still a child. If the sorcerer breaks the protection, it will be ugly and bloody."

"I've watched Father slaughter hogs," Ishta answered.

"A hog is not a man," Tesk said.

"Come on," Garander said, putting a hand on Ishta's shoulder. "Let's go inside. It's getting chilly."

She shook off his hand. "No!" she insisted. "I want to see what happens to Tesk!"

"You said maybe nothing will happen," Grondar said.

Again, Tesk's shoulders bobbed. "Perhaps nothing will. But there is a reason your people know so little of Northern sorcery."

"How interesting!" Lady Shasha exclaimed. "So you cannot live among other people, and no one else can use your magic?"

"That is true," Tesk replied.

"It's as if the magicians who created you *wanted* to make you worthless to anyone else."

"They did," the *shatra* said. "They did not want capturing one of us, alive or dead, to be of any value to your side."

"But you aren't of any possible value to *their* side now," the Ethsharite said. "Their side doesn't exist anymore."

"Then I am of no value to anyone," Tesk said. "You have come here for nothing."

Lady Shasha gave a sort of half-nod, but before she could say anything more Ishta said, "What about the mizagars?"

Velnira, the baron, and Lady Shasha all looked at her. "*What* mizagars?" Velnira asked.

"Those mizagars," Tesk said, pointing at the woods to the northeast.

Garander turned, as did most of the others, and saw dark shapes emerging from the forest.

They were hideous, unnatural things, standing between three and four feet high, with legs that projected out to the side and then bent downward, so that their bellies were almost touching the ground. They did not seem to have necks; their heads were just extensions of their long, barrel-shaped bodies. Their eyes were so small as to be effectively invisible at this distance, while their mouths were huge, practically splitting their heads in half. Their skins were black, and they remained partly under the shadows of the trees, so that it was very hard to make out any further details.

There were four of them, by Garander's count.

"They obey my orders," Tesk said. "I told them to come here today to show you another reason you should leave me alone where I am. For twenty years I have kept them from attacking farmers or travelers. If you force me to leave, I cannot restrain them."

"We can kill mizagars," Lord Dakkar said.

"I am sure you can," Tesk agreed. "But I save you the trouble."

"Tesk," Lady Shasha said, turning her attention from the mizagars back to the *shatra*, "what do you want?"

Tesk seemed puzzled by the question. "I do not want anything from you or your master."

"That's not what I asked," she said. "What is it you *do* want? Why do you stay here? You could have stayed hidden in the wilderness forever, if you wanted to, but you didn't. Why?"

Tesk stared at her for a moment, and just when Garander thought he was not going to answer at all, he said, "I was lonely."

Lady Shasha nodded, as if she had expected that response, but it was Lord Dakkar who spoke next. "I can get you women," he said.

Tesk's mouth quirked in a half-smile. "I do not want women," he replied.

"But you just said…"

"I want companionship, not female bodies." Tesk straightened up. "I want to live as I always have, but to visit with friends sometimes. That is all I want."

"Well, *we* want you to help us learn about Northern magic," Lord Dakkar said. "We can see to it that no one bothers you if you do that."

"No, you can't," Lady Shasha interrupted. "You can't keep everyone away if they're determined."

Lord Dakkar turned to her angrily. "We can do better than *you* can! This is our territory, not part of your hegemony."

"You are permitted to think yourselves independent because the overlords of Ethshar were reluctant to shed Ethsharitic blood in the years immediately after the war, but if you provoke them sufficiently, I assure you that they are capable of reasserting their authority."

"Are you threatening me?" The baron's hand was on the hilt of his sword.

"I am *warning* you, and all your so-called fellow barons, that the patience of the overlords is not infinite," Lady Shasha calmly replied. "Lord Edaran already thinks it was a mistake to allow you so much freedom, but up until now Lord Azrad and Lord Gor have restrained him. They are old men, and long since tired of fighting, but do not assume they cannot be roused to anger. And who knows what their heirs may say, when the time comes?"

"Wait a minute," Garander said. "Are you threatening a *war*?"

"If that's what it takes to establish the Hegemony's authority," Lady Shasha replied.

"You wouldn't take our land without a fight," Lord Dakkar growled.

"It isn't *your* land in the first place!" Lady Shasha snapped. "Ask Grondar!"

"This is my farm," Grondar said, "but I...I think we're Sardironese here."

"There's no such thing as 'Sardironese' outside the walls of Sard-iron," Lady Shasha told him. "This is all Ethsharitic territory. All the World outside Old Ethshar rightfully belongs to the Hegemony."

"Not any more!" the baron shouted.

"You'd fight a *war* over Tesk?" Garander asked, astonished.

"I'll fight a war if that's what it takes to keep the overlords out!"

"Lord Edaran is prepared to fight if that's what it takes to restore order to the northern territories," Lady Shasha said.

"That's crazy!" Garander said. "Father's told me about the war—you can't seriously want to go through that again, and fighting amongst our-selves. We're all descended from Ethshar, no matter what we are now."

"Tesk isn't," Ishta said.

"But the rest of us all are!" Garander said.

"Now that the Northerners are gone, maybe it's time to straighten out the enemies among those who claim to be our own people," Velnira said.

"But you don't *need* to," Garander said. "There's nothing worth fighting a war over!"

"That is not for a mere farm boy to decide," Lord Dakkar said.

"But this is about *Tesk*, isn't it?"

"He's just the excuse, son," Grondar said.

"What?" Grondar had had so little to say that Garander had almost forgotten he was there. Now he turned to look at his father.

Grondar held up a hand. "We'll talk later," he said.

"But..."

Grondar shook his head, and Garander subsided, but now it was Tesk's turn to speak. "You both say you have come to bargain for the magic I hold, yes?"

"That's right," Lady Shasha replied.

"You understand now that I cannot use your money or live in your cities, and that I cannot simply give you my equipment or teach you how to make more."

"I understand you *say* that," Lord Dakkar answered.

"Perhaps we should take time to reconsider our positions," Tesk said. "I will try to think of what I want that you can give me, and how I might be useful to you. You can think of what you want of me that I can give, and what you can offer me, what promises you can make to persuade me. We will meet here again in a few hours' time—at dusk, perhaps?—to resume negotiations."

"That sounds good to me," Grondar said.

"Some time to gather our thoughts might be useful," Lady Shasha acknowledged.

Velnira glanced at Lord Dakkar, who frowned. "All right," he said.

With that, the gathering broke up. Lord Dakkar, Velnira, and the baron's soldiers headed for the baron's camp; Lady Shasha returned to the still-hovering flying carpet, where one of the other passengers offered his hand to help her up.

Grondar collected his family, using his outstretched arms to herd them toward the house. "Come on," he said. "We're going inside. Your chores can wait; we need to talk."

"May I walk with you?" Tesk asked.

Startled, Grondar threw him a glance, then turned up a palm. "As you please," he said.

As they walked, Shella the Younger said, "I don't understand what's going on."

"I do," Grondar said. He looked at Tesk again. "I think you do, too."

"I think so," the *shatra* agreed.

"What did you mean, he's just the excuse?" Garander asked.

"Just what I said," Grondar replied. He sighed. "Lord Dakkar is a young man, too young to have fought in the war. Lord Edaran is even younger, little more than a boy. Young men want to prove themselves. Lord Dakkar wants to show everyone he deserves to be treated as an equal in the Council of Barons. Varag is a small, unimportant town, and the other barons, from Sardiron and Aldagmor and the Passes, probably treat him like a child. As for Edaran, he's been called an overlord since he was nine or ten, but from everything I've heard his mother and his advisors have really run everything in Ethshar of the Sands, and the other two overlords, Gor and Azrad, have run everything outside the city walls. He was treated like a child because he *was* a child, and he wants to prove he's become a man."

"How does fighting over Tesk prove anything?" Garander asked.

"It's not about Tesk," his father answered. "Tesk is just an excuse. Those two both needed *something* to show that they're strong and decisive leaders, men who go out and accomplish things and don't back down, and Tesk is an opportunity to demonstrate their resolve."

"But Lord Dakkar and Lady Shasha talked as if they were ready to start a war!"

"Lady Shasha is probably just doing as she's told; it's Lord Edaran you're hearing when she speaks."

"That's not my point," Garander said. "How could *anyone* want to start another war?"

Grondar sighed. "Because they don't remember the last one. Have you ever listened to the men in the village when they talk about the war?"

"Of course!" Garander said.

"Most of them make it sound like a big exciting adventure, don't they?"

"Well, they..." Garander blinked. That was *exactly* what they did. "But *you* don't talk about it that way," he finished.

"Never?"

Garander paused, remembering.

The stories Grondar told at home were about how horrible the war was—the boredom and fear and horror, dead friends and family, years spent living in crowded, miserable conditions while waiting for battles that never seemed to matter. But the stories he told when he and his friends got together to sample the new beer or prepare a bridegroom for his wedding were different; they were funny, or exciting. He never made himself out a hero the way some of the older men did, but in the village he didn't talk about corpses in the mud, or about huddling under a bush, trembling in fear, while magic fire blazed overhead; he told stories about outwitting Northern scouts, or finding a way around some unpleasant duty.

"I always wanted you and your sisters to understand what the war was like," Grondar said. "I don't think everyone else was as careful. After all, why should they be? The Northerners were gone, so there couldn't be any more wars, could there?"

The bitterness in his father's voice startled Garander. "But there *shouldn't* be any more!" he said.

"But there will be, sooner or later. In fact, I hear there have been wars in Old Ethshar all along—all the self-proclaimed kings and councils fighting over who's the true heir to the Holy Kingdom."

"But...would the barons really fight the Hegemony?"

"If they think they can win, yes. And they probably *do* think they can win, because the Hegemony is run by two tired old men and an untrained boy, and its people have gotten soft after twenty years of peace down there in the warm south."

"*Could* they win?"

"I doubt it." He glanced at Tesk. "Unless maybe they had a *shatra* on their side."

"I am not interested in fighting for either side," Tesk said.

"Neither am I," Grondar said. He looked at Garander. "And I don't want my son to fight, either. I don't want my daughters taken to sew uniforms and bind wounds. I want no part of another war." He turned back to Tesk. "I assume you're going to vanish into the woods, to stay clear of the fighting?"

"I have not decided," the Northerner replied.

Grondar nodded. They had reached their front door, and he paused with his hand on the latch.

"If you do," he said, "can you take us with you?"

CHAPTER TWENTY

Grondar had not been happy with Tesk's response. The *shatra* did not think he could keep the entire family alive and safe if they fled into the hills, and while Grondar knew that was reasonable, he was not eager to accept it. He argued for several minutes.

Finally, though, he had gone inside, with his wife and two daughters, leaving the *shatra* outside.

Garander had also remained outside. He had seen his father look at him and say nothing, and he knew that Grondar approved.

Tesk looked at him, but also said nothing. He began walking toward the woods, not in his usual rapid zigzag, but at a casual stroll. Garander followed him, and for a moment neither of them spoke.

Then Garander asked, "What are you going to do?"

"I have not decided."

"If you do try to disappear, they'll come after you."

"I know."

"If you don't choose a side they'll try to kill you, no matter *what* you do."

"I know." The *shatra* smiled. "Will they send a dragon after me?"

Garander considered that, then shook his head. "I don't think anyone still *has* any tame dragons. They were all supposed to be destroyed at the end of the war."

"Do you believe they all were destroyed?"

Garander thought for a second, then said, "No. But I don't know where they are. I mean, dragons are *big*, aren't they? Where would you hide one?"

"I do not know." Tesk seemed to hesitate for a moment, then said, "I have seen a dragon, east of here. I do not think it was tame."

Startled, Garander asked, "You've *seen* one?"

"Yes. A very large one."

"So my father's warnings about dragons in the woods were right?"

"It was many miles east of here."

"But there could be others, smaller ones."

Tesk moved his shoulders. "I have not seen others."

"What did you do when you saw it?"

"I hid."

Garander nodded. Tesk surely knew his limitations, and even a *sha-tra* wouldn't want to meet a wild dragon.

"So they do not have dragons," Tesk said.

"I don't think so," Garander said. "But they have wizards. *Lots* of wizards."

"I cannot hide effectively from wizards' spells."

Garander nodded again. "So you'll have to choose a side."

Tesk smiled again, humorlessly. "Then only *one* side will be trying to kill me."

"And the other will try to protect you! It's better than both of them trying to kill you."

"I do not know how much they will try to protect a Northern half-demon."

Garander knew the *shatra* had a point. "Can the mizagars help guard you?" They had reached the edge of the forest; Garander glanced around, but saw no trace of the monsters Tesk had summoned earlier.

"They would die trying," Tesk answered. He noticed Garander's gaze and added, "I sent them away. They were an empty threat."

"So you think you're going to be killed no matter what you do."

"It seems likely." Again, his shoulders moved. "All my people died twenty years ago. I have had more time than any of the others, but I cannot live forever."

"Not even with your demon half? Don't demons live forever?"

"Demons do. I will not."

"You might live longer if you chose one side, though."

"I might." Tesk cast a glance at Garander. "Which side do you think I should choose?"

"I don't know," Garander said. "My father always said we were Sardironese now, not Ethsharitic, but...I don't know." A thought was stirring in the back of his mind. "Tesk, you can do things ordinary people can't, right?"

"Yes."

"Can you stop your heart? Without dying?"

"You suggest I fake my death?"

"Well...I was thinking that if we could make each side think the other had killed you..."

"Then they would have a cause for war, would they not?"

"For killing a left-over Northern monster?"

Tesk did not reply immediately. The two proceeded another three or four steps before he asked, "How could this be done? Would they not examine me closely, to be certain? Would they not fight over my equipment?"

"I don't know," Garander admitted. He looked at the *shatra*, studying the rods strapped to Tesk's back. "How much equipment do you still have, anyway?"

Tesk took another step before replying, "That is an interesting question."

"It is?"

"Yes. For twenty years I have been traveling through land where the Empire and Ethshar fought. Soldiers are not always tidy. Sometimes they must flee without warning. Sometimes they die without warning. Sometimes when this happens, they leave equipment behind."

"Yes?"

"I did not want your people to find old Northern equipment. I have been gathering it."

Garander started. "You...what?"

"I have been gathering all the Northern equipment I have found in twenty years," Tesk told him. "I have used my own talismans to find... I cannot think of the word. Caches? Places where equipment was hidden for later use. There is a lot of it now."

Garander was stunned into momentary silence. Then he said, "If Lord Dakkar and Lord Edaran knew that, they would *really* want you. It isn't *all* enchanted so only you can use it, is it?"

"No. There is some anyone can use, and some no one but a Northern sorcerer can use." Tesk stopped, then leapt up into a tree, leaving Garander on the ground below.

"Then..." He looked up at the *shatra*. "If you showed us where it is, and how to use it, maybe my parents and sisters and I *could* survive out here to get away from a war."

"Most of it is either weaponry, or devices that are of no use any more, like the talisman Ishta found. I do not think you want to live in exile in the wilderness, in any case."

"Not really, no. But I don't want to be a soldier, either."

Tesk had no answer for that. He sat back on his branch and leaned against the trunk of the tree.

"I don't want you to be killed," Garander said.

"I do not want to die," Tesk replied. "We cannot always have what we want."

"*Can* you stop your heart?"

Tesk sighed. "Yes. But I do not think that will be sufficient."

"Would you do me a favor?"

Tesk looked down at him. "What is it?"

"Can you go to one of your hiding places and bring back some equipment? Things you don't mind losing, enough to look like it's everything you normally carry. In fact, twice as much as that."

"Why?"

"I have an idea."

Tesk considered Garander's face, then made that odd shoulder motion. "When?"

"I think...I think we'll need them tomorrow morning. Before dawn, if possible."

"I have said I will meet those people again at dusk."

"I know. You'd need to leave after that. You can see in the dark, can't you?"

"I can. But do not depend too much on my magic, Garander. There are many things it cannot do."

"I know. But if you can bring things that look like the things on your back, things as harmless as possible, I think we may be able to save your life. Maybe. I'm not sure. I'm still working it out."

"I do not think they will believe I am dead merely because I do not move. They have heard stories about *shatra* just as you have."

"I know. But there's *another* story I heard once."

"Will you explain this to me?"

Garander shook his head. "I'd rather not, not yet," he said. The truth was that he was afraid Tesk would point out flaws in his plan, and talk him out of trying it at all.

"Perhaps when we meet at dusk?"

"Maybe."

Tesk nodded. "Then I will see you then. For now, I think I will take a nap. It seems I may be traveling tonight."

"Good," Garander said. "Thank you. I'll see you later." Then he turned, and with one final glance at the *shatra* relaxing in the tree, he headed back toward the family farm.

When he emerged from the trees he paused and looked around, taking in the situation.

The sun was getting low in the west, and shadows were stretching across the fields. The flying carpet had set down again, in the field south of the house; its passengers were spread around the vicinity, some standing, some sitting. They seemed to be talking amongst themselves.

The baron's party had mostly regrouped around their remaining tents, and several people were walking around the burned area where the destroyed tent had been, apparently studying it.

Another tent had been moved, though, and set up well to the north of the main group, away from everyone else. Garander was unsure what that was for, and debated whether to go to the house and point it out to his father, but decided not to. There was someone else he wanted to talk to, so instead of turning his steps toward the house he headed for the main group of tents.

As he expected, a soldier stopped him. "What do you want here?"

"What business is it of yours?" Garander asked. "This is my family's farm; I can go where I please."

The sentry looked uncertain. "Wait here," he said. Then he turned and called, "Captain!"

Another soldier turned, and Garander recognized him as Hargal. He had not realized Hargal was a captain.

Hargal took in the situation in an instant, and came over to them.

"Hello, Garander," he said. "What do you want?"

"I wanted to ask Azlia something; is she here?"

Hargal frowned. "What did you want to ask her?"

"About something Zendalir the Mage, the wizard from Ethshar, said." That was not true in any way, but Garander had decided that telling the truth had gotten him in enough trouble lately. He wanted to see whether lying might work better.

Hargal considered that for a moment, then turned up a palm. "This way," he said.

Garander followed for a dozen paces; then Hargal pointed. "That's her tent," he said.

There was nothing remarkable about the indicated shelter; it was a plain tent, not an elaborate pavilion like the baron's. "Thank you," Garander said.

He walked up to the tent, moving cautiously through the camp, hearing a steady babble of voices all around him; he could not make out words, for the most part. This was more simultaneous conversation than he had ever before heard, and not all of it sounded like ordinary Ethsharitic.

At the tent he paused, unsure of the correct etiquette; there was no door, as such, and he could not very well knock on canvas. He cleared his throat, and called, "Hello, Azlia?"

As he waited for a response, Garander looked around and realized that at least a dozen of the camp's residents were staring at him. That was not good. He did not want to draw that much attention. He tried to look casual.

A flap was flung back, and the wizard's face appeared. "Garander?" she said, startled.

"I was wondering if I might have a word with you," Garander said.

She glanced back over her shoulder, then said, "I was just talking to Sammel; would you care to join us?"

Garander frowned. "I thought he was working on Tesk's wand."

Sammel's face appeared beside Azlia. "I looked at it, but it's beyond me," he said. "I turned it over to Arnen of Sardiron." He leaned out and pointed at the tent set off to the north. "He's over there. In case something goes wrong."

That explained why that one tent was isolated. "Oh," Garander said.

"Would you like to join us?" Azlia asked again.

"Ah...actually, I would prefer to speak to you alone," Garander said. "It's about something one of the wizards from Ethshar said."

Azlia looked at Sammel, who turned up an empty palm. "Guild secrets, maybe?"

"It seems unlikely," Azlia said. "I'm curious, though, so if you don't mind?"

"Go ahead. If you think it's any of my business you can tell me about it later."

"Would you like to come in, then?" she asked Garander.

He looked around, then said, "There isn't really much privacy in a tent. Anyone could listen through the canvas. I thought we might take a walk."

Azlia looked up at him, her head tipped to one side. "You have certainly piqued my curiosity," she said. "Should I bring my pack?"

"I think it might be a good idea," Garander said.

"Just a moment." She ducked back inside.

Garander waited, and a moment later she emerged with a leather bag slung on one shoulder. "Where shall we walk?" she asked as she straightened up.

"This way," Garander said, pointing to the northeast, away from the camp and the house and the downed carpet, toward the bushes behind the barn and woodshed.

They began walking, at an easy stroll. The wizard stumbled occasionally; she was obviously not accustomed to rough ground.

When they had covered perhaps a hundred feet she asked, "What's this about, Garander?"

He glanced back at the camp; no one appeared to be following them, though a few people did seem to be watching them—not with the sort of intense scrutiny that might worry him, but with mild interest.

"Tesk and my father think that Ethshar and Sardiron are on the verge of going to war over Tesk," he said.

"I don't know that they'll go *that* far," Azlia said, "but Lord Dakkar certainly doesn't intend to back down."

"My father says he and Lord Edaran want to prove themselves. They were too young to fight in the Great War, so they want a little war of their own."

Azlia frowned. "Your father may be right. But they aren't the sole rulers here; Lord Dakkar answers to the Council of Barons, and Lord Edaran is only one of the three overlords. I don't think Azrad or Gor wants another war, and the Council of Barons certainly won't be unanimous. In either direction."

"Do they *need* to be unanimous? I don't know how the council works."

"No, they don't need to be unanimous. But really, I don't think…"

"Gor and Azrad are old men. What are their heirs like?"

"I…" Azlia frowned. "You're starting to worry me."

"I was…"

Before Garander could complete his thought he was interrupted by a sound unlike anything he had ever heard before, a high-pitched squeal; he and Azlia turned to look for its source.

The isolated tent where the Sardironese sorcerer was studying Tesk's weapon was glowing an eerie blue, but they only had an instant to observe that before it vanished in a flash of red-orange light, with a noise like a gigantic lantern blowing out. It did not explode; it vanished, leaving a circle of bare earth that seemed to shimmer briefly.

Someone screamed, and several people raised their voices. Azlia took one step toward the spot where the tent had been, but Garander caught her arm.

"You can't do anything," he said.

"I'm a wizard," she snapped, shaking off his grip. "You don't know what I can do."

"That was sorcery," Garander said, "and you can see there's nothing left."

"You don't know that!" Azlia insisted. "Not everything is visible." But she did not try to leave again; they could both see other people, including magicians, rushing to the site.

"I'm sorry," Garander said, "but Tesk did warn Lord Dakkar. Was Arnen a friend of yours?"

Azlia shook her head. "I barely knew him," she said.

For a moment the two of them watched as assorted Sardironese explored the area where the sorcerer's tent had been, apparently finding nothing. Garander glanced over in the direction of the flying carpet; he could see some of the Ethsharites watching, as well, but none of them were approaching.

"I thought it would explode," Garander said. "Not do *that*. Whatever it was."

"Magic can do the unexpected," Azlia said. Then she turned her attention from the vanished tent to Garander. "What was it you wanted to talk to me about? This war your father thinks is coming?"

"That's part of it," Garander said. "We think there might be war, and we don't want that. And we don't see any way this can end without Tesk either dying, or taking one side or the other, and we don't want him to die, and if he chooses a side—well, I don't like *that* idea, either." He gestured at the cluster of people where the sorcerer's tent had been. "I don't like the idea of either side doing things like that."

"Oh, that's nothing much," Azlia said. "We already have far worse magic than that. But your point is taken."

"If he won't choose a side, they'll kill him," Garander said. "If he *does* choose a side, the other side will kill him eventually. It'll just take a little longer."

Azlia sighed. "You're probably right." She watched the investigators poking at the ground where the tent had vanished.

This was the moment when Garander had to reveal his scheme. He knew it was a risk; if Azlia decided her loyalty to the baron was more important than preventing a war or saving the *shatra*, this would ruin everything. But he needed a wizard; he needed a particular spell that he had heard about in old war stories. He took a deep breath.

"So we need to make everyone think the other side already killed him," he said.

"What?" Startled, the wizard looked up at Garander.

"We need to convince Lord Dakkar that Lord Edaran killed the *shatra*, and we need to convince Lord Edaran that Lord Dakkar did. That's where I need your help," Garander said.

"What are you talking about?"

"There's a spell my father told me about. Tesk knew about it, too. It makes someone look dead—really horribly dead, with blood everywhere. Ethshar used it during the war to fool Northerners into leaving live soldiers on the battlefield, instead of taking them prisoner."

"I never heard of it," Azlia said.

Garander's heart sank. "Oh," he said. It had not occurred to him that she would not know it; he had somehow assumed that if some ordinary soldiers had heard of it, *every* wizard knew it.

But on the other hand, if it wasn't well known, then it was less likely anyone would guess what was happening. He hesitated, then asked, "Do you think any of the other wizards Lord Dakkar brought might know it?"

Azlia considered that for a moment, then said, "No, not really. There's just the one, a man who calls himself Bardak the Dreaded, and I'm pretty sure he's something of a charlatan, not half the wizard he pretends to be. I mean, a *real* wizard doesn't call himself 'the Dreaded.' That's just unprofessional."

"Oh," Garander said again. His scheme was crumbling practically before it even got started.

"But there are at least two wizards with Lady Shasha," Azlia said. "One of *them* might know."

Garander blinked. "But…they're on the other side."

"What of it? We're all wizards, and we aren't at war yet. I can say I need to talk to them about Wizards' Guild business."

Garander's spirits lifted. Perhaps his scheme wasn't as hopeless as he had thought. "Don't talk to Zendalir the Mage, though," he said. "Talk to the other one."

Startled, Azlia asked, "Why?"

"Because Zendalir is a pompous ass. I wouldn't trust him to keep his mouth shut; he'd probably brag to Lady Shasha about what a good job he did faking Tesk's death."

"Ah." She wrinkled her nose. "Thanks for the warning. It's fortunate that they've brought another." Then she abruptly turned and started marching south, toward the carpet.

"Wait a minute," Garander called, stumbling after her. "Where are you going?"

"To meet the wizards from Ethshar, of course," Azlia called back.

"Should I come?"

She shook her head. "Go home. Talk to your family."

He stopped, and watched her go.

Her suggestion was good advice, he decided; he headed back toward the house.

CHAPTER TWENTY-ONE

His father and sisters looked up when he stepped through the door; his mother was busy with a delicate bit of stitchery and paid no attention. "What was that strange noise?" Shella the Younger asked.

"The baron's sorcerer finished studying that wand."

"You mean he figured out how to make it work?" Shella sat up. "Lord Dakkar's soldiers…"

"He didn't figure out how to make it work," Garander interrupted. "Not unless you consider blowing himself up is making it work."

"He's dead?" their father asked.

"He's vanished without a trace, along with his tent and everything in it," Garander said. "I'm guessing he's dead, but it wasn't an ordinary explosion, it was something strange, so for all I know he's now riding the lesser moon across the sky."

His father frowned. "A man is dead, Garander," he said. "Show some respect."

"Tesk *warned* him," Garander replied.

"Still."

"I'm sorry, Father."

For a moment no one spoke; then Grondar said, "You spoke to the *shatra*?"

"Yes."

"Is he going to flee?"

Garander hesitated.

This was the moment when he should tell his family about his plan, but he could not bring himself to do it. Ever since Ishta found that talisman every time he had revealed a secret, no matter to whom, it had made things worse. He did not trust his parents or sisters to maintain appearances, even if they did not actually tell anyone what was happening.

"I don't think so," Garander said. "Actually, I think he's getting ready to die. He expects the magicians to kill him. Or if they don't he may kill himself, in hopes of averting another war."

"That's…unfortunate," Grondar said.

"He can't kill himself!" Ishta exclaimed. "I don't want him to die! He should go live in Ethshar; the baron's wizards can't get at him there!"

"He *can't* live in a city, Ishta," Garander said. "You heard him. His magic won't let him."

"Well, that's *stupid* magic!"

"Of course it is," her father agreed. "It's *wartime* magic, and wars make everything stupid."

"Can't someone fix it?"

Grondar shook his head, but Garander said, "I talked to that wizard from Varag, Azlia. She doesn't want a war, and doesn't think giving one side a *shatra* is going to be good for anyone, so she's going to see what she can do."

"How good a wizard is she, really?" Shella the Younger asked.

"How should I know?" Garander said, turning up a palm.

"Will the *shatra* come back at dusk, as he said, do you think?" Grondar asked.

"I think so," Garander said. He glanced at the window; the sun was low in the west, its rays reaching the hearth in the east end of the room. "In fact, I think I'm going back out to wait for him."

"I'll come, too!" Ishta called.

"No, you won't," her mother said, looking up from her embroidery. "You'll stay here and help me in the kitchen. When this big important meeting is over we'll still need to eat."

"But Mother! Tesk's *life* is at stake!"

"And your presence isn't going to change whatever happens," Shella told her. She set down her stitchery. "Come on, let's get this started; once everything's cooking you can go watch."

Ishta started to argue, but Garander did not wait around for the inevitable outcome. He slipped back outside, and ambled around the side of the house in the general direction of the flying carpet. As he rounded the back corner, though, he noticed two figures in the shadows. He turned to look.

The smaller figure was Azlia; the larger was a man he did not recognize. They had been talking quietly, but they looked up as he approached.

"Garander," Azlia said. "Allow me to introduce Ellador of Morningside."

The man wore a dark blue robe and a blue velvet cap with red piping; white hair spilled down over his shoulders, and a long white beard hid much of his face and chest. He looked very much like the traditional image of a wizard. "Hello," Garander said, unsure what he should do or say when introduced to a magician.

"A pleasure to meet you," Ellador said. "I understand you live here, and you are concerned about whether this dispute over the *shatra* might trigger a war."

Garander smiled wryly. The man certainly got to the point. "Yes," he said.

"You inquired about the Sanguinary Deception?"

"The...what?"

The old man smiled. "The Sanguinary Deception. The spell that makes a person look very, very dead."

Garander straightened up, and felt his heart beat a little faster. "Yes," he said. "Do you know it?"

"Oh, yes," Ellador replied. "It's quite simple, and once upon a time every wizard in the army was expected to know it. Since the war it's fallen out of fashion, though; it really doesn't have many legitimate uses in peacetime. I'm sure Azlia's master didn't see any reason she would want to learn it."

Azlia made a wordless noise that Garander could not interpret, and he was more concerned with learning whether his plan was practical. The spell he wanted did exist, and this wizard claimed to know it, but was it practical? Remembering Azlia's spell in the root cellar, Garander asked, "How long does it take?"

"Oh, just a few seconds."

Garander's breath came out in a sigh of relief; he had not realized he had been holding it. Then another thought struck him. "Do you have the...materials you need for it?"

"We usually say 'ingredients,'" Ellador corrected him. "And all it takes is a knife, a wizard, and the blood of the person being enchanted."

"That's wonderful!" Garander said, smiling broadly.

"Who did you want it cast on?" Ellador asked. "I'm afraid Azlia had not yet told me that, or why an apparent death would keep these young fools from fighting one another."

Garander had thought it was obvious, but he was tactful enough to stop himself before saying that aloud. "The *shatra*," he said.

Ellador blinked, and sucked a wisp of mustache into his mouth. "Hmm," he said. "You think that its death would mean there was nothing to fight over?"

Garander nodded.

"An interesting thought. It might work. But I'm not sure the Sanguinary Deception will work on a *shatra*—aren't they supposed to be as much demon as man?"

"They're part demon," Garander conceded. "But Tesk says his blood is red, not black like a demon's, so...well, does that mean it would work?"

"It might," Ellador said, stroking his beard. "It might. I can't say for sure."

"It's worth a *try*, isn't it?"

"I don't see how it can make matters worse," Ellador agreed. "What did you have in mind?"

Garander had refined his original plan somewhat. "Tesk—the *sha-tra*—is going to be back to talk to Lord Dakkar and Lady Shasha soon, to hear their final offers. Then he'll tell them that he'll give them a decision in the morning, but in the morning I'll tell each group that he decided he would rather die than serve his ancient enemies, and I'll lead them to his 'body.' Which you'll have enchanted. The spell makes the body look *really horrible*, right? So they won't want to inspect it and make sure he's really dead by cutting off his head or something."

"Well, I can't be sure they won't decide to be thorough, but he'll look very dead indeed," Ellador said. "If it works on a *shatra* in the first place."

"And there's no way to see through it, and tell it's an illusion?"

"Oh, I didn't say *that*," the wizard replied. "But it would take magic. A witch could probably tell, and I wouldn't be surprised if there's some talisman a sorcerer could use to test it. But no one could see through it *without* magic."

That was not quite as impenetrable as Garander had hoped, but he thought it would probably be enough. "And it won't wear off suddenly, or anything?"

"Well, yes, it *does* wear off. It starts to fade a day after the spell is cast. But it will last at least a full day."

"Can he move during that day?" The idea of Tesk being trapped, motionless, for an entire day had some obvious drawbacks.

"Oh, he can move just fine. He'll *look* dead, and won't breathe, his heart won't beat, and sometimes it makes the enchanted person *smell* dead, though that part doesn't always work, but from *his* point of view he'll be perfectly normal. No pain or discomfort. Oh, except that if he coughs, he'll spew blood." He grimaced. "It's pretty ugly."

"I don't think that's a problem," Garander said.

Ellador turned up a palm. "Then I'm willing to give it a try."

Garander grabbed the wizard's hand. "Thank you!" he said, with sincere gratitude.

"I'm still not clear what you think you'll accomplish, but then, I haven't really followed everything that's been going on." He glanced at Azlia. "Your friend here probably thinks I'm a fool, but I agreed to come along in case Lady Shasha needed some sort of wizardry that Zendalir couldn't manage, and didn't really pay attention to any of the details. I just do what they pay me to do." He smiled. "I thought I would mostly be working communication spells, to keep her in touch with Lord Edaran and his advisors back in Ethshar, not dredging up old-fashioned disguise spells from my army days!"

Garander's heart dropped at the mention of payment. "I…can't pay you much," he said.

Ellador waved that away. "Don't worry about it. I'm doing this as a courtesy to Azlia. It's an easy spell. I haven't used it for twenty years… no, not that long; I forgot, we used it as a prank once, about fifteen or sixteen years ago. But not since then."

"Are you sure you remember it?" Azlia asked.

"Oh, yes. I did it dozens of times during the war."

Garander did not find that as reassuring as Ellador apparently intended it to be, but he did not say anything about that. "Can you meet me tonight, after dark?" he asked. "I'll take you to the *shatra*, and you can enchant him."

"Well, I can try," Ellador said. "I told you, I can't be sure it will work on a *shatra*."

"We'll see," Garander said. "Shall we meet here?"

"All right. After dark."

"And if anyone asks what we were discussing here," Azlia interjected, "Ellador and I have been trading spells, and we were talking to you about buying ingredients for them—herbs and feathers and bones."

"Oh," Garander said. "That's a good idea." He looked to the west; the sun was touching the treetops of the windbreak around Felder's dooryard. "We should go; Tesk will be coming to talk to the nobles soon."

"Indeed," Ellador said. "Does *he* know what you're planning?"

"Not exactly," Garander admitted. "But I'll tell him." Then he turned and hurried back toward the meeting point in the west field.

He found Velnira waiting, and a glance back over his shoulder showed him Lady Shasha approaching, as well. He wondered whether she had been able to contact Lord Edaran with one of her wizards not present; perhaps that was something Zendalir could handle by himself, or perhaps one of the other magicians knew some sort of communication magic.

"Well?" Velnira demanded, as Garander ambled up to her. "Where is the *shatra*?"

"How should I know?" Garander asked, startled. "I'm his friend, not his keeper."

Velnira did not look satisfied by this, but had no immediate answer. She simply glared at the farmer's son.

Annoyed by this, Garander asked, "Where is Lord Dakkar?"

"In his tent," Velnira replied. "I am to speak for him."

Garander could not say why, but that made him slightly uneasy. Wouldn't the baron want to bask in his success, if he made Tesk a winning offer?

But maybe he knew his best offer was not good enough, and did not want to see it rejected. Garander grimaced, and turned to watch Lady Shasha march up, accompanied by Zendalir and a plump woman Garander did not recognize but assumed to be another magician of some sort.

The aristocrat curtsied to Velnira and Garander, then ostentatiously scanned her surroundings, making a silent point of Tesk's absence.

"I'm sure he'll be here soon," Garander said.

"Of course," Lady Shasha said, with a significant glance to the west. The sun was below the horizon now, and the clouds above were outlined in brilliant orange.

Garander looked around, to see whether the shatra was visible. He did not see Tesk, but he saw that his father and sisters had emerged from the house and were watching. His mother was not in sight.

And then he *did* see Tesk, emerging from the shadows between his father and the barn. The *shatra* paused and said something to Grondar, startling him; he paused to ruffle Ishta's hair, then strode on toward the waiting emissaries.

Garander glanced at the two women, gauging their reactions. Lady Shasha seemed imperturbable as ever, but Velnira looked distinctly nervous, and Garander's suspicion that Lord Dakkar's offer was embarrassingly inadequate grew stronger.

The threesome waited silently as the *shatra* approached.

Tesk stopped a few feet away and said, "I have come, as I agreed I would." Then he looked directly at Garander and asked, "Why are you here, instead of safe with your family?"

Startled, Garander realized he did not have a good answer ready; the truth was that it had never occurred to him *not* to be there. He had simply taken it for granted that he should be present for any negotiations.

Tesk was waiting for an answer, and at last Garander said, "I'm here to represent my family. After all, this is our land. And I thought you might want a friend present."

"I certainly have no objection to his presence," Lady Shasha said. "While I hope that someday you might call me your friend, I know that as yet the term does not apply, and I welcome the young man in that capacity."

"I don't care whether he's here or not," Velnira said. "Let's get on with it."

That did not sound good, Garander thought. Such gracelessness was worrisome.

"Shall I begin, then?" Lady Shasha asked.

"Go ahead," Velnira said, with a wave of her hand.

"Excellent!" The Ethsharite smiled. "Tesk, Lord Edaran regrets that you cannot enjoy the comforts of his city, and apologizes for any discomfort his ignorance of your limitations may have caused. He would still very much appreciate your services as an advisor in matters magical and military, and access to your devices and your own body, so that his own magicians might study and learn from them. In exchange, he offers to provide you with transportation anywhere you might wish to go, by any means within his power—the flying carpet that brought me, for example, can be placed at your disposal. Perhaps you would like to visit the ruins of your homeland, to see if there is anything to be salvaged there, or if there are any rites or ceremonies for the dead to be performed. Furthermore, given that you have said you seek companionship, he would be happy to send visitors to see you, at whatever intervals and for whatever duration might best suit you, and these visitors shall be of your choosing. If you would like the company of singers, perhaps, or dancers, or storytellers, that can be arranged. Should you be interested in educating yourself in the ways of our people, he would be happy to send teachers—historians, perhaps, or scholars of one sort or another. If there is something you would like to teach *us*, in addition to your magic, that would be appreciated—your native tongue, perhaps, or the history and culture of the Northern Empire as seen from within. We know so little of your people! If you do not wish to see your own language lost to the world, we have students eager to learn it."

As she paused for breath, Garander marveled at the cleverness of this offer. Helping the memory of his people survive might indeed appeal to Tesk, but Garander was sure that the Ethsharites were more interested in knowing Shaslan so they could read surviving Northern documents—especially magicians' records of their magic.

"That is everything we have thought to offer," Lady Shasha continued, "but if there is anything else you desire, we will consider whether we can reasonably provide it. Exotic foodstuffs, perhaps—Lord Azrad's Ethshar is becoming famous for its spice trade, and the small kingdoms that now rule Old Ethshar have developed some interesting cuisine. Fine clothing, if your nature allows it and you take any interest in your appearance. Whatever the wealth of Ethshar of the Sands can comfortably provide can be yours. There must be limitations, of course; you cannot ask us to put any innocents to death, or to perform any extravagant acts of destruction, but Lord Edaran is ready to be extremely generous, and to accommodate your nature as best he can. I await your decision."

Having concluded her speech, she curtsied again, and took a single step back.

Tesk regarded her for a moment, then said, "That is a better offer than I expected." He turned to Velnira.

She threw an angry glance at Lady Shasha, then cleared her throat.

"Lord Dakkar, Baron of Varag, has given due consideration to your earlier statements of why you are not interested in the offer he made earlier, and has concluded that there is no rational way to pay you for your services with anything but your life. Furthermore, since you are a Northern abomination trespassing on the baron's lands, and since no formal peace was ever made with the Northern Empire, the proper thing to do would be to kill you. However, Lord Dakkar is a merciful man, and a practical one. If you agree to assist his magicians in studying your magic, and his soldiers in learning the arts of combat, he will allow you to live. If you do not agree, he will have you hunted down and slain, whether here in these woods, or in the wastelands where the Empire once ruled, or in the streets of Ethshar."

Garander stood silently listening to this, at first in disbelief, and then in anger. No wonder the baron had not wanted to deliver his ultimatum in person! Tesk might have killed him on the spot. In fact, in Tesk's position Garander thought he might go ahead and kill Lord Dakkar anyway, even if it meant fighting his way through a few guards, in hopes his successor would be more reasonable.

"Not a very generous offer," Lady Shasha said quietly.

"It is not an offer at all," Tesk said. "It is a threat. But I do not know whether he can carry out his threat."

"Maybe you can accept *both* offers," Garander suggested.

Both women started to speak at once; then they stopped, looking at one another. Lady Shasha made a gesture indicating Velnira should go ahead.

"Lord Dakkar won't allow that," the chamberlain said.

"Regrettably, neither will Lord Edaran," Lady Shasha said. "His agreement with you must be exclusive."

"I see," Tesk said. He thought for a moment, then said, "Perhaps you will each ask your master to reconsider. If I could accept both offers it might make this easier." He looked up at the darkening sky. "I will think about this. You will know my decision in the morning."

Lady Shasha curtsied again, but Velnira demanded, "What is there to decide?"

Tesk looked at her and said, "Whether I live or die." He turned away. "Garander, walk with me. I wish to say goodbye to your family."

"Of course," Garander said. The *shatra* had not waited for his answer, but was already walking swiftly toward the house; Garander hurried to catch up.

CHAPTER TWENTY-TWO

"You have a plan," Tesk said as they walked. "What is it?"

"I was originally going to say we wanted both sides to think you were dead," Garander replied, "but now I wonder whether you should maybe accept Lord Edaran's offer, and we would only need to convince Lord Dakkar you're dead."

Tesk shook his head. "Lord Dakkar would find out. Lord Edaran's people could not keep their visits to me secret."

"Probably not," Garander admitted. "All right, both sides. Separately, so they won't fight over the body. I'll go to each of them and say I found you dead in the woods. I'll tell the baron's people that you killed yourself rather than give in to his threats, and I'll tell the Ethsharites that the baron decided not to wait and went ahead and killed you. Then I'll bring them into the forest and show them your body—there's a magic spell called the Sanguinary Deception that will make it look like you're very definitely dead, so obviously dead that they won't bother to make sure. And with each of them, you'll have a bunch of weapons and talismans and equipment that they can steal to study, so they won't think they're leaving anything for the other side."

"Hm," Tesk said. "Blaming my death on the baron may not be clever."

"Maybe not," Garander admitted. "So suicide there, too, then."

"Or perhaps you could blame my demon half," Tesk suggested. "Say that it killed me rather than allow me to surrender. Which it might in fact do."

"Oh!" Garander said. "Of course."

"This spell—how does it make me look so obviously dead that they will not cut my head off to be sure?"

"I don't know," Garander admitted. "But if they try, you're fast enough to dodge, aren't you?"

"That would ruin the deception."

"I know. Then we'd have to try something else."

"I see. Do you have another plan to try, if that happens?"

"Not yet."

"I see." Tesk considered that for a moment, then asked, "Will you be casting the spell?"

"No, one of the wizards agreed to do it."

"Then this wizard will know I am still alive."

"Yes," Garander admitted. "I couldn't see any way to avoid that. And it's actually *two* wizards—the first one I asked didn't know the spell we need."

"Can we trust these wizards to remain silent?"

"I think so," Garander said. "They don't want a war. And I've always heard that wizards are good at keeping secrets—they keep the workings of their spells secret, after all."

Tesk nodded.

"Then you'll do it?"

"I have no better plan. I will try it."

"I'll bring the wizard to the woods once it's full dark."

"I will meet you."

"Once the spell is cast, you'll need to get those tools and talismans—enough so that each side will think they have all of them."

Tesk asked, "Will this deception spell interfere with bringing the supplies?"

"I don't *think* so. But we'll ask the wizard. If he isn't sure, maybe we can wait and cast the spell in the morning."

Tesk nodded again. "Bring the wizard," he said. He added, "Do not follow me," and then sped up, changing direction and heading toward the forest to the northwest.

Garander could not have followed at such a pace in any case; he stopped, and saw that he had walked past his own front door without realizing it while they spoke. Tesk had said he wanted to say goodbye to the family, but apparently he had changed his mind, or been so distracted by the discussion of Garander's plan that he forgot.

Garander turned back and headed inside. He found his family waiting for him. "What's happening?" Ishta demanded, before anyone else could say a word.

"The Ethsharites made an offer," Garander said. "A good one—they said they would send visitors, teachers and students, to keep him company, and teach him about Ethshar, and learn about his magic and the Northern Empire."

"And the baron?" his father asked.

"He made a threat. He said he would have Tesk killed if he didn't cooperate, or if he agreed to work for the Ethsharites."

"Won't the Ethsharites protect him?" Shella the Younger asked.

"I'm sure they'll try," Garander said. "If he agrees to their terms, anyway."

"Why wouldn't he?" Ishta asked.

"He doesn't trust them," Garander said. "And he doesn't really want *anyone* learning about his magic."

"Then what's he going to do?"

Garander hesitated. He did not want to lie to his family, but he did not trust Ishta to keep a secret, not even when it might save Tesk's life.

But on the other hand, she had managed to keep quiet about Tesk's very existence for months.

Their father had not, though. Garander threw a quick glance at Grondar, then turned back to Ishta. "I don't know," he said. "I don't think he's decided yet."

Grondar gave him a look Garander could not interpret, then called, "Shouldn't you be getting our supper, Shella?"

Garander's mother started. "Oh, yes!" she said. She grabbed her elder daughter's arm and hustled toward the kitchen.

"Ishta, help your mother," Grondar ordered.

"But I…"

"Go! It will keep you busy and take your mind off your *shatra* friend."

Reluctantly, Ishta obeyed.

"Garander and I will get on with the chores," Grondar called after the women. "Just because we have wizards and aristocrats all over the place doesn't mean the pigs will feed themselves."

Garander was in no mood to tend to the livestock, but he knew his father had a point. He walked back out the door he had just entered, and started toward the barn.

His father caught his arm. "You have an idea of some sort, don't you?" Grondar asked. "I saw you slip away earlier."

"I…" Garander hesitated.

Grondar held up a hand. "Don't tell me. I can't give away secrets I don't know. You can tell me all about it later, when it's all over."

"Thank you, Father," Garander said.

"Is there anything else you need to do?"

Garander glanced in the direction of the flying carpet. "Actually…"

Grondar gave him a shove. "Go do it. Don't tell me anything. And if you can get back in time for your supper, good, but if you can't, I'll tell your mother the hogs were being troublesome."

"Thank you, Father!" Garander repeated, more enthusiastically. He gave a look at the baron's camp, but they would not be able to see much in the gathering gloom, especially if he went around the far side of the house. He hurried to the corner, watching over his shoulder as his father vanished into the barn.

Ellador was not at the designated meeting place, and Garander grew steadily more worried as he waited for what seemed like an hour but was probably no more than a fourth of one. The colors had vanished from the west, and the sky overhead had faded from dark blue to starry black, when at last the wizard's voice spoke.

"I'm glad to see you," he said. "I was afraid you might be delayed."

Startled, Garander looked around but saw no sign of the old man.

"I'm wearing the Mantle of Stealth," Ellador said. "I didn't want Zendalir or Shasha asking awkward questions."

Garander had never heard of a Mantle of Stealth, but guessed it was some sort of invisibility spell. "Good," he said. "This way."

He hoped the wizard was following him, but had no way of telling for certain—his magic apparently hid the sound of his footsteps, as well as rendering him invisible. He was reassured when the old man stumbled and muttered, "Death!" as he struggled to recover his balance.

Garander made his way slowly and carefully from the farm into the forest, making it easy for the wizard to keep up, even in the growing darkness. Fortunately the greater moon was rising, and dull orange light trickled through the trees.

He and Tesk had not specified an exact spot for their meeting; Garander had relied on the *shatra*'s superhuman senses to find him. He wandered almost at random into the woods, more or less aiming at a clearing where he and Ishta had visited with Tesk a few times.

He had not quite reached it when Tesk's voice asked, "Is the wizard coming, or has something gone wrong?"

Garander stopped, and the *shatra* dropped out of a tree almost directly in front of him.

"Nothing's wrong," he said. "The wizard's right behind me."

He *hoped* that was true.

"Gods!" Ellador's voice said, relieving Garander's doubts. "It really is a *shatra*!"

Tesk jumped sideways, and suddenly one of his black rods was in his hand. His head jerked upward, then back down.

"I can smell you," he said. "And I sense your body heat…"

"I'm right here," Ellador said, suddenly appearing in a patch of moonlight between two trees. He was holding a large piece of dark cloth in one hand; he was hatless, and his hair was rumpled.

"He was using a spell to help him slip away," Garander said.

"The Mantle of Stealth," Ellador explained. "It's a simple invisibility spell."

"Ah," Tesk said, lowering his wand—but only partway, Garander noticed.

"I'm Ellador of Morningside," the wizard said. He started to hold out his hand, then thought better of it. "My friend Azlia asked me to help this young man out with a bit of magic, and I agreed."

"I am Tezhiskar Deralt aya Shatra Ad'n Chitir Shess Chitir," the *shatra* replied. "Your people call me Tesk." He still did not put his weapon away.

"I take it you are not comfortable around wizards," Ellador said, pointing at the black rod.

"I am not," Tesk agreed.

"That could be awkward. To perform the spell Garander wanted, I'll need to draw your blood with my own knife. Can you allow that?"

"How much blood?"

"Oh, just a few drops—a pinprick, really. Though if the spell works it will look like far more."

"*If* the spell works?"

"Well, it's probably never been attempted on a *shatra* before," Ellador said cheerfully. "*I* certainly haven't used it on one!"

"Does that matter?"

Ellador turned up the palm of the hand that was not holding the cloth. "Who can say? But the spell is meant for humans, and as I understand it, you are *not* fully human."

"I am not," Tesk acknowledged.

"Then we won't know until we try it."

Tesk considered that, and finally lowered his weapon the rest of the way, though he still did not return it to its place on his back.

"Ideally," Ellador said, "I would draw blood from your throat. Anywhere will do, though, if you can't bring yourself to let me get that close."

"Why would the throat be better?" Garander asked, before Tesk could respond.

"You seemed worried that someone might want to make sure he's dead by cutting off his head," Ellador replied. "Well, wherever I cut him, it will appear the flesh in that spot has been cut open clear to the bone. If I nick his throat, just ever so slightly, it will look as if his neck's been sliced clear to the spine; cutting his head off the rest of the way would be pointless."

Tesk and Garander exchanged glances. "It will?" Garander asked.

"If the spell works at all, yes."

"I like that idea," Garander said.

"It is not your throat," Tesk retorted. "But I see the wisdom in this."

"Then shall we proceed?"

"It will last until morning?" Garander asked.

"It will last until at least sundown tomorrow, and will be gone without a trace by dawn of the day after."

"I am not sure I can allow you to cut me," Tesk said.

"If I meant you any harm, I wouldn't be here, plain to see. I could have kept the Mantle of Stealth, after all."

"It may be that you could not use other magic while it lasted."

"Well, yes, in fact that's true, but really, why would I be *here*, instead of using a spell that would kill you from afar?"

"Yes," Tesk acknowledged. "Your words are convincing."

"Then will you trust me to draw some blood from your neck?"

"I am not sure I can allow it."

"But you just agreed…!"

"I am not sure I *can* allow it. The demon may object."

Ellador looked startled. "There really *is* a demon inside you?"

"Yes," Tesk replied flatly.

"You doubted it?" Garander asked.

"Well, I haven't ever seen anything like it before! No one in Ethshar ever knew how to merge a man and a demon."

Garander had nothing useful to say to that. Instead he suggested, "What if Tesk held your wrist while you make the cut?"

"That might help," Tesk said.

"All right," Ellador said. He drew the knife on his belt, and took a step toward the *shatra*.

Tesk's hand came up so fast that Garander did not see it move; the black rod was just suddenly *there*, pointed at the wizard's heart.

Ellador stopped. "I can't work the spell without your blood," he said.

"I know," Tesk said. Slowly and carefully he returned his weapon to its place on his back; then he reached out and gripped Ellador's wrist.

Ellador's face went pale, the change visible even in the faint moonlight. "Do you need to hold it so tight?" he asked.

"I apologize," Tesk said, and Garander thought he could see the struggle on the *shatra*'s face as he forced his fingers to loosen their hold.

"That's better," the wizard said, as Tesk's grip relaxed. "Now, guide the blade to your neck."

Tesk jerked the wizard's hand closer, forcing Ellador to stumble forward, and then the tip of the shining dagger touched the *shatra*'s throat.

For a moment nothing more happened; both men stood motionless, staring at one another. Then Ellador jabbed, and Tesk's fingers tightened; the wizard let out a gasp of pain. Garander started toward them, but before he could intervene Ellador had stepped back, and Tesk had released him.

"I am sorry," the *shatra* said. "I warned you. Do you want to try again?"

Ellador began massaging his wrist with his other hand, but looked at Tesk, startled. "Why would I want to try again?" He held up the knife. "That's enough blood right there."

Garander could barely see the speck of dark red on the tip of the blade. "It is?" he asked. He looked at Tesk's throat, and saw the tiniest of scratches, no bigger than a spider's bite.

"I told you I didn't need much," Ellador said, and Garander thought he sounded a bit smug. "Now I need to mark you with it." He dabbed the index finger of his other hand on the dagger, then reached out and drew a faint line across Tesk's throat with the blood. The *shatra* did not resist.

"A few more marks might be useful, but that one will probably do," the wizard said. Then he waved the dagger in a peculiar zigzag motion, and said something that did not sound like anything that should come from a human throat.

Garander was about to ask a question when the dagger began glowing faintly purple. He stared as the wizard continued his incantation.

Then Ellador finished his chant with a flourish, and lowered the dagger. Garander turned back to Tesk, to see what he thought.

Then he stopped, and swallowed to keep from vomiting.

Tesk's throat had been laid open clear to the spine, and thick, dark blood was spilling out. The *shatra*'s face was ashen gray, with bluish blotches on the cheekbones; blood dribbled from his nostrils and the corners of his mouth. He was obviously dead—but still upright, still moving. "Gods!" Garander exclaimed.

"Oh, good," Ellador said, smiling. "It worked."

"It…" Garander said, but was unable to force more words out.

"I do not feel anything unusual," Tesk said, and thick blackened blood ran from his mouth with every word. The effect was appalling.

"There's no reason you should," Ellador said. "But if you look in a mirror, you'll see. And if you need more blood for some reason—say, you don't think there's enough on one of your arms—just cough, and you should have plenty."

Garander swallowed again.

Tesk looked at him. "I feel no different," he said.

"Believe me, you *look* different," Garander told him.

"I've done what I promised," Ellador said. "I'll be going back to camp now."

"Yes, of course," Garander said, still staring in horror at Tesk. "I'll go with you, so you don't get lost."

"Thank you," the wizard said. "I'd appreciate that."

Tesk said, "My appearance is different?"

"Oh, yes," Garander said. "All you have to do is lie still, and no one will doubt you're dead."

"You don't have a heartbeat or a pulse," Ellador added helpfully. "And no one can hear you breathe or see your chest move."

"I do not feel different," Tesk said again.

"We have to go," Garander said. "You go fetch those supplies we talked about, and find someplace convenient where I can show you to people. Maybe cough some blood on the stuff. I'll see you in the morning, and we can arrange the viewings."

"Viewings?" Tesk snorted, spraying clotted blood from his nose. "You make it sound like an exhibition."

"That's what it is," Garander said. "Now, go get your things!"

Looking slightly annoyed, Tesk turned and leapt up into a nearby tree, then vanished in the spring foliage.

Garander did not watch him go; he did not want to look at the ghastly illusion the spell created. Instead he took the Ethsharite wizard by the arm and said, "This way."

CHAPTER TWENTY-THREE

"Velnira! Come with me, please!" Garander tried to sound genuinely desperate.

The baron's chamberlain looked up from her breakfast, blinking in the bright morning sun. "Why?" she asked. "What is it?"

"It's the *shatra*!"

Her eyes narrowed. "What about it?"

"He…it…it's terrible!"

Velnira set her plate aside, and asked Burz, "What's he talking about?"

"I don't know," Burz said. "He just said it was urgent, and I knew he was in on all the talking, so I let him past."

She looked questioningly at Garander.

"Something terrible has happened!" he said. "I think he may be dead."

Her eyes narrowed. "The *shatra*? Dead?"

"I…I think so."

"What about his magic?" she asked warily.

"You mean why didn't it protect him? I don't know! His talismans are still there, so—come and see!"

Velnira frowned and got to her feet. She told Burz, "You're coming with us." She pointed to another soldier, a man Garander did not know, and said, "You, too." She ordered a third, "Inform the baron, and see which magicians are available. Have the magicians ready, in case I send for them." Then she turned to Garander. "Show us," she said.

Garander turned and trotted eastward, glancing back over his shoulder to make sure the others were following. Burz took the lead, then Velnira, and the other soldier brought up the rear as the farm boy led them across the field and into the woods beyond.

"I was coming to see whether he wanted to talk to anyone this morning, and I found him," Garander said as he pushed through the underbrush. "I came straight to you—I thought the baron ought to know."

"You haven't told anyone else?" Velnira asked, as she stumbled over a fallen log.

"No," Garander said. "I'm a loyal subject of Lord Dakkar, so I came to you first."

"Hmph."

Then Garander brought them around the trunk of a big oak, and there was Tesk, lying on his back in a pool of blood, his head flung back across a fallen branch, his helmet half off, and his throat exposed—both the outside of his throat, and the inside. Raw red flesh and a glimpse of white bone lay open in a shaft of sunlight, and the bits of skin around the wound that weren't covered in blackening blood were grayish-white.

Even though Garander knew it was an illusion, he shuddered at the sight. He heard Burz choke, and Velnira gasped and stepped back at her first glimpse of the downed *shatra*.

"I think one of the mizagars may have turned on him," Garander said. "Or maybe his own demon, because he was talking to Ethsharites."

"He looks like he's been dead for *days*," Burz said.

"We spoke to it last night," Velnira said. "Maybe it's decaying quickly because some preserving magic is gone, and it's making up for all those years time was kept at bay."

Garander was pleased that he did not need to make that suggestion himself; he did not want to appear to have all the answers, as that might arouse suspicion. He was just a farmer, after all, not a magician or scholar.

"Go fetch the magicians," Velnira ordered the soldier behind her. "Tell Lord Dakkar that the *shatra* is dead, and we await his instructions."

"Should he tell Lady Shasha?" Garander asked. "She ought to know, too, shouldn't she?"

Velnira threw him a sharp glance, and then looked at Tesk's body—and at his equipment, scattered on the ground around him. "Make sure none of the Ethsharites see you," she told the soldier. "We want to keep this quiet for now. Don't let anyone see you or the magicians when you bring them back—maybe one of them can work a spell to ensure that."

"I'll do my best," the soldier said, with a bob of his head. Then he was gone, crashing through the underbrush.

"All his weapons are still here," Burz remarked. "Whatever killed him didn't rob him."

"Maybe there's a protective spell on them," Garander suggested. "Or maybe it really was a mizagar—they wouldn't have any *use* for all those tools and talismans."

"Maybe," Velnira said.

"What should we do?" Garander asked.

"We wait," Velnira told him. She gestured at a mound of dead leaves. "Have a seat, if you want."

"I know you don't want to tell Lady Shasha," Garander said, "but shouldn't I tell my family?"

"No," Velnira snapped. "Sit down." She suited her own actions to her words, slumping back against the base of a tree.

Garander hesitated, then found a spot of his own, not on the dead leaves, but nearby. He glanced up at Burz, but the soldier seemed content to stand.

"Poor Tesk," he said, looking at his friend's body again.

It was hard to believe that the *shatra* was *not* really dead; he looked ghastly. In addition to the slashed throat, blood ran from his mouth and nose and stained his clothing from neck to navel. Blackish rivulets had run down his side and pooled on the ground beneath him.

"Hard to believe he's dead," Burz said.

Velnira turned her head to stare at him. "Are you mad? *Look* at him!"

"Oh, I know he *is* dead," Burz acknowledged. "I just don't understand how he *could* be. I saw him fight; by the gods, I fought him myself. He was faster and stronger than anything I had ever seen before. If he had wanted to kill me, he could have done it at any time. But here he is, dead as a stone. If this was a mizagar's work, then those things are even more dangerous than I thought."

"It might have caught him off guard," Garander suggested. "After all, he thought they were on the same side."

"That's true," Velnira said, "but it might have been one of those wizards from Ethshar."

"Why would *they* kill him?" Garander asked. "They were trying to *hire* him!"

"Maybe he told them no," Velnira said.

"Oh," Garander said. "You think that's it?" He tried to decide whether he wanted the Ethsharites blamed for this. He probably did not; it might serve as a pretext for conflict.

There was something ludicrous in the idea that the barons might start a war with Ethshar to avenge the killing of a left-over Northern monster, especially when Lord Dakkar had announced last night that *he* would have the *shatra* killed if Tesk did not cooperate, but that did not mean it was impossible.

Velnira did not answer, and after a moment of awkward silence Garander asked, "Would a wizard leave his throat like that? I thought wizardry…well, that it either wouldn't leave any marks at all, or that he'd be completely ripped to pieces."

"I don't know," Velnira said, obviously nettled. "Ask the wizard when she gets here. Or he. Or they."

Another uneasy silence settled over the threesome. Garander wished that they would get on with whatever they were going to do; he was worried that someone from Ethshar of the Sands would come looking for Tesk and stumble on the party.

He also feared that Tesk might shift position. He knew no ordinary man could stay so motionless for very long. Tesk, of course, was no ordinary man, but still, Garander could not help worrying.

It seemed like hours before the soldier returned with Sammel, Azlia, and a woman Garander did not recognize, but at last they came stomping through the forest, making what seemed to Garander like far more noise than necessary.

"*There* you are!" Velnira said. "What did Lord Dakkar say?"

"He won't be coming himself," the soldier replied. "He thought that would attract too much attention."

"And of course, he's worried that it might be a trap," the unfamiliar woman said. Startled, Garander took a closer look at her.

She was short, and a bit plump, dressed in a red tunic embroidered in white, green, and gold over a respectable ankle-length green skirt. She was wearing boots—far more sensible for tramping around the forest than the shoes Velnira, Sammel, and Azlia had on. Given the soldier's instructions and the fact that no one had remarked on her presence, Garander assumed she was a magician of some sort, but her clothes gave no indication of what *kind* of magician. Wizards traditionally liked hats and robes, while her head was bare and her clothes ordinary; although he had never met either one Garander had always heard that theurgists wore white and demonologists wore black. She might be another sorcerer, like Sammel or the man who had vanished after tampering with Tesk's weapon, or she might be a witch, or something else entirely.

Whatever she was, Sammel glared at her and held two fingers to his lips in a shushing gesture. Then he lowered the fingers and looked at Tesk.

"Well, there's not much question he's dead," the sorcerer said. "I don't think even a demon could keep him alive in that condition."

Azlia glanced at Garander and said nothing.

"Is there some way you can tell whether the demon is gone?" Velnira asked.

Sammel frowned. "I'm a sorcerer, not a demonologist."

"Do we have a demonologist?"

"Not that I know of. Certainly not in Varag, and I don't recall anyone in the delegation from Sardiron who looked like a demonologist."

"Some demonologists prefer not to announce themselves," the unknown woman said.

"Well, if someone's keeping it secret, then we can't invite him," Sammel retorted.

"So we don't have one," Velnira said. "It's up to you, Sammel."

Sammel grimaced. "You saw what happened to Arnen."

Velnira nodded. "Be careful," she said.

Moving cautiously, Sammel approached the fallen *shatra*. Azlia, Velnira, and the two soldiers watched him intently.

The strange woman, though, watched Garander; he shifted uncomfortably, then glared back.

He had expected her to look away, but she did not; instead she beckoned to him, and stepped back, away from the others.

Intrigued, Garander gave the others one quick glance, then followed the stranger as she stepped behind a big oak.

The minute he joined her, she whispered, "You know he's not dead."

"Who are you?" Garander asked.

"My name is Zatha the Witch. You're Garander Grondar's son?"

"Yes."

"You know he's not dead. Why are you doing this?"

Garander threw a glance at Tesk. Sammel was carefully lifting one of the larger talismans from the *shatra*'s side.

"So they'll leave him alone," he said. "Lord Dakkar threatened to kill him; well, he can't kill him if he's already dead."

"Where did you get the spell?"

Garander hesitated. It was none of the witch's business. "Why do you want to know?" he asked.

"I want to know who knows he's still alive. The more people who know a secret, the more likely it will come out."

"A wizard from Ethshar," Garander said. "And Azlia knows. No one else."

"Will Sammel notice anything, do you think?"

"I don't know. *You're* the magician; *I* don't know whether a sorcerer can see through a wizard's spell. Until you called me over here, I didn't know *witches* could."

"Oh, this is exactly the sort of thing we're good at, but sorcerers? I don't know. If Sammel had seen anything, though, he'd have spoken up by now, so you may be safe."

Garander looked over at the rest of the party. Sammel had retrieved several devices and passed them to the two soldiers. The Sardironese seemed more interested in looting the body than in Tesk's condition.

"Is that stuff booby-trapped?" Zatha asked him.

His head whipped back to face her. "No! We wanted peace—that's why we're doing this. We were afraid those idiots would start a *war* over him."

"Ah!" Zatha nodded. "And I'm sure Lord Dakkar would have tried, but the other barons aren't all as hot-headed and stupid as he is. So those things are harmless?"

"I didn't say that," Garander whispered. "They're real Northern equipment; they aren't any safer than the one that killed Arnen. But they aren't any *less* safe, either. The idea is to let the baron think he's gotten *something* for his trouble."

"Clever! And the Ethsharites?"

"We have more equipment hidden away. They'll get their share."

The witch nodded. "What if they decide to take the body with them?"

"Which? The Ethsharites?"

"Or my people, either one."

Garander threw Tesk a glance. "He won't allow it. He's alive and conscious. If anyone tries to move him, he'll probably kill them."

"It seems to me that's a flaw in your plan."

"It's a risk," Garander admitted. "I did the best I could."

"You did well," she answered soothingly.

"Are you going to tell them he's alive?"

She snorted. "Why would I do *that*? I don't want them to capture your *shatra* or start a war any more than *you* do, even if my reasons are different."

"Thank you," Garander murmured.

She nodded, then stepped out from behind the tree and walked straight toward the rest of the group. Garander hurried after her, terrified that she had just lied to him and was about to expose his scheme.

"Don't move the body," Zatha said, as she strode up next to Sammel. "I sense danger. I think it would explode if disturbed. After all, the Northerners didn't want anyone to study the *shatra* and learn their secrets."

Startled, Sammel turned to her. "Are you sure?"

"No, I'm not sure—I'm a witch, not a sorcerer or a demonologist. But I sense danger."

Sammel frowned, then handed the last of the Northern artifacts to Burz. Kneeling over Tesk, the sorcerer pulled his own pack off his shoulder and fished in it for a moment before bringing out a gleaming metal talisman.

"What are you doing?" Garander asked.

"I'm checking…" Sammel held the talisman over Tesk's chest; a spot on its surface glowed yellow. The sorcerer sucked in his breath, then returned the talisman to his pack.

"You might be right," he told Zatha. "There's sorcery still active in his body, even though there's no sign of life."

Velnira stepped back; the two soldiers looked to her for instructions.

"If you're planning to move the body, give me time to get clear," Sammel said, straightening up and moving away.

"That won't be necessary," Velnira said. "We have his equipment, and we know he's dead. Let us take it to the baron; if he wants anything more, he can say so."

"Good," Burz said, hefting a bundle of Northern sorcery.

"Come on," Velnira said.

"I'll go tell my family," Garander said.

Velnira dismissed him with a wave, and marched off through the trees. The two soldiers followed her, carrying their loot; Sammel came close behind, lifting his pack back onto his shoulder.

Azlia hung back, watching Garander; Zatha moved to one side, as if attending to some private business of her own. Garander hurried to the wizard's side.

"Thank you," he whispered. He glanced toward the witch. "Zatha could tell he was alive, but she says she won't tell anyone."

"Is he really going to be all right?" Azlia asked. "He looks *horrible*!"

"He's fine," Garander said. "I talked to him before I went to get Velnira, while we were setting everything up. He's fine. Thank you."

Azlia hesitated a second longer, then turned and followed the others.

Then Zatha was there beside him.

"Good work," she said. "I'll try to put a little subtle pressure on Lord Dakkar, to get him to pack up and go home; I'm sure you don't want him around."

"Thank you," Garander said. "Thank you for everything!"

CHAPTER TWENTY-FOUR

Garander did not go back to the house to tell his family; he waited until everyone was safely out of sight, then knelt down and asked Tesk, "Are you all right?"

"I am fine," he replied, lifting his head; if Garander had not known it was an illusion, he would have wondered how the *shatra* could move enough air through his ruined throat to get the words out. Tesk sat up, and shook clots of red-black blood from his arms.

"We need to get more equipment," Garander said. "Then I'll bring the Ethsharites."

"I know this," Tesk answered, looking around at the trampled ground. "We should use another place."

Garander had not really thought about that, but a single glance made it obvious that Tesk was right. "And we should make it look like something has dragged you away," he said. "In case Velnira or Burz comes back."

Tesk considered this for a moment, then stood up. "Lie down," he said.

"What?"

"Lie down where I was. I will drag you away."

"Me?"

"Yes. I am stronger than you and heavier than you."

"Stronger, yes…" Garander said, looking at Tesk's lean figure.

"And heavier. I am not human. There are things inside me that weigh many pounds."

Garander had to concede that could be true, and he reluctantly lay back on the bloody earth.

He was startled, though, when Tesk did not grab him by the arms, as he had expected, but by the neck. "*Hai!*" he protested.

"Do not struggle," Tesk ordered. "You are pretending to be my corpse, being dragged by a beast such as a mizagar."

"Urgh," Garander said. Tesk was not trying to strangle him, but the powerful hands around his throat could not help but make it difficult to talk. He tried to relax as the *shatra* dragged him between two trees, and several yards along the forest floor. He closed his eyes, so as not to look at the hideous pallor and phantasmal blood of Tesk's enchanted face and body, and found that made it easier.

When Tesk finally released him Garander opened his eyes, sat up, and rubbed his back. "I'm going to have bruises," he said.

"Probably," Tesk agreed. "Now let us prepare again."

It took almost an hour to find a suitable spot and arrange Tesk and another collection of Northern equipment there, but finally they were both satisfied with the tableau they had created, and Garander hurried off to fetch the Ethsharites.

Lady Shasha did not bring any guards, but when Ellador offered to accompany her she made no objection. That made matters much simpler for Garander; he and the wizard checked Tesk for signs of life and gathered up the various sorcerous devices, and only needed to fool a single observer.

Of course, Lady Shasha appeared to be brighter and more alert than Velnira, but even so, having one of her own trusted magicians assuring her that the *shatra* was indeed dead was sufficient to convince her.

"It couldn't be a sorcerous illusion?" she asked.

Ellador made a few meaningless gestures with his dagger, then assured her, "No, my lady."

That appeared to satisfy her. She did ask Garander to help carry the equipment back to the Ethsharite campsite, and to thank his parents for their hospitality, and he could not see any reason to antagonize her by refusing. She apologized for not saying her own farewells, but said that Lord Edaran would want to receive the news—and the talismans—as swiftly as possible.

Delivering the Northern devices took some time, so it was an hour or so before Garander was able to return and allow Tesk to once again drag him away.

There was scarcely another hour remaining before noon when Garander finally left the forest and returned home to do his much-delayed chores.

He saw that the baron's party was breaking camp and packing up, clearly preparing for departure. The Ethsharites, who had kept almost their entire camp on the flying carpet, were already gone; he could see them far to the south, a black speck against the midday sky.

His father found him there, staring at the distant carpet. "Where have *you* been?" Grondar demanded. "What have you done?"

"Good morning, Father," Garander said.

"One of the baron's soldiers told me they're leaving. He said their business here was done, and they won't be back."

Garander nodded.

"What happened to the *shatra*, then? Did he go with them? Or with the Ethsharites?" He gestured toward the southern sky, where the carpet had now vanished over the horizon.

Garander shook his head. "He's dead," he said. "That's why they're going."

"*Dead?*" Grondar said, his eyes widening. "How? What happened?"

Garander bit his lip; he had not thought about how his parents would react to the news. Grondar looked more upset than he had expected. "I…I think one of the mizagars turned on him. Maybe it didn't like him talking to all those people."

"How did you find out?"

"Um…I went into the woods looking for him, early this morning," Garander said. "I found his body with the throat torn open."

"You did? Where?"

"In the forest. I told you."

"Show me!"

"But I haven't done my chores, and it's almost noon!"

"That can wait! Show me!"

This had been no part of Garander's plan; he hesitated, wondering if perhaps he should tell his father the truth, but that had rarely worked out well where Tesk was concerned. He mentally turned up a palm and said, "This way."

He hoped that Tesk was well clear; he did not want to try to explain any anomalies to his father. Of course, the *shatra* would probably hear them coming.

He could have gone to either site, but he chose the one he had shown the Ethsharites, since it was slightly closer. He only remembered at the last minute to feign surprise at the disappearance of Tesk's body.

"He was here!" he said, pointing at the blood-soaked moss and flattened undergrowth. "He was right here!"

"He isn't here now," Grondar said. "Are you sure he was really dead?"

"His throat was ripped open! I could see his spine; his head was half-off!"

"Then where did he go?"

"Well, he certainly didn't get up and walk away," Garander said. "Either some animal got him, or some of our guests stole the body for their magicians to study." He pointed to the trail he and Tesk had made. "It looks as if *something* dragged him away."

Grondar frowned. "That shouldn't have happened. He deserved better. I was going to build him a pyre."

"His demon part might not have liked that," Garander said.

"Huh," Grondar replied. "I hadn't thought of that. Maybe *it* woke up and walked the body away."

"Could it do that?"

"How should I know? I'm no demonologist." He shook his head.

They both stared at the bloodstains and other marks for a moment longer, then turned and headed back toward the house.

They were perhaps halfway home when Grondar said, "Ishta will be heartbroken."

"I know," Garander answered.

"She'll suspect something, with all the visitors leaving."

"I know." He hesitated, then asked, "Do you want me to tell her?"

Grondar did not reply immediately, but then said, "I think that might be best. You saw the body, and I did not. She may think I still hate Tesk for being a Northerner. She may accept it better from you. But I'm her father; it's my responsibility."

"I don't mind," Garander said. "I think she *will* take it better from me."

"Then I will leave it to you." Garander thought he heard relief in his father's voice, though of course Grondar tried to hide it.

When they reached the house Grondar sent his son to the barn to feed the livestock and muck out, with instructions to come straight inside to eat as soon as he was done. Garander obeyed.

He was feeding the pigs when Ishta appeared. "Father said you wanted to see me," she said.

Garander had been thinking about how to deal with this. He did not want to see his sister crying over Tesk, but he did not want her to give away any secrets, either. "I did," he said.

"Is it about Tesk?"

He nodded.

"Is he all right?"

"The baron thinks he's dead," Garander said. "So does Lady Shasha."

Ishta sucked in her breath. "They do?"

Garander nodded again.

"Do *you* think he's dead?"

"I'm not going to answer that right away."

"So you don't. What's going on, Garander?"

"If they all think he's dead, they'll go away and stop bothering us."

"I know. I saw them leave. But is he all right?"

"I showed them his corpse," he told her. "I helped them steal all his equipment. Then they left him in the woods—they thought his body might be booby-trapped, so they didn't try to move him. But if anyone goes back to look, they'll find what Father and I saw—the body is gone. Something dragged it away."

"Garander, you're scaring me!"

"They all think maybe a mizagar killed him because he was getting too friendly with enemies of the Northern Empire. Or maybe it was his demon. Whatever it was, it ripped out his throat; there was blood everywhere. And whatever it was came back later and dragged the body away."

"Garander!" He could see her eyes starting to well up.

That was good. He wanted her a *little* upset, so she could fool their parents.

"But the thing is," he continued, "how could they *both* steal all his equipment? Velnira had two soldiers carry away armloads. Lady Shasha had me and one of her wizards help her carry everything."

"What?" Ishta tried to blink away the incipient tears.

"Isn't it just a little convenient, him dying like that?" he went on. "But both sides will think it must be real, because of all the magical stuff they took. He wouldn't let that happen if he were still alive, would he?"

"Garander!"

"But what if he had extra equipment? There were Northerners all around here once, and they must have left supplies behind, and Tesk would know about them."

She just stared at him as he hung up the now-empty feed bucket.

"Did you ever hear Father talk about a spell the Ethsharitic army used to use to fool Northerners into thinking that soldiers were dead, when they weren't? It turns out one of Lady Shasha's wizards knows it; he says it's called the Sanguinary Deception."

"You *fooled* them!" Ishta burst into a smile.

Garander held two fingers up to his mouth.

"So Father doesn't know?"

"He might tell the baron if he thought Tesk was still alive."

The smile vanished.

"You'll need to be *much* more careful than before," Garander said.

Ishta nodded.

"Don't wipe away those tears."

She nodded again, and smiled feebly.

Lunch was a somber affair. Ishta did not say a word, and as soon as the meal was done and the table had been cleared she vanished into the room she shared with her sister.

The baron's party had gone, leaving the west and north fields a mess; the Ethsharites had done considerably less damage. Grondar and his son went to work cleaning up the debris.

That took most of the afternoon, and for the most part father and son worked side by side in silence. The sun was low in the west when they headed back toward the barn to dump the bags of trash and put away their hoes and rakes.

They had just stepped inside when Grondar said, without preamble, "He's not really dead, is he?"

Startled, Garander said, "What?"

"He's not dead. It wouldn't be that easy. Even if it *was* something Northern."

"I don't know," Garander said.

"And the others—they wouldn't have just left. They came here for Northern magic."

"All his things were gone," Garander said.

"But they *both* left," his father insisted. "If one of them had found the body first, they would have taken everything, and the other side would have put up an argument."

"Maybe they agreed to share."

"That fast? No." He shook his head. "I don't know what you did, son. I don't *want* to know. But he's alive, isn't he?"

Garander looked his father in the eye and said nothing.

Grondar nodded. "Good," he said. "Don't say anything. Then I *can't* tell anyone anything, no matter how tired or drunk or careless I get. Does Ishta know? Because at lunch…" He did not finish his sentence.

"I didn't tell her everything," Garander said. "I didn't want her to look too happy, but I didn't want to make her miserable needlessly, either."

"Well done. But she'll need to be very careful if she visits him anymore."

"She knows."

Grondar nodded again.

"Good," he said again.

And that was that.

EPILOGUE

Garander convinced Ishta not to go looking for Tesk until the spell had worn off, and for once she did as she was told. The spell wore off on schedule, though, and within three days of the staged death scenes Ishta and Tesk were once again chatting happily in the forest.

Despite concerns about what might happen now that the *shatra* was gone, no mizagars were seen in the area then or for many years thereafter.

There were no reports of any great magical discoveries in Varag or Sardiron; instead there were occasional stories of sorcerers dying in various horrible ways when their experiments went wrong.

No reports came from Ethshar of the Sands by any ordinary routes, but every so often thereafter Garander would have a dream in which Ellador would appear to him to update him on the latest news, or sometimes simply to talk. He had no *proof* at first that these dreams were magical sendings, but Garander was certain that they were just that; the dream-Ellador said he was using something called the Spell of Invaded Dreams to let Garander know what was happening.

Lord Edaran, the dream-Ellador said, had wanted to send magicians to retrieve the *shatra*'s body, but had been dissuaded by Ellador and his friends, who had reported that the body had been destroyed.

Lord Edaran had also talked about perhaps sending a punitive expedition into the baronies to avenge the *shatra*'s death, which he somehow blamed on the incompetence of Lord Dakkar's magicians, but by this time word had reached the other two overlords of what was going on. Azrad and Gor made it very clear to their young partner that there was to be no war unless the barons were actually stupid enough to invade the Hegemony—which they were not.

Experimentation on the captured equipment, Ellador reported, was conducted with *extreme* care, using every sort of protective spell. Whether anything ever came of it he could not say.

In time, Grondar and Shella's three children grew up. Garander remained a farmer, becoming an equal partner with his parents; he met and eventually married a merchant's daughter by the name of Peretta the Clever, and became the father of five children—three daughters and two sons.

Shella the Younger married Karn Kolar's son, but the marriage did not last; after she left him she wound up living in Sardiron, where she became a noted dressmaker, married a captain in the city guard, and bore him three sons.

Tesk remained in the forest, visiting occasionally with Garander, Ishta, and later Peretta; neither Grondar nor either of the Shellas ever saw him again.

And Ishta, with Ellador's assistance as arranged in Garander's dreams, went to Ethshar of the Sands, where she apprenticed to a demonologist. Her original intent may have been to find a way to separate Tesk's human and demonic parts, but although she was successful in her chosen field, and visited him every so often, she never achieved that particular feat.

ABOUT THE AUTHOR

Lawrence Watt-Evans is the author of four dozen novels and over a hundred short stories, including the Hugo-winning "Why I Left Harry's All-Night Hamburgers." He has been a full-time writer for more than thirty years and lives in Takoma Park, Maryland with his wife and an overweight cat.

His web page is at www.watt-evans.com, and readers of this book may also want to check out www.ethshar.com.

Lightning Source UK Ltd.
Milton Keynes UK
UKHW011953150319
339243UK00001B/169/P

9 781479 404643